Beyond Contempt

Jeff Zwagerman

Black Rose Writing | Texas

ISBN: 978-1-68433-374-5
PUBLISHED BY BLACK ROSE WRITING
www.blackrosewriting.com

Printed in the United States of America
Suggested Retail Price (SRP) $19.95

Beyond Contempt is printed in Book Antiqua

This book is dedicated to my sister Joan, the comma Nazi. Without her constant barrage, I would string together countless sentences and other assorted errors and omissions. Thanks for kicking me in the posterior. I know you have always wanted to do it.

Beyond
Contempt

Prologue

Men moet de dag niet prijen voor het avond is
Don't praise the day until it is evening.
---Dutch Proverb

Sara Jane De Graff, now called Jayne Grafton, delivered a five-pound baby girl. She might have been bigger, but she was born a month early. If she had been born on time, the chances were that Jayne Grafton would have died. Having a baby later in life was always a risk to both mother and child.

Jayne was torn up inside, and the doctor had said it was touch-and-go trying to stop all the bleeding. Her actual mother, Millie DePont, had never left her side. Millie had given her daughter to her older sister to raise early in her life. Millie hadn't paid much attention to the newborn after the nurse told her that the baby was just perfect. It was a mistake she had been trying to correct since she had reconnected with Jayne.

Jayne was in a drug-induced haze and comprehended bits and pieces of what was happening around her. Mostly, she just slept. Millie thought it was commonsense keeping her immobile. It might help her to heal her torn insides.

The damage to her reproductive organs was severe. The doctor, whose name was Carol, kept what she could and removed what she couldn't. She told Millie that Jayne would be going through menopause unless she took drugs. Millie hadn't understood everything until that point. She understood that, however. It was not good news for Jayne, and she would be damned if she would tell her.

"That's a subject you'll broach with Jayne when the time is right," Millie said to the Carol.

"It's my job, Millie." They'd been best friends for years. "Breaking news like that is always difficult. It's not the hard part though. The hard part will be living with it for the rest of her life. That's where you come in. Now you need to get off your high horse and decide how you will go about it. If you need to talk strategy, I'll be here." Carol walked away.

Millie smiled. Carol's ability to put her in her place had cemented their friendship right from the start. Not everyone in the community could stand up to Millie, and when someone showed some spunk, Millie took notice. Millie looked over at Jayne and wondered where all this would be heading.

The door to the private room opened, and Carol came back partway into the room.

"That baby needs to be held and nurtured. That would be your job until her mother is able. It's time you pulled your weight if you plan to keep hanging out here."

"Stop being so damn bossy. It's irritating," Millie said.

"Oh, I'm just getting started. Some major decisions need to be made right now. Since Jayne can't do it, those things need to fall on your shoulders. Such as they are."

"Such as? And by the way, kiss my ass," Millie said, pretending to be angry.

"Let's start with her name. Do you have one?"

Millie hadn't thought much about a name, and Jayne hadn't shared any ideas if she had any.

"Hadn't thought much about it."

"Well, are you going to be calling her Baby Girl Grafton for the rest of her life?"

"I get your point, but that's not my decision, now is it." It wasn't a question.

"This baby is a healthy little girl, and she can't stay in the nursery very much longer. Are you going to be equipped to take care of her in your home until Jayne is able to look after her?"

"You don't have to be so damn aggravating about the whole thing," Millie said.

"It's my job to be aggravating to someone who's the biggest asshole in the county." Carol was not backing down.

"Just the county?" Millie asked, with a bit of sarcasm in her voice.

"I wouldn't know. I don't know many people outside the county, but my guess is that you could hold your own with anyone who sported the asshole banner."

Millie knew she could never best her friend, so she just smiled.

"I guess I'll go and hold the baby. Point me in the right direction."

"High time. Just follow me to the nursery," Carol said, pushing open the door.

"I might need a bit of coaching. I don't have any experience in child rearing." Millie was feeling some trepidation.

"All you need is to ask for help. We have capable people to help the ignorant like yourself." Carol smiled, and led the way to the nursery.

Carol left her at the door. The nurse on duty showed Millie a rocker in a small room just off the nursery and went to get the baby. When she returned, she showed Millie how to hold the child and placed a cloth on her shoulder.

"What's that for?" Millie asked gruffly.

The nurse knew about Millie's reputation, and she wasn't intimidated.

"She needs to be fed, and that's for when she spits up."

"What the hell? Does that always happen?"

"She's a newborn. So, yes it happens." She handed the baby to Millie.

"Why is she all wrapped up like a mummy?"

"It's called swaddling. A newborn child needs to feel the comfort of the womb. This is the closest thing we have to make the transition to life on the outside."

Millie realized how little she knew and how much both she and Jayne would need to learn about child development. It was a daunting thought. Then she noticed the little girl in her arms.

She was beautiful. Her eyes were open, and Millie had a feeling they were going to be blue. Millie just knew it. She searched for any resemblance to the family but decided it was too early to tell. Then she started to cry. Millie looked up helplessly at the nurse who laughed at the face she was pulling.

"She needs to be fed. I'll go fix a bottle." The nurse turned to leave.

"What am I supposed to do with her in the meantime?"

"Comfort her. Pat her on her back. Just use your head, and don't act so helpless."

The comment pissed Millie off, because she wasn't used to being talked to by someone she felt held a lesser place in her world. It made her stop and reevaluate that position. It was an elitist attitude, and she needed to make sure this new little child would never learn that she had a silver spoon in her mouth.

Millie took the child, placed her on her shoulder, and patted her on her back. She stopped crying. Millie smiled. The first success of what she hoped were a series of successes for the both of them.

1

Much to Zander's relief, Aubrey hit it off with his former lover, Ingrid. Danny Bloemendaal, Ingrid's husband and Zander's high school friend, told him that he was a lucky man. Zander already knew that. The reunion and Aubrey's introduction was a huge success. Danny and Ingrid insisted that Zander and Aubrey spend the night at their farm. Zander at first declined. He wasn't able to hold his ground against the constant barrage by everyone in the room.

After thanking Danny's sister, Betsy, Zander and Aubrey followed Danny and Ingrid to their farm. Aubrey was staring out of the side window of the pickup. Zander noticed that she was unusually quiet.

"Is there something wrong?"

"Why do you ask?" Aubrey asked, trying to sound unconcerned.

"If this is too weird, we can always find a hotel."

"I'm interested in your past life. Ingrid is a real knockout, and I can see why you were attracted to her."

"The key word is "were," I think," Zander said.

"Don't worry, I'm not threatened by Ingrid. She's a wonderful person and quite a hoot to be around."

"What is it then?" Zander asked, trying to be gentle.

Aubrey turned to Zander.

"I've had this feeling that we're being followed."

Zander knew what she was saying. He had felt it also.

"Do you think it's the State Department?" Zander asked, not knowing what secret organization was behind the men who had been following them since they left Florida.

"I think it might be them," Aubrey paused, "Hell, I know it's them."

"What do you want to do about it?" Zander asked.

"Nothing. Pull over." Aubrey was firm.

Zander pulled the pickup over to the side of the gravel road they had been travelling. Zander looked out as he put the truck into park. It was the same spot where Quentin Stryker had hit the car he was driving with Ingrid. It was the place where he had almost lost his life. Zander thought there might be something ironic going on.

"You need to promise me something," Aubrey said firmly.

"Maybe I should know what that is before I say yes," Zander replied, smiling.

"This is no light moment we are having here. I want you to know that up front."

"Okay." Zander was concerned.

"It will be just a matter of time when these people will find us and take me."

"Not without a fight from me," Zander exploded.

"That's what you will not do. You will do nothing. These people are not to be trifled with, ever. My guess is they will grab me and be gone before you even realize it. They won't want to involve any more people than necessary."

"But..."

"Shut up and listen. Nothing can be done about it. They have too many resources. I'll be okay. They will give me a job to do in Cuba, and when that's finished, I'll return and find you."

"I can't do this."

"Zander, listen to me. If you have any love for me at all, you'll do as I say. Anything else would be disastrous for both of us."

Zander turned and put the pickup into drive. He was pissed.

Aubrey slid over and knocked the gearshift back into park and put her arms around Zander.

"Do you love me? Do you care for me? Do you want to continue our relationship?"

"You know I do." Zander's shoulders dropped.

"Then please just believe in me. I know how this would end if you go off the deep end. I couldn't bear the thought." Aubrey kissed Zander.

Zander returned the kiss, and there was nothing sexual about it. It signified a deep understanding the two possessed.

Zander embraced Aubrey when the kiss ended.

"When do you think this will happen?"

"I don't know. I just know it will be soon. They have been watching me for some time, and they haven't done much of a job covering their trail. That means they are almost ready to make the move."

"This is the United States of America. This can't happen. We're citizens, and we have rights."

"Don't be naïve. This kind of shit happens all the time. Crawl out from the rock you've been living under." Aubrey laughed.

Her laugh made Zander feel better.

"So, what am I supposed to do?"

"Nothing. This doesn't concern you," Aubrey said.

"We've got to have a plan for after." Zander hated thinking about life without Aubrey.

"I'll need someplace to contact you when the job is over."

Zander thought.

"That would have to be the Branchwater Saloon in Frisco, Colorado. If I'm not there, you can talk to someone called Fats. Otherwise, you could call the number on my card. It's an answering service that I check periodically." Zander handed Aubrey his card.

Aubrey studied the card for a few seconds and smiled.

"This is so cheesy. I like it. This is what I'll use to contact you. I don't know this Fats guy."

"We're going to meet him. Frisco is our next stop after we visit guys at the Glass Onion in Omaha."

Aubrey put her arms around Zander's neck and pulled the gearshift into drive.

"First, we need to spend the evening with your friends."

"They're your friends too," Zander said, looking at Aubrey.

"Agreed."

They drove on to Danny and Ingrid's home.

By the next morning at 8:00, they were on their way to the Glass Onion. Zander couldn't wait for all his bar buddies to meet Aubrey. He was quite sure she would knock their socks off.

Neither Zander nor Aubrey saw the black SUV fall in behind their pickup as they exited onto I-29 from highway 75 in Sioux City.

2

Aubrey's charm over older men hadn't waned since Zander had first met her. All the boys in the bar circled her, and Aubrey seemed to enjoy their attention. Zander sat back smiling at these old coots with their tongues hanging out. Nobody wanted to get old, and Aubrey had the gift of making men feel much younger.

Jasper had his eye on Zander. He was trying to decide if Zander was enjoying the scene playing out or if there was some jealousy involved. Zander caught his eye.

"What?"

"She's a keeper, and you just sit here letting these idiots fawn all over her," Jasper said.

"Sometimes to keep someone in your life you've got to give them space. You need to let them go."

"I don't understand that at all." Jasper turned away and grabbed the coffee pot on the back bar. "You want a refill?"

"Might as well. It doesn't look like we'll be leaving for a while." Zander moved his glass mug to the edge of the bar.

The mug had the Glass Onion etched into the clear glass. Zander liked drinking out of them, because they were unique. Jasper poured the coffee right to the very top of the mug.

"I won't be able to drink that without a straw." Zander stood, put his lips to the mug to try to suck down the coffee to an acceptable level, so he would be able to move the mug closer.

The coffee was extraordinarily hot. Zander burned his lip and spilled most of the top third of the mug on the bar. He pulled back and sat back down.

"Nice going," Jasper said, as he lifted the mug and ran a bar rag under it to soak up the spilled coffee.

"Why is that shit so hot?" Zander asked through his teeth.

"Who wants to drink cold coffee?" Jasper asked, and then filled the mug back up to the very top.

"Hey, stop doing that," Zander said, putting a napkin to his lips to try and take away the sting of the hot coffee.

Jasper laughed.

"Just trying to help you take your attention away from this beautiful woman and give you a little shot of reality." Jasper put the coffee pot back on the burner.

"I think my lip is shredded," Zander said, trying to make Jasper feel sorry for him.

Jasper pulled a paper towel off a roll, reached into the ice bin, and put a few cubes into it. He handed it to Zander.

"Thanks." Zander put the ice to his lip. He hoped he wouldn't get a blister.

"What's your plan?" Jasper asked, sitting behind the bar across from Zander.

"What?" Zander tried to understand the question.

"Where are you and the Mrs. going from here?"

"My plan was to go to Frisco but..."

"But what?" Jasper was interested.

"I don't know if we'll make it. At least maybe not together." Zander hung his head.

"I think you'd better tell me what's up," Jasper said.

Zander told him the entire story from meeting her at Everglade City, Florida, to the moment they walked into the Glass Onion. Jasper was quiet until Zander finished. Zander thought it was unusual for Jasper to keep his mouth shut for that length of time. His story must have been intriguing.

"So, what's your advice?" Zander asked, breaking the silence.

"I've got nothing." He paused and looked over at Aubrey. "But I think you'd better do something."

"She says I can't get involved."

"And?"

"Well, of course I'll get involved. You know me. I can't let something like this slide with Aubrey." Zander was looking at Aubrey.

"Is she the one?" Jasper asked.

"Yes. I believe she is."

"So, what will you do?"

"I'm not sure. I've been turning this over in my mind. I think I might have some ideas, but I can't do anything until they abduct Aubrey."

"That surprises me. It sounds reactive to me. I've always known you to be proactive," Jasper said.

Zander stared at the mug of coffee and decided to leave it right where it was.

"You don't know Aubrey. Besides, I don't have the resources of these suits. They've got equipment right out of some science fiction novel."

Jasper nodded, "Then reactive is about your only option. Just remember, if you need anything, we're always here."

Jasper was implying the entire bar, but Zander knew he was talking about himself.

"Thanks Jasper. If I need anything, you'll be the first one I'll call."

Jasper broke out a broad smile. Zander couldn't help but realize how unusual it was. Jasper tried to portray himself as an old curmudgeon.

Aubrey broke away from her admirers and sat next to Zander.

"You going to drink that coffee?"

"Have at it," Zander said, thinking how he might enjoy seeing how she would maneuver the mug without spilling half of it on the bar.

Aubrey reached for the mug and in one quick motion, brought it up to lips and drained as much as Zander had spilled.

"What the hell? Wasn't that hot?" Zander asked.

"Sure, but everyone knows women have a higher pain threshold than men." Aubrey took another swallow and settled in next to Zander.

"See what I have to deal with?" Zander asked Jasper.

"Yep, and you are one lucky man," Jasper said.

"Well said." Aubrey laughed.

"Finish your coffee. We've wasted enough time at this place. We need to move on," Zander said, standing.

Aubrey pushed away the mug of remaining coffee and stood.

"I'll be with you as soon as I use the ladies room." Aubrey moved toward the bathroom but let her hand run up Zander's left side resting it briefly on his shoulder. Then she was gone.

"I'll say it again. You are a lucky man. Just don't screw it up." Jasper winked.

"That's what I'm worried about."

"With your track record you should be worried," Jasper said.

"Thanks for the vote of confidence." Zander always enjoyed the bar banter and the banter with Jasper. He knew he would miss it.

"Just keep us in the loop. You know how to use the phone, and you know my schedule here at the Onion. I need to know what's going on." Jasper stood, and grabbed Zander's arm.

Zander nodded.

"I'll do what I can, but this might get dangerous. I don't want to do anything that might harm Aubrey."

"Understood. Just don't want you to forget about us," Jasper replied.

The comment made Zander uncomfortable. He wasn't used to having Jasper say things that sounded sentimental. There was no time to respond, however. Aubrey came out of the bathroom and grabbed his hand.

"I'm ready to go."

"Hey you have wet hands. I hope that's water and you just didn't dry off when you washed your hands," Zander said, wiping his wrists on his pant leg.

Aubrey just laughed.

"Jasper, you are out of towels in the ladies' room."

"Thanks. I'll get right on it."

Both Zander and Jasper were thankful for the easy way out of the bar. Neither liked to say goodbye. Zander looked at Aubrey, and she smiled. Zander would remember to ask her later if this was her plan all along.

Ten minutes later they were making the move from I-680 to I-80 and then west toward Frisco. They weren't alone on the trail, however.

3

Just west of Kearney, Nebraska, Zander decided to pull into a rest area. He hadn't used the bathroom at the Glass Onion and his bladder was overflowing. Aubrey just laughed but decided not to pass up a chance to stretch her legs. They parked to the left of the restrooms. Zander found the men's room, and Aubrey walked over to look at what was in the vending machines.

The black SUV had pulled into the truck and trailer parking area. The men watched as the couple slid out of the pickup. When Zander went into the restroom, both men jumped out and rushed Aubrey before she knew what happened. One of the men wrapped his arm around her chest and covered her nose and mouth with some kind of cloth soaked in something that made Aubrey quiet. The other man picked up her feet, and together they pushed her into the rear of the SUV. In a matter of thirty seconds the black SUV was back on I-80. They traveled to the Odessa exit and doubled back heading east. When they passed the rest stop, the driver saw Zander walking toward his pickup. He smiled and pointed. The passenger nodded and settled in for a long drive. It had been a successful abduction.

When Zander came out of the bathroom, he noticed that Aubrey wasn't where he had left her. He walked back to the pickup, but seeing no sign of her thought that she might have changed her mind about using the rest room, so he leaned against the front of the pickup. The rest stop had very few cars in the lot. He looked across to the truck parking area and noticed one eighteen-wheeler. Zander thought the driver might have been napping in the sleeper.

He had a bad feeling. He sprinted over to the women's restroom and called out for Aubrey. No answer. He barged into the bathroom and frantically looked from stall to stall. No one was in the place. He ran back out and circled the entire building calling out for Aubrey.

A few people in the picnic area glanced over but no one responded. Zander ran through the building's open area calling Aubrey's name. He was at wit's end and in complete panic. The door to the eighteen-wheeler opened and a guy jumped out.

"Hey, are you looking for a woman?"

"That's pretty apparent don't you think?" Zander was hot.

"Easy man. I was just getting up and rolled over to look out the window. I saw these two guys in a dark colored vehicle grab a woman and throw her into the back."

"How long ago?'

"I don't know, no more than ten minutes."

"Did you get a license plate?"

"Sorry. Everything went so fast. I just caught a glimpse, and then they were gone."

"Describe the vehicle." Zander was fidgeting.

"I don't know. Dark. Blue or maybe black. It was one of those big things that look like a box. Chevy, I think, but might have been a Ford. They took out of here on two wheels."

"Thanks," Zander said over his shoulder, as he ran to his pickup.

He thought he might have a chance to catch these assholes if he pushed. By the time he merged back onto I-80 his speedometer showed the same number as the road he was travelling. He pushed it to almost a hundred, but the pickup started to shake, and it scared him. He dropped down to ninety-five and kept it that way until he was almost to North Platte. He realized that he would have caught anyone traveling the speed limit long before this point. These people were too smart to do the obvious. Zander thought they might have turned back to the east or left I-80 altogether. He knew he was screwed.

Zander slowed his pickup to the speed limit. He checked his gas gage and knew he needed to fill up. The next exit was North Platte, he took it and stopped at the first gas station he saw. He had been paying cash for everything since he and Aubrey had left Florida. He hadn't wanted to leave a trail that would put Aubrey in jeopardy. Since it was no longer an issue, he took out his credit card and put it into the pump.

He put the nozzle into his tank and decided to wash his windows. Zander was going through the motions, but his mind was fogged over. Trying to make some sense of what happened and what Aubrey had told him previously had him totally confused.

Zander remembered from his college days that there were three stages of a loss or breakup in a relationship:

1. Grief
2. Anger
3. Acceptance

Zander hadn't lost Aubrey. She had been taken from him, so there was no time for grief. He was vacillating between anger and acceptance because of what Aubrey had told him. That alone was enough to make him angry, but then he realized that Aubrey had given him no wiggle room about what he could do. It kept him in that fog. He spent the next few hours heading to Frisco.

Exit 201 on I-70 jumped out at him, and he jerked the pickup into the exit lane. He was driving too fast to make the turn, and he hit the brakes hard. He skidded as the pickup reached the stop sign. Zander knew he had to get it together, or he might never make it to the Branchwater. It was a miracle he had made it across Nebraska in his condition.

His haziness lifted. He needed to talk to Fats. When Zander was feeling his worst, he could always count on Fats to help him through. He took his foot off the brake and headed into Frisco. In less than ten minutes, he was parked at the bar. Everything appeared to be the same. That was of some encouragement for Zander. He needed everything to remain in his comfort zone.

It was late, and the outside lights should have been on. They weren't. Zander walked up to the door and noticed the lights weren't on inside either. A taped sign on the door said: "Closed. Plumbing Problems."

That seemed odd to Zander. He figured Fats would keep the place open no matter what the problem might be. He couldn't stand not making a buck.

Zander decided to go around back. Since the bar was in the middle of the street, he drove his pickup through the alley, and parked next to the back door. He still had a key for the door on his key chain. He put it into the lock, and the door pushed open. Zander was on high alert. Something was just not right.

He reached into his boot and pulled out the stun gun. He needed to be ready for whatever might jump out at him.

It was dark in the bar, but there was a bit of light coming out from under the storeroom door. Zander moved trying not to make any noise. He pushed open the door, hoping that it wouldn't squeak.

The light was dim coming from one overhead 60-watt bulb, but he could see two figures sitting with their backs to him on some extra bags of salt they had used for the water softener. Zander squeezed through the door opening making sure not to open it any further. He walked with the stun gun raised. It appeared to be a man and a woman at first glance. The man had his arm around the woman's shoulder. Zander's thought was to take out the man first and deal with the woman after.

Zander stopped. The two sitting on the salt bags were Fats and Fran. He let out the air in his lungs he had been holding. Fats heard the sound and turned around.

"We're closed man. Didn't you read the sign?"

"Yeah I read it. What's going on around here?"

Fats jumped up.

"Ah, Jeez Zander. You scared the living crap out of me."

Fran raised her head but said nothing. Zander thought she looked terrible.

"What are you two doing sitting in the dark back here? There's money to be made, and what's with this plumbing problem?" Zander asked.

Fats got up and moved over to a tarp lying in the corner. He pulled it back, and Zander saw the top half of a woman without much of a face. His knees got very weak.

"That looks like a dead woman," Zander said, without much emotion.

Fats nodded.

"She's the plumbing problem. She leaked blood all over the barroom floor." Fats looked at Fran. "All over Fran as well. This hasn't been the best of days."

Zander needed to sit down. He opened the door wider and pulled in an old chair from the back and brought it over to where Fran was sitting. He sat down and looked into her eyes.

"Can you tell me what happened?" He asked her.

Fats came back and sat next to his girlfriend. He put his arm around her once again.

"She's in shock, man, and can't talk."

"You tell me then," Zander commanded.

"She saved my life." Fats touched her cheek with the back of his free hand. "Fran shot her with one of the pistols I had under the bar before this woman could do the same to me."

"Who is she?" Zander asked.

"It's a long story and from my past. I've never told anyone about it but Fran."

"Well, now you're going to have to tell me."

"When the time is right, I'll tell you the whole story. It's a long one and will take much time and bourbon. Right now, we've got to clean the bar floor and get rid of the blood. Then this bitch under the canvas has to go up to the old mine airshaft and join "The Rooster." She'll make him some fine company."

Zander sat back and knew he was very tired. This was more than most people could handle in one day and wondered what other tragedies might be just around the corner.

He wouldn't have to wait very long.

4

Millie made her way into the hospital each day to give her daughter, Jayne, some support. Jayne's body was starting to heal, but her mind would need more healing before being dismissed from the hospital. Millie would see to it that Jayne was not discharged a minute before she was ready.

While Jayne slept, Millie sat in the nursery and rocked the baby. She had no idea that she was bonding with the child. The baby still had no name, and it was starting to bother Millie. Every kid needed a name, and the quicker they heard it, the sooner they could start reacting. It wasn't her call. She knew she couldn't push Jayne, or she would just dig in. Millie knew no one with a stronger will than her daughter. The thought made her smile, Millie was no pushover either, and so the apple never fell far from that particular tree. With so many things going on in the hospital, Millie failed to see a young woman watching her each time she came to the nursery.

Holly Harris was an employee of the hospital. She always wanted to be a nurse, because she liked to help people. Holly wasn't the brightest bulb in the string of Christmas mini lights. In fact, if you found one of those white bulbs that just barely warmed the filament that would be Holly. She had tried to get her LPN certification but never could pass the tests. If that bothered her, she never let it show. She was a sweet young thing, and everyone liked her. Her personality made up for what she lacked upstairs.

She was hired by the hospital to keep the nursery functioning. It would free up the nurses to do the things they were trained to do. She took the job seriously and was good at it. She made sure there were supplies ready and available for the nurses each day. She cleaned the entire area twice a day and made sure each infant had clean garments. She did everything the nurses pushed on her, and they all loved having her there for that reason.

Holly loved her job even though it paid very little. If she couldn't be an actual nurse, this would have to do. She watched Millie as she rocked the newborn. She knew who Millie was and where she came from. Everyone in the area knew about Millie. Holly couldn't help feeling a bit of jealousy seeing Millie rock the baby.

Holly's story was a sad one. She was born to a sixteen-year-old who was no more than a child herself. No father to be found, and the young mother had Holly in the bathtub by herself. Holly's mother bled out on the bathroom floor because of complications.

Her parents found her and called the paramedics. It was too late. Holly's mother died on that cold bathroom floor. The next day, Holly's grandparents wrapped her in a blanket and put her in a cardboard box. They made a trip to Perry and dropped the box at the fire station. They couldn't bear to look at the baby-all they saw was that she was the cause of their daughter's death.

It was lucky for Holly that this all took place in Florida. If it had happened in one of the northern states, she wouldn't have survived the elements. The fire department was of the volunteer variety, and many of the fire fighters only came to the station when the alarms sounded. Holly lay at the door for almost a full day, until a curious little boy on his bike stopped to see what was in the box. The boy rode to the police station to report his finding. The police rushed the baby to the hospital hoping that the baby would survive. One of the officers, who had children of his own, found it strange that the baby never cried. He knew she was in poor shape, but she just stared at him with wide eyes. It bothered him, and he checked on Holly over the next two weeks. When the doctors declared that she had turned the corner and was a healthy baby, the officer lost interest. He had a family of his own and couldn't feed another mouth on his salary. He felt bad for her but went on with his life.

Holly was alone. The hospital staff named her Holly, because Christmas was just a few days away. She had no last name, so someone came up with Perry. It was the town where she had been born, and it was as logical as anything. Holly stayed in the hospital until the staff decided she was thriving, and then she was turned over to the local social worker.

This part of Florida was no stranger to orphaned children, and the social worker was quick to place the child with the first foster parents that showed interest. She was passed around from household to household without ever finding a permanent landing.

Most children would be disheartened and even angry. Holly never showed any emotion. She had a smile for everyone, but there was something just a bit off about her. That was the reason no one ever adopted her.

Holly forged on. She developed early. Her baby fat dropped substantially, while her body started showing all the right curves. She wasn't what people would call pretty, but she had an interesting face, and the permanent smile was quite disarming.

When she entered high school, the older boys noticed her. Holly had never experienced much attention. It was new to her, and she liked being a part of something. Unfortunately, she became just someone who was passed from guy to guy. They would meet her at some secret place and have their way with her. Then they would drop her off where no one would see them. This went on for quite some time, until Holly got a terrible STD. She had no idea what was happening, so she failed to get treatment. It would have been possible to cure the disease without doing damage to her reproductive organs, but it was far too advanced.

Holly would never be able to have children. She learned the hard lessons, but she had become a pariah. None of her classmates wanted to be around her. She had no girlfriends, and she no longer trusted any of the boys who faked attention to get something in return.

About that time, she became a candy striper at the local hospital in Perry. She would go every day after school and on Saturdays and Sundays when they let her. She felt she belonged to something. She had very little life outside the hospital. Her foster family was taking her in for the money, and Holly had to be careful to keep her bedroom door locked and avoid the constant barrage of unwanted advances by her foster father. When she told her foster mother, she got slapped across the face. Holly supposed it was her fault, so she took to wearing baggy clothing to try and avoid showing her body.

Holly's life would have been sheer misery for most. She took things in stride and changed her behavior to keep her life afloat somehow. She was one of those people in society that fall through the cracks. But she was a survivor, and that made people show less concern for her situation.

She seldom missed school. She was one of those students who sat in the back not making trouble but also not adding much to the classes she took. Try as she might, her grades always hovered around the failure area. Her teachers passed her anyway, because she never caused trouble, and she was always there. Maybe if one of those teachers would have gotten to know Holly, her life could have been different. Maybe if one of those teachers could have referred her to the guidance counselor, and as a mandatory reporter, the counselor could have made sure things would have been different. Then again, maybe not.

Holly's life seemed to just chug along, not changing much and not very productive. Her first three years of high school followed the same pattern. She volunteered at the hospital during the summer months and returned to the same schedule when school started once again.

Her senior year things started to change for the better. She turned eighteen and the hospital, seeing what a good thing they had with Holly, hired her on a part time-basis for minimum wage. Holly was elated. It was the first real money she had ever earned, and it felt wonderful. Things seemed to be working out.

Unfortunately, that's also about the time she met Harris.

5

Harris lived somewhere north of Perry and South of I-10. The family had a series of old trailers east of highway 221 in what the family called the compound. The compound was situated on swampy land that nobody wanted. It suited the family, because they owned no land. No one seemed to care that they were squatting. The land was worthless, and no one in his or her right mind would ever live there. During the rainy season, the road to their settlement was impassable. It wasn't a road at all but a dirt path that ran a few miles into the swamp.

Harris would have to walk the two miles to the highway in hip boots, which he would leave under a bush before he would get on the bus to go to school. Harris was still naïve enough to think he had a chance in life. His name alone should have given that away.

Harris's full name was Harris Harris. His father though it would be a fine joke to give him that name. The Harris family all had first names that began with the letter "H." His father's name was Henry, but everyone that knew him called him an asshole, including his family. No one had the guts to say it to his face, however. His sons called him Papa Henry. In their minds, however, Papa meant asshole. When they were out of earshot they would call him Asshole Henry. It was a dangerous game they played. If one of them ever slipped up and called that to his face, there would be hell to pay.

His mother's name was Helen, and most people thought Henry had married her because her name started with an "H." Baby-making happened over their years together. How much love was involved in the process was anybody's guess.

The couple had no daughters but popped out sons without much effort. Their first child was named Harold. He was the first of seven boys. They included Harvey, Herbert, Howard, Harley, Hunter, and of course, Harris. Three small graves were outlined at the edge of some swampy ground away from the compound. The stillborn births involved two boys and one girl. No names were given and no markers were on the graves. Helen had taken it hard after she lost the baby girl. She hadn't shown much interest in anything after that.

The family was what everyone called "dirt poor." Others could be heard using the term "white trash." They tried to raise food to eat in the swampy land and were somewhat successful. They were into collecting junk and stealing whatever they could. They were quite artful at both. None of Harris's brothers had gone to high school. Harris was the first and determined to do what no one else in his family had ever done.

Then he met Holly. They sat next to each other in senior English class. Harris found it impossible to get up enough nerve to even say anything to Holly until five weeks into the semester. Holly gave him a huge smile, and Harris was smitten. Holly was happy just to have someone who was willing to talk to her. It was a relationship that was meant to be. At least that's what it seemed from their perspective.

When it came close to semester's end, Harris proposed to Holly. He gave her some cheap ring one of his brothers had found breaking into a vacant house. The ring had been lying in the corner of a bedroom. The former renters dropped it in their move. The ring had a big rhinestone diamond that could have been purchased at any five-and-dime for fifty cents.

Holly loved it and said yes. Harris had a plan to get married over Christmas break, and then the two would go back to school and finish the year and graduate.

There was an old trailer in the compound that no one was using, and although it was rough, Harris thought they could fix it up a bit and make it livable.

Helen welcomed Holly with open arms. She would become the daughter she never had. Henry paid little attention, until Harris shared his plans.

"You ain't school housin' if you get married. We got mouths to feed, and she's an extra. Time you got to work." Henry scowled at Holly and pointed. "Her too."

"Name's Holly. She's already got a job at the hospital."

Henry liked what he heard.

"That's some good news, anyway. What's the last name?"

"Perry," Holly said, and looked down.

Henry snorted, "My ass. Well, you keep that name anyway when you marry my boy."

Holly gazed at Harris not understanding. Harris knew why the old man had said what he did, and he would try and tell her when the time was right. Whenever that might be.

Everyone in the compound lived off the grid. The Harris family had no existence at least by government standards. No banking accounts or credit cards existed. Everything was handled with cash.

No Social Security numbers, so there were no taxes. No sanitary sewer bills, because they used outhouses. No water bills, because they had their own wells. No mail delivery and no post office boxes, so no one could send them anything. Of course, there were no phones anywhere on the property, and the one source of electricity was from a gas generator. They used the generator to power the well pump and fill a large wooden water tower that Henry had put together with the help of his boys. That was the single modern convenience the compound could boast, running water. The trailers had light from kerosene and battery-powered lanterns.

Henry had outlawed candles much earlier after almost losing one of the trailers. Harold, his oldest boy, fell asleep before he remembered to snuff one out. It burned up a tablecloth before he woke up and threw a five-gallon bucket of piss over the fire, effectively putting it out. It seemed Harold was too lazy to go out and use the outhouse, and the bucket was his own personal urinal. The kitchen table always seemed to have a strange odor after the incident.

Harris' family life mirrored that of people from the early 1800s. This wasn't the 1800s, and they lived in Florida around a tremendous amount of population and tourism.

Holly looked around and felt that with all its flaws, this would still be better than where she had come from. She could tell that Harris' father was totally in charge. She wondered what role Harris would end up playing in the family business. She realized that there was no knowledge of what the family did for their business. If it worried her, she never let anyone know.

Henry decided the wedding would be the next day. Holly was shocked. She had always dreamed about getting married in a big church with a huge reception afterward. It had just been a dream, since Holly had no friends or relatives. She noticed that all the boys called their father Papa Henry. Trying to fit in, she did the same.

"Papa Henry, can I ask my foster parents to come to the wedding?"

"I ain't your papa, so you will never call me that. No one else is invited. This is a Harris family affair. I will marry you at the pond tomorrow at 3:00." Henry turned around. "Come on Boys, days a-wastin'. We got things to do."

The boys followed their papa toward one of the flatbed trucks. They had some junk to recover from one of the farmers down the road. Henry and the two oldest got into the truck. The others piled into the bed. Henry started up the truck and then noticed that Harris was still standing with Holly. He turned off the ignition, opened the door, and looked over at Harris. He crooked his figure in a summoning manner, and Harris ran over to the truck.

Henry hit Harris on his head with a closed fist knocking him to the ground. Holly let out a short scream, and Helen put her arm around her and pulled her away from the scene.

"When I tell you to come. You come. You ain't at that school no more. You do as I say, boy." Henry stared at Harris.

Harris got up rubbing his head.

"I can't go with you today. You set the wedding for tomorrow, so we got to go and get her stuff."

Henry rubbed his chin and then moved toward Harris. Harris raised his arms in a defense motion in case Henry was going to hit him again. This time Henry kicked him in the groin. Harris went down again.

"Don't sass me, boy. I won't stand for it. You got a point there about getting her stuff, but you need to ask permission."

Henry got into his truck. The Harris brothers were smirking as they drove by him lying in the dirt. Harris lay on the ground moaning, wondering if he would ever be able to feel anything down there again.

Holly waited until the truck drove off and broke away from Helen's grip. She raced over to where Harris was laying and knelt down.

"Oh, Harris, are you okay?"

Harris opened his eyes and frowned at Holly. His look frightened her, and she recoiled.

"No, I'm not okay, you dumb bitch," he yelled, as he rolled over.

Holly fell back and sat in the dirt stunned. Harris had never spoken to her that way before. She wondered what secret darkness this family was hiding. It was all too much for her to handle.

She felt a hand on her arm pulling her to her feet. It was Helen, and she was brushing the dirt from Holly's dress.

"Don't mind Harris," she whispered. "He's embarrassed at what Papa Henry did to him. It makes him look weak in front of you, and he doesn't know how to handle it."

"What do I do?" Holly asked.

"Nothing. Just leave him alone. He'll come around. Let me make you some coffee, and we'll have a little talk."

They sat in the trailer for almost an hour, before they heard a truck start up. Helen got up and stared out the window.

"Harris must be feeling better. He's driving one of the trucks over here."

Holly stood up and took a step toward the door. Helen stopped her.

"Sit down. Let him come to you," Helen said, and poured herself another cup of coffee.

"I don't understand," Holly replied.

"Men are a funny bunch of little boys. They think they need to do things on their terms. A smart woman lets them." Helen filled Holly's cup.

Holly never liked coffee, but she figured she needed to fit in somehow. This could be a first step with Helen.

Harris burst into the trailer.

"Come on, let's go get your things."

Holly peered at her cup unsure how to proceed. She was hoping that Helen would cue her in somehow.

"Did you hear what I said?" Harris sounded frustrated, and Holly hoped she wouldn't cry. She wondered again what she had gotten herself into.

"Sit." Helen commanded Harris.

Harris took a glimpse at her, and then took a chair next to Holly. Helen put a cup in front of him and filled it with coffee.

"Apologize," was all she said, and sat down.

It was uncomfortably quiet for a few moments.

"But…" Harris tried to blurt out something, but Helen stopped him. "Now."

Harris glanced over at Holly, took her hand, and gazed into her the eyes.

"I'm sorry for what I said to you out there." The apology was sincere.

Holly wondered how Helen had managed to turn everything around. When she glanced at her, Helen prompted Holly to say something with a short nod of her head.

"I'm sorry that happened to you. It wasn't right. You're a man, and you deserve better than to be treated like a dog." She looked at Helen, and she smiled.

Holly had passed her first test. Always make your man feel like he's the one thing that counts. It would be something Holly would have to rely upon.

6

Harris and Holly bounced around in the truck on their way back to Perry. Flatbed trucks-four of them-were the vehicles the Harris family owned. Two of them were purchased used, with cash, from a dealer. The licenses and registrations were paid with cash, so there was no insurance or paperwork on either vehicle. The other two trucks were put together from parts they stole from various junkyards. Henry was good at fixing vehicles, and it was a skill he was trying to get his sons to acquire without much success. They found some old license plates in a junkyard and used them. If they needed to go any distance they used the legitimate plates and kept the other two trucks close to home. No one paid much attention to the trucks anyway.

Harris was unusually quiet on the way to pick up Holly's things from her foster family's home. Holly had no idea of what to say, so she kept her mouth shut. When they came to the Winn-Dixie, Harris pulled into the parking lot.

"What's going on Harris? Why did we stop here?" Holly asked.

"I thought we could pick up some boxes for your things."

"I don't have much. Mostly just clothes," Holly replied.

"We need to pack everything in boxes. This truck doesn't have the best way to haul personal stuff. I can rope down the boxes so we don't lose them."

"That's a good idea, Harris. I would never have thought about it." Holly was trying out the advice Helen had given to her.

The comment made Harris relax, and he smiled.

"I guess that's why I'm here."

"You are the best. You are too good to take any abuse from your family," Holley said.

Harris' face clouded over, and Holly wondered if she had spoken out of turn. Harris turned to face Holly.

"My family will pay for what happened today. You deserve more than what they have to offer."

"So do you, Harris."

Harris put his arm around Holly and kissed her on the lips.

"Let's get some boxes," Harris said, and pulled her through his driver's door. "How many do you think you'll need?"

Holly thought. "Three or four at the most."

"Do you have a dress for the wedding? I have some money. I could buy your something nice."

Holly had a prom dress she bought from the Goodwill the year before. She thought that would be just right for the occasion.

"Thanks Harris, but I have something that will work. How about you? What will you wear?"

Harris smiled. "It's a surprise. You'll see tomorrow."

"Oh, I like surprises." Holly smiled as they walked into the store looking for boxes. She was happiest when just the two of them were together.

When they arrived at Holly's foster home, she was relieved to see that her tormentor wasn't home. His wife opened the door, and Holly told her why she was there. Her foster mother was furious. She could see the dollars walking out the door, and it made her angry.

"My husband won't stand for it. You can't leave without the social worker releasing you."

"I'm eighteen, so that would be wrong," Holly said, not backing down.

The woman raised her hand intending to slap Holly for her insolence. Harris was quicker and grabbed her arm before she could swing it around.

"There won't be any hitting today. Holly will be getting her things, and I'll be helping her," Harris said without emotion.

"Maybe I'll call the police. You would be trespassing, and they'll throw your skinny little ass in jail."

"You should do that. Holly told this skinny little ass about your husband's behavior toward her. I'm sure the community would love to hear about the sexual abuse coming from this house," Harris said.

The woman stared at Harris. She knew what had been going on and had chosen to ignore her husband's aberrant behavior. The last thing she needed was to have people find out about what he had done.

She moved away from the door, and Holly and Harris entered. They went right to the cramped attic that had served as Holly's room. The door used to have a lock but it no longer worked. Holly knew who had disabled it and compensated by trying to stay away from the house as much as possible. She would never tell Harris what her foster father had done to her. She would never tell anyone.

When all her things were packed into the boxes, the couple carried them out, and Harris strapped them to the back of the truck. The woman was watching them through the door. Holly decided to confront her one last time.

"I'm sorry your husband is such an asshole. You deserve better." Holly turned and walked to the truck and got into the cab.

The woman stared with hatred in her eyes. Harris noticed and decided to make a little confrontation of his own.

"Your husband is a sexual pervert. I'm sure Holly hasn't told me everything he did to her. If you want your life to go on the way it was, you'll let this go. Convince your husband it would be in his best interest to follow your lead." Harris knew what he had just said was a threat, but he failed to care. All the adults in his life had been stealing his strength and control. He decided that he was going to take his power back, and he would help Holly to get her strength back as well.

The trip back to their compound was much better than the trip out. Holly sat next to Harris with her head on his shoulder. She smiled in anticipation of a better life. She was certain that she deserved it.

When they drove into the compound, the couple went to their trailer to unload the boxes. Helen watched them as they worked with anticipation of their new life together. She felt bad for Holly. She felt those same emotions when she first came to this place. She also knew it wouldn't be anything like they imagined. Helen knew she should intervene but was clueless to know how without all hell raining down. So she did what she had been doing for so long. She ignored it and went about her own dismal life. If she had been a stronger woman perhaps her life would have turned out like she had always dreamed.

• • •

Harris slept without Holly the night before the wedding because he thought it would be bad luck. Holly got the bed, and Harris slept on a ratty old couch in the living room. When Holly woke she got dressed and went out to find Harris. The trailer was quiet, and there was no Harris to be found. Holly assumed he had errands to run on their wedding day, so she went about finding her prom dress in the midst of the boxes.

The dress was a simple off-white shift. It had a high empire waist and was low cut in the front. It showed all of Holly's curves, and she thought she looked stunning in it. She could remember turning a few heads at her junior prom. She hoped Harris would like it.

Holly hung the dress in the closet and took a damp towel and brushed a few places where the dress had some wrinkles. She knew they would be gone when the dress dried. The dress was the nicest thing she owned and was happy to wear it for her wedding.

The wedding was to take place at 3:00 with Henry presiding over the ceremony. Holly found it difficult to know what that meant, because she thought there had to be a minister at the ceremony to make it official. The Harris family had never followed customary protocols. Since her life hadn't been what most would call conventional, there was no real concern.

Harris came back to the trailer about an hour later. Holly had been trying to straighten things up, and put a female touch on the place, without much luck. She had very little to work with in that regard. Harris noticed, however.

"It looks good in here," Harris said, looking around.

"Thank you." Holly blushed, and then noticed a garment bag over Harris' shoulder. "What's in the bag?"

"You'll see," Harris said and then smiled.

He went into the bathroom, and Holly heard him moving around. He called out.

"Okay. Close your eyes, and I'll tell you when to open them."

Holly followed his direction. Harris came out of the bathroom and moved in front of Holly.

"You can open your eyes."

Holly stared at the person in front of her. Her first impulse was to laugh, but she caught herself just in time. Harris was dressed in a baby blue tuxedo, baby blue tux shirt, and baby blue bow tie.

"Wow," was all she could say.

"Do you like it? I got it from Mr. Wallace in the theatre department at school. I saw it hanging in the costume area when I was doing some stage construction for him."

Holly hid her smile.

"You look good." She thought he looked like some circus performer but didn't want to hurt his feelings.

"Thanks. Are you going to get dressed, so I can see what you are wearing?"

"No, it's bad luck to see the bride dressed before the wedding."

Harris was unsure about what to do. He just looked at Holly.

"Why don't you go and have lunch with your parents. Afterwards, I'll see you at the pond just before the wedding," Holly said, while pushing him out the door. "After you have lunch, would you ask your mother to come here and help me get ready?"

Harris liked what Holly had said. He liked his mother and hoped she and Holly would be friends.

He found his way to their trailer and invited himself to lunch. Henry hadn't returned from whatever he and the boys were doing that morning, so Helen was happy to have Harris share some time with her.

Henry and the boys returned just as Harris and his mother were finishing lunch. They piled into the trailer and sat around the table after Harris and Helen got up. It was time to be fed, and Helen went about her business.

Harris tried to leave the trailer as his brothers entered, but they weren't having any of it.

"What in hell are you wearing?" Harold shouted waving his hands up and down. "You look like some kind of bird."

Everyone laughed but Henry.

Helen went over and cuffed Harold on the ear.

"When you are in my home you will watch your language. Sit down and keep your mouth shut. Harris borrowed that suit from his school for the wedding. Seems kinda funny to me that my youngest child is the first to find a wife. Maybe you should borrow the suit and see if it works for you."

Harold's brothers all tried to hide their grins because Harold had a temper. None of the boys wanted to be confronted after lunch by their eldest brother. Harold sat down and stewed. Some day he would stand up to his mother, but he still feared what his father would do to him.

"We had a good morning," Henry said to Helen.

"Were you able to get the things I asked for?" Helen asked, as she filled his plate.

"It's in a bag in the truck. I don't like picking up women's things."

"You wouldn't have to if you would let me go along."

"Can't do it. Too dangerous."

Helen had no idea what that even meant. Henry kept her away from whatever his business entailed. That was acceptable to Helen, because it gave her much needed time that she could spend alone.

Helen knew about the bootlegging business, however. A still was hidden somewhere nearby, and Henry and the boys had been making moonshine and selling it illegally. The family had made a market for the stuff in that part of Florida, and it had become one of their primary sources of income right behind their theft and pilfering. The junk business was the legal part of what they did and the least profitable.

Harris had been too young to take part in the illegal side of what they did, but now that he was getting married, Henry would be expecting him to step up. Harris wasn't stupid, and he knew what was going on with his father and brothers. He knew what was expected of him, and he hoped he could make enough money to take Holly away from all the madness. It would not be without of risk, however.

7

Helen fed the family and then went over to help Holly get ready for the wedding. Harris went outside and found his way to the little area where the wedding was to be held, sat down on an old log, and threw stones into the pond. He was happy to have Holly in his life but was questioning whether he should have just gone to the justice of the peace to be married. He had very little money, or he would have run away with Holly and never come back.

Harris was stuck, and he knew it. It made him depressed on what should have been the happiest day of his life. He had to try and shake the feeling because Holly deserved better.

Helen helped Holly get ready and then returned to her trailer and started ordering everyone around.

"Boys, I want you all to get back to your trailers and put on your Sunday best. This is a wedding, and we all need to look our best for both Harris and Holly."

Of course, none of the Harris family ever went to church, so Sunday best was a big joke to the brothers. They decided to find something appropriate to please their mother. Henry would wear a waistcoat with a clean white t-shirt and black pants that he had purchased at a second-hand store for his own wedding back in the day. It no longer fit him because the girth of his belly had increased dramatically. He could still pull the zipper on his fly about halfway up. He would wear suspenders so he wouldn't lose his trousers.

The brothers were excited for the wedding, because Henry had promised that a good supply of moonshine would be used to celebrate. The moonshine was used on special occasions because it was worth too much for Henry to waste on the family. The brothers had a taste for it and stole a mouthful whenever possible. This would mean that today they could drink as much as they wanted, and they wanted much. A tarp on the flatbed truck hid a five-gallon crock of the moonshine just waiting to be used for the celebration.

The brothers moved a wooden picnic table to the spot where the wedding would take place and then placed the crock of moonshine on the table. An assortment of drinking ware to hold the moonshine bordered the crock. All the brothers wanted was to crack the cork and get the party started, but no one had the courage. Henry hadn't given them permission, and he dictated everything concerning the family.

The ceremony, such as it was, started on time, just as Henry had specified. Helen had walked Holly to the pond. When they reached Harris, Helen turned and faced Holly. She whispered something in her ear and then turned and joined her sons on the periphery.

Holly turned toward Harris and took her place on his right. Harris thought he noticed something in her face for just a moment, but then it was gone. He put his arm around her to help settle her nerves. He wanted her to feel safe.

Henry read something from a book he pulled from his coat. It wasn't a Bible and what he read was some rambling diatribe. It seemed to be about man's dominance over women and how they needed to obey and be subservient to their husbands. Holly's understanding was minimal and wanted the ceremony to be over. Harris felt the same way and was visibly uncomfortable standing in front of his family. He wondered what Holly was thinking about it all. He hoped she wouldn't be angry with him for subjecting her to his family and their unorthodox behaviors.

Henry ran out of steam and pronounced the couple married. The brothers rushed to the picnic table to get the party started. Henry stopped them.

"Fill the glasses for the wedding toast."

The brothers filled whatever was handy, as he had demanded. When everyone had some moonshine, Henry made the toast.

"To the married couple, may the woman bring happiness to the man. May she be fruitful and multiply. May she also bring in money from her work in town."

There were a number of "Here, here's," but everyone wanted to rush into drinking from the overflowing glasses. Holly had never heard a stranger toast from anyone. She looked at Harris, and he smiled and winked at her. If he was trying to dismiss what she had just heard, Holly wasn't buying it. She wondered why the toast involved her and not Harris. No mention was made of them as husband and wife.

Harris gave her a cup of the moonshine, and she took a small sip. It burned all the way down. Holly hated it and placed the cup on the picnic table. Helen came over, picked up the cup and put it back into her hands.

"Drink up, dear. You'll need much more of this if you plan to survive the night." Helen's voice had been soft, so no one but Holly could hear what she had said. Holly looked at her, remembering the words she had whispered to her just before the ceremony started.

Harris' brothers were slapping him on the back and filling his glass with moonshine every time he took a sip. It seemed that everyone's goal was to get Harris drunk. Holly sat on the picnic table and watched as her husband laughed uncontrollably at nothing at all. She thought her wedding night with Harris was looking like it would be quite uneventful. She was wrong.

Around five that afternoon, Harris passed out. He was not as familiar with the effects of moonshine as his brothers, and that had been their plan all along. Hunter and Harley carried Harris to the couple's trailer and put him to bed. The party was over for him.

Helen decided the party was over for Henry as well. She helped him back to their place hoping to put him to bed. Henry got himself into a recliner and promptly fell asleep. Helen stared out toward the pond and wondered if Holly would be able to survive the night. She dropped her eyes as she shut the door. Helen had troubles of her own. She had tried to warn Holly earlier, when she had whispered to "run like hell."

Harold and Harvey had both been married and neither of the marriages lasted more than a week. Their wives had run like hell. Harold's wife lasted two days and Harvey's was gone the next day. Helen never liked either woman, and it was fine that they left. She liked Holly, however, and hoped that she would find a way to make it work with Harris. He was her baby and the best of the lot. Her husband hadn't had the time to destroy his gentle personality. Maybe Holly could help keep her son from joining the Harris family legacy.

Helen heard some hoots and hollers coming from around the pond. She went over to her transistor radio and turned it on. She found a station and turned up the music to mask out the sounds that would surely be coming later. She went to the cupboard, found a jug of moonshine Henry kept hidden and poured a full glass. She would need it to get herself through the night. The Harris family tradition was not for the weak of spirit.

After Hunter and Harley put Harris in his bed, they snuck off to the trailer they shared together. They weren't all that interested in what happened the rest of the evening. They were more interested in some alcohol-fueled sex between themselves. The older brothers all knew about their perversions and ignored them. If they kept it to themselves, no one would be the wiser. They were careful around their father. They knew there would be hell to pay if he ever found out. Helen had walked in on them once, and they couldn't tell if she had been shocked or disappointed. She told them not to ever let their father see them that way. They never did.

Harold, Harvey, Herbert, and Howard did not share their unusual appetites. Harold and Harvey had some experience with women and shared a bed briefly with their wives. Herbert and Howard knew nothing about women, but they were eager to learn.

The four boys had been talking about the wedding for some time. The plan was to get Harris drunk and then have their way with Holly. Of course, the oldest would be first and then on down to the youngest. It was the biggest joke of all, since the actual husband was the youngest. Poor Harris wouldn't be getting anything at all on his wedding night. It made the boys laugh uncontrollably.

Holly was afraid of the look in the brothers' eyes. When they began pawing at her, she made sure that her glass was never without moonshine. She would need to be numb if things turned out the way they were looking.

Someone unzipped the back of her dress and Holly's bare shoulders became visible. It sent the boys into a lustful rage. Two them picked Holly up and moved to one of the trailers. Which trailer they picked never mattered, because the boys were beyond rational thought. There was no resistance. She knew better. She had been in this position before although never with four males. She knew it would be rape, and she also knew she was powerless to stop it.

Harold was the oldest, so he was first. He pulled down her dress and ripped off her underwear. He never bothered with her bra and was inside her before he even had time to throw her on the floor. Holly was hoping it would be over, and she at least had that piece of luck. Harold had been in such hysteria that he had an orgasm. He rolled off laughing, and then threw up on the floor. It missed Holly, and by the time she got up, Harvey was moving her to the bedroom. He was a bit gentler with her and paused long enough to take off her bra. It was another short run for the second brother. The other two brothers were watching and liked what they saw but were both too drunk to even manage an erection.

Harley tried to kiss Holly, while Hunter felt her breasts. Holly showed no response to their advances, and soon enough both the boys were on the floor snoring soundly.

Holly had survived the onslaught. She went outside and headed to the pond with her clothes in her hands. She put her underwear and dress on the picnic table and waded into the pond to clean off what the boys had left on her and inside her. She just wanted the stink of their touch off her skin. Harris would not be finding any traces of his brothers. The pond might have had alligators or snakes, but Holly was beyond caring. The coldness of the water helped her shake some of the effects of the alcohol. After inspecting herself, she was confident that her body was clean enough for her husband.

Holly climbed out of the pond and was about to reach for her bra, when a hand caught her wrist. She was pulled around and found herself looking right at Papa Henry.

"Have you been busy this evening?" Papa Henry asked, trying to sound concerned.

Holly said nothing and dropped her head.

"I want to personally welcome you to the family."

Henry pushed her back onto the picnic table and pulled down the zipper on his fly that was halfway down to start with. He never bothered with any other of his clothes and was all over Holly. Henry had time to sober up before he took his turn and was taking his sweet time with his new daughter-in-law. Holly thought she would be sick but gazed up at the darkening sky and held her breath.

It seemed like an eternity before Henry made a little choking sound in the back of his throat and collapsed on Holly. At first she though he was dead. She wished he was dead, but after a few moments, Holly realized he had an orgasm. It disgusted her, and she had nothing but contempt for the entire family. She hated Helen. Helen had told her to run like hell before the wedding, and Holly realized she must have known what was going to happen. The family had become horrible for Holly, but it was nothing to what she was feeling toward Helen. She was beyond contempt.

"Now you're officially welcomed to the family," Henry said with a toothy grin. "You best keep this to yourself, or it might become a regular thing."

Holly said nothing but returned to the pond. She decided she would remain there until Papa Henry left. It wouldn't matter how long it took.

The sun had fallen below the horizon and nightfall had begun to set in, when Helen heard the door to the trailer slam. She got up and peered out the window. Helen saw her husband walk toward the pond. Enough light existed to see what he was doing. For the first time, Helen felt anger stir in her chest. She knew her husband and what he was capable of. Strangely, her anger was not directed at him. The anger came from within. She was angry with herself for allowing all of it to happen. She could have done something to stop it, but she was too afraid to allow herself to make a stand. Now it was too late.

Helen sat on her bed trying to decide what she should do next. In times past, she would have gotten herself ready for bed, and she would think that everything would be better in the morning. Not this time.

Helen went out the back door and skirted around her husband who was staggering back to the trailer. She watched him enter and close the door, and then she ran down to see if there was anything she could do for Holly.

8

Holly had nothing to say to Helen. She couldn't believe Helen could allow her family to degrade her without stepping in. Helen was trying hard to explain her side of everything, but Holly quit listening. She walked to the trailer and wondered if she even had a place in this family. She would never allow anything like this to ever happen again.

Holly went into the trailer, and as Helen tried to accompany her, Holly slammed the door in her face. Helen turned and sat on the steps and cried. Holly heard her crying, and it made her smile. Why should she be the one to feel the pain? It made her stop and think about Helen. It could be that there was more to her than Holly could process. It was something to ponder, when she found herself less angry.

Holly got ready for bed and took her place next to Harris. Nothing would be happening that night. It was fine with Holly. They had been experiencing their share of sex for quite a while, and that would serve to help her block out the memories of what had just happened. Holly wondered if her life could continue with the history of abuse that had been a constant. It was still nagging at her, when she fell asleep.

Holly woke up to the sound of Harris throwing up somewhere outside of the trailer. At least she was thankful for that small favor. She wouldn't have to clean up his vomit today. She wondered if her life was over, as she pulled the sheet over her head. Harris came back into the trailer, and Holly heard him making noise in the kitchen. Soon she could smell coffee brewing on the Coleman stove. She decided to get up and face the day. It was early, and she noticed that there wasn't any sound coming from the compound. Everyone was nursing hangovers. That meant she might have some time before Harris would be expected to get to work.

Harris saw her when she walked into the kitchen. He dropped his head.

"I'm so sorry, Holly. I should never have drunk that much. I promise never to do it again."

Holly went over and filled two mismatched cups with coffee. She handed one to Harris. They drank their first sip in silence. The coffee was extremely hot and Holly thought it felt good going down. It might burn away the events of the previous day.

Harris burned his tongue.

"Shit, that's hot."

Holly smiled. She couldn't stay mad at Harris. It wasn't his fault, after all.

"Feeling a little sick today?" Holly asked.

"I didn't know I knew anyone named Ralph until today."

Holly was confused, "Ralph who?"

Harris mimed throwing up.

"I must have used his name fifteen times. RALPH." Harris said the name with such emphasis that Holly couldn't help but laugh.

"What will happen today?" Holly asked.

"No work today. The family always takes the next day off after any wedding."

Holly knew why.

"So what will we do today?" Holly couldn't even remember what day it was. It didn't matter with the Harris family. Not one day had any more meaning than any other. This would be one of the few holidays the family would ever observe. The significance of its depravity would never be erased from Holly's mind.

"Papa Henry thinks you need to have your own vehicle. People shouldn't know that you are living here. It wouldn't be wise if someone dropped you off everyday in one of the flatbed trucks."

Holly's mind started racing. She hadn't been expecting that Papa Henry would let her have her own car. Then she stopped and shot a look at Harris.

"Who's going to pay for it?"

"Well, I have a little money, but you told me you have a savings account." Harris had to tread lightly.

"So, who will own the car if I buy it?" Holly asked.

"You will. My family can't register it. It has to be in your name."

"What is my name, anyway?" Holly knew, but she needed to bait Harris.

"Holly Perry. You have to keep your last name. Hopefully we can change that when we get some money saved up."

Holly knew that it would fall on her shoulders. Henry wouldn't be paying Harris much of anything. That's how he kept his boys in check. They couldn't leave the compound, because no one had the wherewithal to make it on their own.

"What day is it?" Holly had no idea.

Harris thought about it.

"It might be Monday."

Holly thought that was right.

"Good, I don't have to be to work until tomorrow morning. We could go look for a car today."

Harris liked the idea.

"That would work. How much money do you have?"

"There is almost two thousand dollars in the bank," Holly said. She had a little over five thousand dollars total but kept two thousand in the bank. So it wasn't a lie. It just wasn't the entire truth. Holly knew she had to rely on herself and until she could trust Harris totally she wouldn't be sharing everything.

"I have around five hundred, so we will have to find something around that amount. I don't think it will be much of a vehicle," Harris said.

"As long as it runs. I don't need anything but transportation to the hospital and back." Holly wanted Harris to think about the car and not about her finances. She had the rest of the money hidden inside the big stuffed alligator she had always kept on her bed. She knew it wasn't the best place to keep more than three thousand dollars, because everything at the compound was fair game. After the preceding day, that included Holly as well.

"I'll get a truck, and we'll go find you a car." Harris was excited.

"I'll put on some clothes, and you can pick me up in a few minutes," Holly said and started for the bedroom.

"Maybe I should clear it with Papa Henry first," Harris said.

"Do what you need to do. Just don't take too much time. Remember, you told me this was a holiday of sorts."

Harris left and hoped his father was either asleep or gone. When he knocked on the door, his mother answered.

"Where's Papa Henry?" Harris asked.

Helen opened the door wider and pointed to the recliner. Henry was snoring.

"He drank more after." Helen was careful not to say what "after" meant.

"I want to take Holly into town to look for a car," Harris said.

"Go now. He could wake up at any moment."

Harris turned and sprinted to one of the flatbed trucks and drove over to pick up Holly.

She was waiting and soon the pair was bouncing down the lane on their way to Perry. They would stay away from the compound for most of the day, enjoying their time together. Holly knew these moments would be few and far between, so she would make the best of the time they had.

Harris talked about how to make enough money to be able to leave the family. Holly listened and was heartened to hear that Harris still wanted them to leave together. Time would be of the essence, because she knew it wouldn't be long before one of the brothers told Harris what had happened on their wedding night. She had no idea how he would react and decided not to find out.

After searching most of the morning, the couple settled on a Ford Pinto station wagon. It was orange with some wood grained quarter panels. The exterior was in good shape, and the exterior was showing little rust.

Holly checked out the interior and found it to be acceptable. Harris started the engine and crawled all around underneath the car. It had over a hundred thousand miles, but the motor sounded tight. Harris proclaimed that it was a good buy. He was excited to find out that they could have it for eighteen hundred. That meant he wouldn't have to use any of his own money.

When Holly suggested that she contribute eight hundred dollars and he put in his five hundred, Harris was going to explode. Holly could see the darkness in his face, and it scared her.

"This will be your car. Why should I pay anything?" Harris asked, but Holly knew it wasn't a question.

"I suppose I could do the whole eighteen hundred dollars, and we could keep your money for emergencies."

"That would be a great plan," Harris replied, as his face began to relax.

Holly had noticed that the car would have a number of hiding places for the rest of her money, and that made her feel better. Now her bank account would have a few hundred in it so the family wouldn't be getting their hands on more than that.

Holly knew that she needed to figure out a plan to hide some of money from her job so the Harris family couldn't steal everything from her. She wasn't getting the best feeling from Harris at the moment, and that made her sad. He had been the one thing she thought she could always rely upon. She knew she would need to proceed carefully.

After the couple visited the bank, and Holly withdrew enough money to pay for the Pinto, they doubled back to the auto dealer and completed the deal. He would take care of the paperwork, and she could return the following day and get the title, registration, and license plates when she picked up the car. It meant Harris would have to take her back into town, and he liked that idea. Holly was feeling better about the entire transaction as well.

On the way back to the compound Holly put her arm around Harris. When they turned onto the lane to take them to the compound, she removed her arm and slid over. There was no explanation as to why she had done that, but she thought it was better not to tempt fate. The family was unpredictable, and she would try to blend in whenever possible. She was a survivor after all.

9

Holly was dressed and ready to leave at 6:00 a.m. the next morning. She had to wake Harris.

"Harris, we need to get moving. I need to be to work by 7:00."

"What time is it?" he asked, still half asleep.

"Almost 6:00."

"Shit. Papa Henry will skin me if I'm not ready for work and standing at his door by 6:30."

Holly said nothing and moved toward the door. Harris pulled on his clothes and was in the truck with Holly in less than five minutes. Holly had to laugh at him. He looked terrible. His hair was sticking up all over and his eyes were puffy. Harris decided to laugh as well.

The marriage consummation had taken everything out of him. It had seemed to go on all night. Just when they had finished one session, one or the other wanted to do another round. They would both be too tired to get much done this evening. The memories would have to be self-sustaining.

Harris pushed hard to get Holly to work. He was more concerned about not being late himself. Papa Henry would be watching him now that he was no longer in school. Harris wasn't so concerned with the tongue-lashings, but the beatings were hard to tolerate. He avoided them at all cost.

Holly directed Harris to the employee entrance.

"I'll be back after my shift," she said, as she opened the truck's door.

"How will you get your car from the dealer?" Harris asked.

"Don't worry about it. I'll either get a ride with someone, or I'll walk. I'm used to walking, and it isn't all that far."

Harris knew it was over five miles, but he decided he had his own problems. Holly would have to fend for herself. Holly, on the other hand, had no plans to find a ride. The walk would be good for her, and it also would mean less time that she would have to spend at the compound.

Harris put the truck into gear and sped off. Holly watched him go and realized she hadn't given him a kiss goodbye. She wondered if it had any significance, as she walked into the hospital.

It was a typical busy day with people hustling around trying to meet the needs of the patients. Holly found her way to the nursery and put her things into a locker. She went about her appointed chores with a lighter heart. Holly enjoyed the repetition of her daily routine. Being a creature of habit suited her personality.

When she reached the nursery itself, Holly noticed that Millie DePont was once again rocking the baby. Holly had spoken to her once and called her Miss Amelia. Millie hadn't corrected her and dismissed Holly with an odd look.

Everyone in northern Florida knew Millie DePont. No one knew her at all, but everyone said they did. It was fashionable to pretend that people had a relationship with the area's most powerful woman.

Holly never considered herself worthy of Amelia DePont's attention. She was content to watch her rock the baby and couldn't help feeling some pangs of jealousy once again. She would never have her own child, let alone be able to rock a grandchild. Life was never fair for the have-nots. Holly wasn't complaining, but she knew it was the truth. Sometimes things weren't fair in life, and this was a big one.

Holly went about her day with a heavy heart. Her workplace had been the one bright spot in her life and hated feeling this way. It gave her much little for the future. When her shift was almost over, Holly slipped back into the nursery and fussed with the babies. She made sure they were changed and swaddled. Four babies were left in the nursery, so her job went along without much fanfare. When she came to the little girl that Miss Amelia had been rocking, she stopped and picked her up. Holly wanted to rock the baby the way Miss Amelia had earlier.

The baby never moved and clung to her chest. Holly would have given all she had to able be to nurse this helpless baby. She knew it could never happen, and it made her sad. Large tears streamed down her cheeks, as she snuggled the baby as closely as she dared. She wiped the tears away, so they wouldn't fall on the baby. She stopped and wondered what the child was named. The child wore a wristband and when Holly glanced at it, all it said was Grafton. She couldn't believe there was no first name and wondered what she would call her if she were hers.

Holly was still pondering a name, when she heard someone coming from across the hall. She placed the baby back into her crib and pretended to swaddle her when Millie walked in.

Millie walked over to the crib and removed the child without saying anything to Holly. Holly made an exit from the room, as Millie sat and began rocking the baby. Holly could hear Miss Amelia singing softly to the child.

She decided to go to her locker and get her things. In her coat pocket, she found the business car for the car dealership. She had a long walk ahead and wanted to be sure they would be open. She used the phone at the nurses' station to call and find out what time they closed.

Holly talked to the salesman, and he told her the car was ready. She could get all the paperwork from the receptionist. They were open until 9:00 that evening. Holly was relieved. It was 4:00, so she would have plenty of time and wouldn't have to hurry. It would give her time to think and do some dreaming. The way her life was shaping up, she needed some dreams to keep her going.

As she walked, her thoughts involved getting away with Harris. If she could get a job at some other hospital far enough away from the Harris family, they might have a chance to make it work. She had that money hidden in the alligator that might get them by. Now they had a car, so maybe with some planning, they could figure out a way to change their lives. Holly knew she had to find a way even if it wouldn't include Harris. Thinking about that part pained her, however, because she thought she loved him. She couldn't imagine living a life without him being in it.

The car dealership was in sight, but Holly stopped and stared at the sky. The thought that had crept into her mind had frightened her at first, but soon enough she was embracing it and wondering if it could be the answer to everything.

She would need to be careful how she presented it to Harris. There was nothing she wanted less than to scare him off before she could prove to him how it could save them.

When she reached the car dealer, she was pleased to see that the car was ready and waiting for her. Even the license plates had been mounted properly. The woman at the desk was pleasant, and within fifteen minutes, she had signed everything and been given a file folder full of paperwork.

Holly got behind the wheel and threw the folder in the back seat. She would go through everything when she got home. The thought that the compound was now her home made her shake. It wasn't her idea of anyone's home. Bad things happened there, and she wanted out.

She hadn't been planning to make such a fast trip back, but she wanted to share her idea while it was fresh in her mind. If she waited too long, she might have second thoughts.

Holly drove the speed limit and turned onto the lane that led to compound. She drove slow enough to try not to kick up much dust, to avoid drawing attention to herself or her new vehicle. It would be nice to have some time with Harris to present her idea.

As she drove into the clearing, Holly could see that the men had not yet returned. She felt relieved. It would give her time to make dinner for Harris. It was something she had forgotten about. The plan was to stop at the Piggly Wiggly on her way back and pick up items for dinner. She hoped there would be something in the trailer to put together for the two of them.

Holly drove next to her trailer and fished the folder out of the back seat. It was important to her to remove the keys from the ignition. It was her car, and any other family member should never think they could take it anytime they pleased. She went into the trailer and straight to the bedroom. She placed the paperwork and her keys on a table next to the bed. Then she changed her clothes into something more comfortable and less industrial.

After looking into the mirror to make sure she looked presentable, she went back into the kitchen. Sitting on the Coleman stove was a pot. The burner had been turned to simmer. A note was left on the table. Holly picked it up and read what it said.

The Harris men expect food to be on the table when they come home. I'm here to help if you need me. All you need to do is ask. It's just tuna and noodles. It's comfort food, and I thought you might need some comfort after…. You'll find peas in the garden. Why don't you pick some and boil them as well? They seem to go well with the tuna. Harris will think you prepared his first meal. I think that's important. Helen.

Holly read the note. It was a very nice thing to do. Maybe she had judged Helen too harshly. She would try and remember to thank her.

The peas were picked and shelled when the Harris men returned. Holly was washing the peas in a bowl next to the sink, as Harris entered the trailer.

"It smells wonderful in here. What's for dinner?"

"Tuna and noodles and peas." Holly motioned toward the bedroom. "For dessert I thought it would be the two of us."

Harris laughed and fell into a kitchen chair.

"I don't know if I have the energy. Last night took almost everything out of me, and today Papa Henry did the same."

"So, what did you work at today?" Holly asked as she put the peas into a pan and placed them on the Coleman stove's other burner.

"Please don't ask me that. I don't want to say, and you don't want to know," Harris answered.

Holly could tell that he was trying not to involve her in the family business, and that made her love him even more. She knew whatever they did, it was more than likely illegal. The more Harris disliked what he did, the easier it would be to share her idea with him. She decided to wait until after dinner when he had eaten and was more relaxed.

When dinner was finished, and the dishes were washed and out of the way, Holly took Harris' hand and led him out to the pond. It was good place for them to be alone. Holly tried to ignore what had happened to her on her wedding night, as they sat on the picnic table where the rape by Papa Henry had taken place. It served to make her resolve that much stronger. Holly decided not to waste any time and get right to the point.

"I want us to leave this place as soon as possible," she said.

She had Harris' attention, and he looked her in the eyes.

"That's what I want too, but we can't just pull up and leave without having some kind of plan."

Holly would never share her stash of three grand in the alligator. She remembered that she wanted to hide it in her new vehicle. That would be easy enough when Harris went to work with his family.

"I know we need to plan. I'll have a good check from the hospital coming this week. We could take the money and find a nice place away from here. I could get a job at a hospital, and you could find work almost anywhere. You have skills that most employers would want." Holly was trying to appeal to her husband's ego.

Harris sat back and stared out over the pond. He needed a little time to wrap his mind around what Holly had said.

"Maybe in a month or two, we could make the break," he said.

"A month or two? We can't wait that long." Holly's voice was firm.

"Why would that be?" Harris asked, with a bit of irritation in his voice.

Holly told him about seeing Miss Amelia in the hospital with a baby. Harris wondered what it had to do with what they were discussing.

"I don't know how this baby is related to her. The last name on the bracelet is Grafton. She seems quite uncomfortable when she's with the child."

"What's this got to do with anything?"

"I told you that I can never have children," Harris nodded, and Holly went on. "This could be the baby we could never have together. I could take it from the hospital when nobody was looking, and we could leave and never come back."

Harris just stared at her.

"Say something," Holly said, after an uncomfortably long time.

"You want to kidnap a baby from a hospital? What kind of bullshit idea is that? We could go to jail for a long time."

"Not if we don't get caught. We could go far enough away to a big city where no one would ever know us." Holly had panic in her voice.

"This isn't something that could be done on the spur of the moment. It would need a lot of planning."

"We don't have enough time for all that. The baby won't stay in the hospital all that much longer. Once they take her home, we won't have a chance." Holly was somewhat encouraged by the fact that Harris hadn't walked away.

"Amelia DePont has a lot of resources available. She is the wealthiest person around these parts. This would be very dangerous if something would go wrong."

Harris stopped talking. Holly waited for him to continue, but Harris was lost in his own thoughts. If they played their cards right, this could be a real windfall for the family. It might put him into better graces with Papa Henry. The needs of the family always came first, and even though

Holly wanted to leave, she was part of the family now. She would do what they decided.

Harris got up and left Holly sitting on the picnic table. He needed to talk to Papa Henry.

10

After some discussion about the naked female body under the canvas in the Branchwater's back room, it was agreed that Fats would take Fran back to the cabin. Zander would stay and tend to the bar until closing. Fats would join him when he felt Fran was mentally strong enough to be left alone. Together, they would once again make the way back to the old copper mine's airshaft to get rid of the body. They had some practice in that regard.

Zander enjoyed his time spent in the bar during the day. It took his mind off things he couldn't control. He was excellent at pouring drinks and talking to the patrons, and that would be enough for the present. Keeping busy kept his mind from wandering back to Aubrey and what might have happened to her. The bar kept him from becoming frustrated and losing control.

It was almost mid-afternoon when his old friends, Bert and Jo Williams, came into the bar for coffee. Zander and Fats had purchased the bar from them years ago, and they had remained friends. Zander was quick to comment on Jo's perky breasts whenever the opportunity showed itself.

"Well, my stars, look who has returned to us from parts unknown," Jo said, as she hooked her arm around Zander and pulled him to her chest.

"Your stars are quite ample it seems," Zander said, with a muffled voice from between Jo's breasts.

"You are still incorrigible." Jo laughed, as she released Zander.

"But he isn't wrong," Bert said and ducked, when Jo swung her arm around trying to connect with his chin.

"Looks like those big boobs are still hampering you from connecting with Bert," Zander said grinning.

"You're just jealous that you've never found a real woman like me." Jo turned around showing off her firm body.

Zander knew she was proud of her body for a woman of her age. In fact, Jo had told him so on countless occasions. Zander smiled at her even though he had lost his own real woman. Everything was still too raw to share with his friends.

"Where's Fats today? I suppose he's on furlough because you've returned," Bert said, as he took a barstool and sat down. Jo stared at him, and he realized the error of his ways. He jumped back up and helped Jo with her barstool.

"Fran wasn't feeling well. He took her back to the cabin. I think he's coming back as soon as he thinks she's feeling better." Zander thought it might not be prudent to involve his friends with the story behind the corpse in the back room.

"It doesn't matter. We can see him anytime. You, however, are seen so infrequently in these parts, that it should call for a celebration," Jo said.

"That sounds like something that might interest me," Zander said.

"Well, let's make a plan," Jo said.

Zander knew it wouldn't be that evening because of his promise to Fats. He was on body duty, and it had to be that night or bad things could happen.

"Let's see how Fran is feeling before we make any commitments."

"That's what I've always admired about you, Zander. You continue to put your friends first."

"You might give me too much credit."

"Nonsense. Remember who knows you. We've been through a lot together."

"That's the truth," Zander said, and poured them both coffees.

"See? You know what your friends want before they even have to tell you."

"It's just coffee. Besides, it's too early in the day for a drink."

"Says you," Bert said, and ducked again as Jo tried to hit him in the jaw.

Zander laughed out loud. Jo was always trying to hit Bert, and as far as Zander knew, she never had found the mark. They were a couple no matter what, and Zander knew they loved each other without exception. Their little song and dance was just for show. Just seeing how they were with each other, Zander was pretty sure they had a robust sex life.

"Hey, I thought you two were going to move to Florida," Zander said.

Bert and Jo had made a trip to the Villages somewhere between Ocala and Orlando. It was a fifty-five and older place.

"We changed our minds. We made a visit, and it's nice. Always something to do and people to meet."

"What's the problem?" Zander asked.

"There aren't any young people. Did you know that no one in the entire place has ever listed their birthplace as the Villages?"

"Why would that be?"

"It's just people our age and older. No one was ever born and raised there, so there are never any young people. Young people keep us young, so we're not ready to make that drastic of a move."

"I don't know, seems like a great place for someone as sedentary as yourself."

"Keep talking. I'm starting to remember how nice it was when you were MIA."

The comment caught Zander off-guard. Jo noticed her joke had hit a nerve.

"I'm sorry I said that." Jo took Zander's hand.

"It's not that. It just reminded me of something."

"What's would that be?" Jo kept holding his hand.

Zander knew he couldn't get out of an explanation. He wasn't sure he wanted to keep it a secret anyway.

"It's just that I found someone, and now I've lost her."

"What does that mean?"

Zander dropped his eyes.

"You've got my interest. You need to tell me everything. You know I won't be leaving until you do."

Zander knew it was true. He spent the next 25 minutes in an abbreviated version of what had happened to him in Florida. He was exceptionally detailed when he spoke of his relationship with Aubrey.

Jo was uncharacteristically quiet during Zander's presentation. Bert listened intently and was already forming a plan before Zander stopped speaking.

"Do you trust this Max fellow?" Bert asked.

"He's trustworthy. Why?"

"It seems to me, that from what you told us, that he has many resources. You should contact him and see if he could help you."

Zander thought about how Max had helped them in Key West and saved Mona Kane from a certain death at the hands of Sara Jane. His stomach turned at the thought of the name. That entire debacle was the result of Fats' meddling in Zander's life. He needed to remember to have a discussion about that little fact with Fats when the right time presented itself.

"That might be a good idea. It's something to consider anyway."

"Nonsense. You need to contact him. The trail might already be cold. You'd hate yourself if there was something you could have done and you failed to do it." Jo was firm.

Zander couldn't argue.

"I don't know how I could contact him. I had his information in a cell phone, but I got rid of it when Aubrey and I made our break."

Jo ran her fingers through her hair.

"If I were you, I'd ask Fats for his help. If I remember right, he had a contact following you when you went down there."

Zander just looked at Jo. He realized she knew much more about what happened to him than she first let on. That damn Fats never could keep his mouth shut.

"It seems like anytime I involve Fats in anything, the whole world seems to know all about everything," Zander said, trying to sound annoyed.

"That's what friends do. Even if you don't want their help, they give it to you anyway. Our lives need those folks that insert themselves into our business, because without them, it would be a pretty sad existence. You've had enough of that in your life already. It's time to reach out, and let people help you for a change," Jo said, and grabbed both of Zander's cheeks.

Zander couldn't help but smile. No one had done that to him since he was a child.

"Thanks, mom. I'll get right on it as soon as you give me my face back."

Jo released him. "You need to get this Aubrey character back here and into your life. She sounds like someone I should get to know."

"That would be the plan. I'm not sure she would be ready for all my nosey friends, however." Zander tried to sound sincere, but his face gave another interpretation.

"Just remember to keep involving your friends in your life, and quit trying to be so secretive. It just gets in the way." Jo turned to Bert. "Come on, we've wasted enough time on this knuckle head."

They both got up from the bar stools and moved to the door.

Zander let his eyes follow after them and blurted out "thanks" which surprised even him.

"Talk to Fats. Get the ball rolling and then let me know when you want me to get your homecoming celebration going. I'll need to some time to get all our friends on board with schedules and everything."

Zander nodded and watched Bert and Jo leave through the front swinging bar doors. He needed to get off his dead ass and stop feeling sorry for himself. Aubrey deserved better. He was still thinking about it, when Fats walked in from the back door.

"Fran retired to find some repose, so I removed myself for a few minutes to see if you needed assistance."

"I don't know, every time you to try to help me everything seems to go to hell."

"I would prefer to make a protestation to this statement, but I cannot."

"I should think not."

"I wish not to start a donnybrook at this moment in time. A cadaver needs our attention before it becomes mummified in our storage area."

Zander rubbed his face with his left hand. He had almost forgotten the body in the back room. He tried not to think of the smell it would create if left there for very long. He had smelled dead bodies in the past and decided he would rather not repeat the experience again.

"What's the plan, Fats? I assume you have thought about how you wish to solve your little problem."

"Little? Did you see the size of that woman's chest? There's nothing insignificant or negligible about the massiveness of those female mountains."

His friend was one of a kind, and he just couldn't stay angry.

"Go back and stay with Fran. Come back at 11:00 with your pickup, and we'll deal with the body after we lock up."

"I will do as you command. However, would you do me a service in the meantime?"

Zander hated commitments, especially when Fats asked for them.

"What would that be?"

"Find some lubrication we can use belatedly to burnish the decedent."

Zander had no idea what Fats had just said. He thought it sounded like some kind of perversion.

"What are you saying? I hope it's not what I think it is. I've heard about people with corpse fetishes. You are not one of them, I hope."

"I am flabbergasted at the thought. Please don't speak of that vision now or anytime in the future. It makes me want to discharge the contents of my stomach through my mouth."

"So why the lubricant?"

"The size of Vera's ta ta's has given me reason for concern."

"I assume that Vera is the dead body in the back. I don't need to know her name, and in fact, the less I know the better off we all will be."

"All you need to know is the size of those babies." Fats held up his hand to mime the size of Vera's breasts.

"Okay, why don't you just tell me what this dialogue means?"

"When we remove the remains and reach the mine's airshaft in the wilderness, we won't be able to dispose of the protoplasm without making the upper body slippery enough to reach the ultimate goal."

Zander understood.

"I see what you are saying. Would a bottle of vegetable oil from the kitchen work?"

"I believe it to be the ultimate solution, my man."

"Good. Go home and come back at 11:00. Don't forget your pickup."

Fats gave him a Boy Scout salute and was out the door before Zander could say another word.

Zander watched him leave. No doubt about it. His friend was weird.

11

Holly went back to work thinking about the baby without talking any more about it with Harris. She assumed he thought it was a bad idea. Maybe it was, but she couldn't help fantasizing what it would be like having a child of her own to nurture and raise. The honeymoon, such as it was, appeared to be over.

Her hospital work was even better than usual. She got to hold a few of the babies and feed them a bottle. The last to get her attention was the Grafton baby. Holly noticed the child's wristband had been changed. On closer examination, she saw that the child had a first name. Sandra Grafton was typed neatly on the little band around the baby's wrist. It was a disappointment to Holly. She had envisioned naming the child when it became hers. It was a silly idea because the last name would be changed anyway. After the morning with Harris, her dreams would not be realized anytime soon.

Holly went about her tasks with a heavy heart. Her life had seemed to be filled with so much promise just a short time ago. Now she wondered how she would be able to survive in the toxic Harris family.

Her thoughts became depressive as she drove home from work. The word "home" wasn't something she had ever considered growing up in foster care. When she felt she had it within her grasp, it seemed to be slipping away faster than she could hold on to it.

Holly drove to the trailer she and Harris shared. The beat-up metal framework wasn't even their own. They were allowed to live in it by Papa Henry. Holly wondered what she would have to do for him in the future just to keep living there. That thought served to deepen her depression.

When she stopped the car, the door to the trailer opened and Harris bounced down the steps to the car. He opened the door. Before Holly could get out Harris put his arms around her, and they fell across the front seat.

"Welcome home Holly, how was your day?" Harris asked and then kissed her.

When Holly caught her breath, she said, "It's better, now that I'm with you."

"I might have some news that will make you even happier. Come inside and let me show you."

They untangled, and Harris got out of the car while helping Holly up. They went into the trailer, and Harris shut the door. Holly had forgotten about her day at the hospital and was eagerly anticipating what surprise was waiting for her.

Harris went into the bedroom and returned with a bag. He set it down in front of Holly, and she wondering what to do next.

"This is for you. Why don't you take it out and look at it?" Harris asked.

Holly opened the bag and pulled out a large backpack. She looked up at Harris with a puzzled look on her face.

"It's a backpack," Harris said, smiling.

"I can see that. What's it for?"

"It's for you. You'll need a place to hide the baby when you take her from the hospital."

Holly was speechless and stood with her mouth open just looking at Harris.

"Have you had a change of heart? I thought you wanted the child," Harris said.

"You didn't say anything, so I thought you didn't like the idea."

"I had to think about it for a while, that's all." Harris dropped his head.

Holly wondered if there was something he wasn't saying but decided not to press the issue. She had a huge weight lifted from her shoulders. She would have a child after all.

"Should I do this tomorrow? Wait, have you thought where we would go after we take the baby?"

"Listen Holly, we have to take this slow. You need to make sure that everyone sees your backpack at work. We can't take any chances that would draw attention. This can't happen right away."

"We can't wait very long, or the mother will be leaving the hospital with the baby. If that happens, we won't have a chance."

Harris thought about what Holly had said. He never considered that the baby might be leaving the hospital that soon.

"How about you try and find out when she will be released?"

"I can try, but that's the doctor's decision. The nurses don't know anything until they are told."

"Then talk to the mother or the grandmother. Maybe you can get the information from them."

Holly thought she might be able to make small talk with Miss Millie when she came to the nursery to hold the baby. She seemed to have warmed up to her the last few days.

"Maybe that will work. Miss Grafton had a hard time with the delivery, so we may have a week at the most."

"Good. That will give us time to make our plans. Just make sure everyone sees you come and go from work with that backpack."

"Okay. I'll do my best," Holly said, and led Harris toward the bedroom. It was time to continue the honeymoon.

When they were finished and lying in each other's arms, Holly realized that her life had taken a turn for the better. She would have a baby soon, and together she and Harris would be leaving this terrible place. She smiled when she thought about how Papa Henry would take the news when he found they had run off.

Harris was the first to get out of bed. He fumbled with his clothes and dressed himself. Holly remained on the bed still cooling down from the sex. Harris glanced at her, as he got dressed.

"You should always be naked just waiting for me to come home."

"Things would have to change as our child grew up, don't you think?" Holly said, playing right along.

Harris' face went dark.

"Maybe this idea of having a kid is a stupid one."

Holly got up and put her arms around Harris. Her naked body pressed against his fully clothed one.

"Don't say that. Our life will be complete with a child that we can love. We need to break the cycle of misery in our lives. We have to give someone a better life than we received.

"I don't know what you mean," Harris said, and removed Holly's arms and pushed her back on the bed.

Holly began to cry.

Harris questioned how to react. Holly was the first woman he had ever known, and he was ill equipped to handle her emotions. He simply turned and went out the bedroom door. Holly heard the trailer door slam a few seconds later and she cried even harder.

After twenty minutes, Holly decided to get out of bed and get dressed. She was hoping that Harris would have returned so they could talk things through. She was never told where he went, but she decided to have dinner ready when he did return. All she could find in the cupboards was some tomato soup. She pulled out two cans and looked at them. This was no way to live. Staying in the compound meant she would need to stop each day and pick up things to eat from the grocery store. Who lived without electricity? Apparently the Harris tribe felt it wasn't prudent to have any government interference in their lives.

Holly opened the cans and put the contents into a pan. She ran some water from the sink and filled the cans with water to mix with the soup. At least they had running water coming in from the wooden water tower. It was a leaky old thing but seemed to work. It was the one time the family used the generator. They would start it up when the tower's water level got low. Papa Henry was always demanding that everyone cut down on the water consumption. He wanted everyone to use the pump at the well. Holly never did. It was her single act of defiance.

She was mixing the water with the tomato soup, when there was a knock at the door. Holly first thought it might be Harris, but she knew he wouldn't be knocking. She put down the spoon she had been using and answered the door. She could see it was Helen through the window. Her heart sank. Dealing with her right now was an intrusion, but knew she had no choice. She opened the door and stood in the doorway.

"Yes?"

"Can I come in?" Helen asked politely.

Holly hesitated and then just moved away leaving the door open for Helen to enter. She went back to stirring the soup.

"You know, it works better when you put some heat to it. The tomato chunks dissolve much easier." Helen was trying to be helpful.

"I'm just trying to save on the gas. It doesn't take as long to heat up when I do it this way," Holly said without any emotion.

"Not much of a meal for our working men."

Holly turned with her hands on her hips.

"It's all we have right now. Maybe if we had some electricity, we could have a refrigerator." There was just a hint of anger in her voice.

"You are dripping soup from that spoon in your hand," Helen said.

Holly turned and put the spoon back into the pan. She kept her back to Helen.

"Why don't you join us for dinner this evening?"

"I don't know where Harris is right now. Besides, I've already open these cans, and I don't want to throw it out."

"I see. Harris is at our trailer right now."

Holly turned with a puzzled look on her face.

"That's why I came to see you," Helen said.

"I told you, I'm not coming for dinner."

"Harris told us what you are planning. I'm just here to tell you not to do it. Nothing good will come from this. It would serve to get us all in trouble."

Holly was exasperated. She couldn't understand why Harris would tell anyone about their plans to anyone in his family.

"We aren't going to involve anyone in this family but Harris and me."

"You are so naïve. We are involved whether you like it or not. I'm here to tell you this is a very bad idea, and it won't turn out the way you think. I'm telling you all this at a great risk to myself."

Holly had no idea what she was talking about. It was beyond her scope of thinking. Abstractions had never been something Holly could grasp.

"I'll do whatever Harris says. He's my husband, and I love him."

Helen looked at her sadly.

"He loves you too. For now, anyway. If I were you, I would get into that little car of yours and leave. I would never look back."

Helen got up and left the trailer. Holly let her eyes follow after her and wondered what she was telling her. She decided to go back to preparing the soup. That was something she could understand.

Thirty minutes later, Harris returned as if nothing had happened. The soup has been simmering on the Coleman stove. Holly turned it up so it would be hot when she served it.

"I'm sorry about dinner. It's all I could find. I'll try to remember to stop at the market after work from now on."

"The soup will be just fine. In fact we'll be just fine when all this business with the baby is complete."

Holly put a bowl of soda crackers on the table. Harris took one and started munching on it. Holly decided not to tell Harris about his mother's visit. She would try not to upset him. It was impossible to know where she stood with Harris any longer. It bothered her that he would share their plans with Helen. She wondered what other family members were in on the secret.

It wasn't a secret any longer.

12

Harris got up before Holly was awake. He made some coffee and found a few eggs from the chicken coop and was frying them when Holly came out of the bedroom.

She noticed the backpack on the chair near the door. Harris saw her look at it.

"I put some of your stuff in it. You can put whatever else you take work into it. Just remember what I told you. Everyone needs to see that you take this to work everyday. If you draw attention to it now, it won't draw attention later."

Holly nodded and sat down to be served her coffee and eggs. The thought of having a baby excited her. It wasn't without apprehension, however. Holly was nervous about getting caught stealing the child from the hospital. It was compounded by her lack of trust in anyone in the Harris family. That included her husband. Things just weren't working out the way she had designed them in her mind. Taking the child was the first step. She would need support from Harris if this was going to work, but questioned whether he could be trusted at the moment. It made her want to just walk away.

"When do we do this?" Holly couldn't make herself say the word "kidnap."

"Well, I suppose it's going to have to be soon. We can't let them leave the hospital. It would screw everything up," Harris replied.

"Friday might be a good day. Everyone on the staff seems to be concerned with the weekend, and they might not be paying as much attention."

Harris thought about what Holly had said.

"It might be a good idea, but I was thinking about late Saturday. Don't they have less staff on duty?"

"That's true for the late shift," Holly said.

"Then you need to volunteer for that shift. In the meantime, get that backpack in front of everyone's face between now and then." Harris stood and moved toward the door.

Holly wasn't finished. She stood and faced Harris.

"What are we going to do after that? Do you have a place we can go?"

"Let me worry about that. I have a plan."

"Don't you think I should know what it is, since I'm taking such a huge risk?"

Harris stopped and turned. Holly saw his face cloud over. He took two steps, raised his open palm, and caught Holly on the face. She staggered backward and fell against the table. Some of the dishes fell to the floor breaking on impact. Holly righted herself and rubbed her cheek. She decided not to let Harris see her cry. She wouldn't give him the satisfaction.

"I make the decisions for the both of us. If I think you should know what is going to happen, I'll tell you. Don't ever question me again."

Holly looked at Harris without showing any emotion. Harris was a little confused with her reaction. He pointed down at the broken dishes.

"Clean up that mess."

Harris bolted out the door and slammed it for his brand of punctuation. Holly decided not to see where he was going. She thought she knew. The moment when Harris struck her changed everything. Now she needed to rethink what her role would be.

• • •

Each day Holly went to work, and each day she became more depressed. Harris would share nothing with her, and the Saturday deadline was looming. She knew she was damned. She wanted the child but never wanted the consequences that might go with abduction.

Saturday came around, and Holly decided it was time to make a stand. She would do as Harris demanded, but after she took the child she would go to the police and explain what she had been forced to do. She knew if she had the child in tow the police would be more likely to believe her story.

Harris had been watching her the past few days and seemed restless. Holly wondered if her demeanor had signaled something. She hoped not.

Holly's shift was from four to midnight. She started getting ready for work at 3:00 and was happy to see that Harris hadn't shown his face. At 3:30 she decided to go to work. When she went to her car, Harris was in the driver's seat waiting for her.

"Get in. I'm driving you to work."

"I thought you didn't want to draw attention to all of this," Holly said, trying to hide her concern.

"Change of plans."

Holly went around the car and found her place on the passenger's side.

"What's going on?"

"It's just a little matter of trust. I want to make sure you do as you are told. I'll be driving you and the baby home later."

Holly spent the trip to the hospital in silence. She kept going over everything in her mind and just couldn't get a real grasp on anything. Harris kept his head looking straight ahead and said nothing.

They reached the hospital, and Harris parked the car in the employees' lot adjacent to the entrance. He turned and spoke to Holly.

"At 11:40, just before your shift ends, you will take the baby and put her in the backpack. Try not to make any noise. You'll use a back entrance the employees use to smoke. I'll be there to pick up the baby. You'll go back to work and clock out at 12:00 like usual. Before you do, go back to the same entrance. Your backpack will be under one of the tables. Your car will be in the parking lot with the keys in it. You drive it back to the compound like usual."

Holly thought the plan was stupid.

"Since you brought me to work, wouldn't it be better to pick me up as well?"

Harris thought about punching her in the face. He knew that she couldn't have marks on her for people to notice, so he just grabbed her by the hair.

"Have you forgotten what I told you? I'm in charge here, and you will do as I say."

Harris never said "or else," but Holly got the message anyway. She removed herself from the car and entered the hospital. At least she wouldn't have to be around Harris for the next few hours. That was one bright spot in a myriad of very dark ones.

Holly's shift seemed to race by and before she knew it the clock read 11:30. She decided to go to the nursery and check on the babies. Hoping in her heart that the Grafton baby would be gone. Hoping for things never paid off for Holly.

Sandra Grafton was sleeping peacefully in her crib. The hospital was quiet, and Holly decided to take the baby to the smokers' doorway in her arms. The backpack would not be used, because she worried about smothering the child. It was late, and she knew there wouldn't any smokers that time of the night. Holly stood in the doorway with the door cracked open, until she saw her car drive up to the edge of the picnic tables. Harris stayed in the car, and Holly went out to him.

Harris was angry.

"Where's the backpack?"

"I didn't need it. It's all very quiet tonight. I didn't want to smother the baby."

"Put her in the back and throw something over her."

Holly placed the baby on the back seat floor. She was swaddled in a blanket so Holly knew she would be fine.

"You need to drive slowly so you don't harm her."

"Shut up and get back in there."

Harris took off and was out of sight before Holly could turn around and re-enter the hospital. She had an awful feeling.

At midnight, Holly clocked out and said goodbye to the night nurse. She walked out of the hospital with her backpack just like usual. When she reached the employee parking area, she searched for her car.

It wasn't there.

Holly had no idea about what to do. It was too far to walk back home, and she couldn't ask anyone for help without giving away the location of the Harris compound. She went over to a bench and sat down. She would need to think this thing through.

Thinking things through helped make things clearer in Holly's mind. This time there wasn't any clarity. She had no idea about how to proceed. She checked her watch and saw that it was just past 12:30. She had been sitting on the bench for almost a half hour. Holly wasn't one to panic, but there was something working deep inside. It concerned her so much that she started to cry. It was an emotion that was foreign to Holly. She reached into her backpack to try to find something to wipe her eyes. Holly found a small package of tissues. A car turned into the parking lot as she was opening the package. It was her car, and it Harris was driving.

Holly got up and sprinted toward the vehicle dragging her backpack on the ground. She no energy to even lift it to her shoulders.

Harris parked the car in a vacant slot and kept the motor running. Holly went over to the passenger side and tried to open the door. It was locked and Harris was just staring through the windshield. She knocked on the window to try and get his attention. Harris squinted at Holly and lowered the side window.

"I should have just left you here. You can't seem to follow directions can you?"

Holly said nothing.

"That little stunt with the backpack could have messed this whole thing up. What if someone had seen you take the baby out the door? I'm not planning to go to prison because you are too stupid to follow a few simple directions." Harris was fuming.

Holly decided it would be in her best interest to keep her mouth shut. Harris had hit her a few times, and it hadn't been a pleasant experience. She waited until he was finished berating her.

"I'm sorry Harris. You are right. I'm sorry I'm so stupid."

Holly said the words to help Harris to calm down. She could never believe any of them. Although, she realized she was stupid for getting involved with the Harris family in the first place. Maybe she was just too naïve. In any event, the apology seemed to make Harris a little calmer. He opened the door for Holly.

"Get in," he growled.

"Where's the baby?" Holly asked, quietly.

"She's safe with the family. I'll take you to her. What's her name?"

"Sandra Grafton. That was on her bracelet. You and I will have to come up with a new name."

Harris had a vacant look on his face but failed to say anything. He put the car into gear and moved toward the entrance of the parking lot. Before he could pull out into the street, both he and Holly saw three police cruisers coming their way with lights blazing and sirens wailing.

One of the cruisers pulled in front of Harris' car effectively blocking him. Harris put the car into park, and Holly could see panic creeping over his face.

"Harris. Pull yourself together. Let me do the talking. Just relax. This could be just the thing that helps to eliminate us as suspects. Harris looked at Holly and took a deep breath but said nothing. Holly liked that. She was in control, and that was always better.

The officer came to the car and knocked on Holly's window. She found the switch and lowered it.

"Hello, officer. How can we help you?"

"What are you doing here this time of the night?"

"I work here at the hospital, and my husband is picking me up. My name is Holly and he's Harris."

"I'll need you two to get out of the vehicle and step to the front."

Holly and Harris got out and moved to the hood of the car.

"What's going on officer?" Holly asked.

"I'll ask the questions. I'll need both your licenses and registration."

Harris pulled out his billfold and handed his license to the officer. He checked it over with the help headlights from Holly's car and handed it back. Then he nodded at Holly.

"My license is in my backpack and the registration is in the glove box."

"Get them please and bring out the backpack."

Holly retrieved the items and handed everything over. The policeman took his time going through the backpack and looking at the paperwork. He handed everything back to Holly. He turned and looked right at Harris.

"Pop the trunk."

Harris reached into the car and pulled out the keys. He went to the trunk and opened it finding nothing inside but a spare tire and a jack. The officer shined a large flashlight into the trunk to get a better look. When he finished, he did the same to the interior of the car. Holly thought he must have been a good police officer, because he seemed very thorough. She was very relaxed and hoped her behavior would help Harris to remain calm.

When the officer finished with his search, Holly decided to speak.

"Can you tell us what's going on?"

"There seems to be an abduction of a child from the hospital."

"Oh no, that's terrible. I need to get back in there. Maybe I can help." Holly was good at role-playing.

"Not tonight. No one is going in or going out unless there is an emergency. We are locking the place down until we can figure out what happened."

"I understand," Holly said.

"You will need to be available for questioning tomorrow."

"My shift starts at noon. You can find me here, or I could come to the police station earlier."

"No, we will want you to walk us through your shift. Hopefully, this will all be settled before that."

"I hope so. Can you tell me which baby was taken?"

"I'm sorry, I can't discuss anything with you until tomorrow."

"Okay, I'll see you then." Harris and Holly got back into the car and waited for the police officer to move his vehicle.

When they were safely on the road, Holly sat back and smiled. She changed her mind about the police officer. He wasn't very thorough at all. No one would allow potential suspects or witnesses to leave the scene like that. It would give them time to work out their stories.

One thing was certain. Holly wasn't planning on returning to work. The night's encounter had changed all that.

13

Jayne woke up from a deep sleep. She heard some commotion in the hallway outside her door. She found the button to summon the nurse's station and pressed it. No one came. Jayne was used to being the center of attention because of Millie's status in the community. She never had to wait for anything.

"What's going on out there?"

No one responded. Jayne's mid-section still hurt like hell. She wasn't excited to get up and find out what all the commotion was about. Just getting out of bed to use the bathroom still took effort. This would be something unneeded right now but "not knowing" had always been a huge motivator in her life. If she took it slow, she just might be able to make it to the door without pain. It was worth a try, and she was getting sick of being an invalid.

Jayne swung her legs past the collapsed steel rack of her hospital bed. It was a meticulous and cautious process. Her feet touched the floor as the door burst open, and Millie flipped on the overhead light.

"What do you think you're doing? Get back into bed." Millie said the words but there was no life in them.

"What's going on out there? Sounds like the entire place is in a panic," Jayne said.

Millie sighed and sat in the recliner next to the hospital bed. She rubbed her temples with both hands.

"Jayne, there's something you need to know. Your child has gone missing."

The words hit Jayne right between the eyes, and she fell back on the bed. Millie got up and helped to move her legs back onto the bed. Neither said a word. Millie couldn't stand the silence.

"The police think it's a kidnapping." Millie's face fell.

"Kidnapping? Why? Who would want my child?"

Millie thought about what she should say.

"Somebody who wants to get into my pockets. We didn't keep a very tight lid on your relationship to me."

Jayne felt the anger rising in her chest.

"Has there been a ransom demand?"

"Not yet. But I'm sure it will come. The staff thinks someone took Sandra between 12:00 and 12:30. One of the aides saw her, before she checked out at midnight."

"What time is it now?"

"It's after two."

"And you are just telling all this to me now?"

"I just found out myself. No one noticed anything until 12:45 when the nurse made her rounds."

"I should have been told." Jayne was hot.

"What would you have done? You can hardly get out of bed."

"Why would they call you before they told me? I'm the mother for God's sake."

"Maybe because people know me, and I have resources. They don't know you and don't know how you would react."

"Where are the police in all this?"

"They are following protocol. The FBI has been contacted." Millie looked down.

Jayne realized that Millie wasn't telling her everything.

"What else?"

Millie looked over and thought about how much she should tell Jayne. The police told her that the first twelve hours were crucial. After that, the chances of finding the child alive would diminish with each passing hour.

"I'll be speaking with the FBI as soon as they arrive. We need to expedite the process of finding her. The longer it takes, the worse the odds for the child."

Jayne couldn't explain the panic she was experiencing. She hadn't bonded with Sandra. In fact, she knew Millie had been doing a better job in that respect. It was just that this was her child, and now someone took something that belonged to her. She couldn't tolerate the thought. She sat up and spoke to Millie.

"What does Zander know?"

The question took Millie by surprise.

"I've not told him anything about you or the child. Have you been in contact with him?"

"Of course not, and I expect it to remain that way."

"Then there wouldn't be any way he could be involved in this. He's the baby's father, so I'm not making any promises about what may happen in the future. We may need his help before this is all over. Right now, we've got concentrate on the problem at hand without these other distractions."

"I feel so helpless."

"As does everyone else. Just so you know, I've enlisted Hector and the other men in my employment to comb the area and keep their eyes open. If anyone talks about this they will know."

"It's something, I guess."

"It's everything until we know more. The sheriff wants to know if you are up to answering some questions."

"It looks like there won't be any more sleep tonight. Send him in."

Millie stood and reached over and took Jayne's hand.

"We'll get through this. Nothing bad will happen to little Sandra, I guarantee it."

"But it already has, hasn't it?"

Millie dropped her hand and left the room without saying anything else to Jayne. Nothing else was to be said.

The sheriff was waiting outside the door talking to the nursing staff.

"She's all yours," Millie said.

"How's she taking the news?"

"As expected."

"I'll try to go easy."

"That won't be a problem. I just hope she goes easy on you." Millie smiled tiredly at the sheriff. "Do you have anything more for me?"

"Not right now. I'll get in touch if the FBI needs anything."

"I'll be going home, then. My guess is that if this is a ransom, someone will try to contact me there."

"We've already put in the request for a phone tap, so you might hear some clicks when you try to use the phone."

Millie left the hospital. Her tired feet were a distraction. When she got to her car, she noticed someone sitting in the driver's seat. She walked closer and saw that it was Rosita, Hector's wife.

"Rosita, what are you doing here?"

"Hector didn't think you should be driving tonight, so he brought me over to take you back home."

"I don't know what I would do without you," Millie said, as she climbed into the passenger's seat of her Cadillac.

"We know," Rosita said, and smiled to break the tension.

"You know, Rosita, I've got about everything anyone could want in this life. But I'd trade a hundred of these Cadillacs to get my grandchild back."

"Maybe that's what these animals want. I can't understand why anyone would take a child."

"Desperation maybe. I just don't know. Most of us never think that way."

Rosita put the car into drive, and they rolled along the highway towards Millie's estate. They were both silent during the ride. When they reached the main gate, Rosita opened the window to put the key into the override for the gate. Millie stopped her. She saw a paper sticking out between a few bars in the wrought iron gate.

"Rosita, stop please. Something is stuck there on the gate."

Millie retrieved the paper. She pulled out an envelope and took it back to the car.

"Turn on the dome light please, Rosita."

She did so.

The envelope was addressed to Miss Mildred DePont. It was hard to read because her name was spelled out in newsprint with different sized letters and fonts. It was something Millie had expected. The content of the letter was brief. Something about the baby being safe, and she would be contacted with the terms at a later time. The last sentence said she should not involve law enforcement.

Millie got back into the car.

"Rosita, drive me back to the hospital. I need to talk to police." Millie never liked being told what to do. She would be in control, so this contrary behavior might have been predicted if these kidnappers had known her better. That was a clue in itself and something she would share with the FBI.

After visiting with law enforcement, Millie went back to Jayne's room. She was back in bed but had raised the mattress to almost a sitting position. Millie charged into the room and sat down on the chair next to the bed.

"Can't sleep?"

"How about you?" Jayne asked.

"Good point."

"There was a letter stuck on my gate when I got home."

"A ransom?"

"Not yet. Just a threat of one."

"Can I see it?"

"The FBI has it. I'm sure they'll share it with you when they're ready. It doesn't tell us much."

"What if they ask for a huge amount of money? What will we do?"

"You'll do nothing. I'll pay the damn thing. Then when we get Sandra back, I'll find them and make them pay."

Jayne liked what she heard. It was the realization that she and her mother had many things in common. Revenge was an emotion that ran first and foremost with them both.

"Just make sure you let me help you with that part of it," Jayne said.

Millie glanced at her but said nothing. The larger question of what had a bigger influence on personality always seemed to pop up. Some felt that environment was the bigger factor, but from what Millie observed, it was genetics. Millie shared much with her daughter, even though she hadn't been there for Jayne's formative years. It made Millie wonder if Sandra would be more like them or her father. The thought made her sit up.

"I'm going back home. I can't let Rosita keep waiting for me. I'll be back tomorrow."

"It's already tomorrow."

Millie checked the clock on the wall.

"So it is. I'll be back before noon."

On the drive back, Millie thought more about the father. She had the number of his answering service and weighed the idea of calling it. She would try and sleep on the idea for a few hours. It wasn't something she would do on a whim. When other people became involved there were always consequences. This would be concern because Zander knew nothing about Jayne's pregnancy or the delivery of his child. That was something to ponder.

As she crawled into bed, she already knew what would be done. That decision allowed her to fall asleep.

14

Fats walked into the Branchwater at 11:15. A few locals were sitting at the bar, but the rest of the place was empty. Zander was sweeping the floor and moving tables and chairs back into place.

Fats took his place behind the bar and decided to address the remaining customers.

"Drink up you soothsayers of doom. It is past time for the apocalypse, and you should find repose with your family of dominion."

The few guys at the bar were used to Fats' diatribes. They finished their drinks, however. It was never any use trying to discuss things with Fats when he made up his mind. Things just got more convoluted when they tried.

Fats locked the door after ushering the threesome out the front.

"Are you ready to erase the evidence this fine fortnight?" Fats asked Zander.

"Did you bring the Cameo?"

"Of course not. That vehicle is a classic, and what is more germane, it doesn't possess four-wheel drive. We will use your pickup for this clandestine project. You also have a cover on your bed of transport which will serve to enshroud the cadaver."

Zander quit what he was doing and handed Fats the broom.

"Planning to sweep this whole thing away cleanly, are we?"

"But of course. With your help, naturally," Fats said.

"Why does it always feel like I'm the one putting myself out there, when the problems are generated by you?"

"Kismet. Happenstance. Consequence. Destiny. Predestination. Harvest the euphemism which is most appropriate."

"What do you do, memorize the Webster's dictionary so you can impress me with your vocabulary?" Zander asked, not letting Fats try to baffle him with his bullshit.

"Not just you. What would be the point? You know me."

Zander had made his point, and Fats calmed down.

"Fran is settled in for the night. We were watching a movie, and she fell asleep. I'll be back at her side before she wakes."

"How's she doing?" Zander asked.

"Thanks for asking. She's doing better. We talked about everything, and she knew she had no other options. I told her we would make this all go away, so I suppose we'd better do what I promised."

Zander couldn't help but like his strange friend. The fact that he put himself into almost all of his friends' business did serve for a huge amount of frustration. Zander knew his heart was in the right place. He had been saved a few times by Fats' interferences. He wasn't about to tell him more than necessary, however.

"How do you wish to proceed?" Zander asked, because he wanted Fats to take the lead.

"What do you think?" Fats responded how Zander thought he would.

"Oh no. This is your mess. I'll help you out, but you make the decisions."

Fats scratched his chin.

"I think we should clean up the place and get ready for tomorrow. After midnight, we can take the body up to the mine's airshaft."

Zander nodded in agreement. Together they worked until 12:15. Zander filled a glass with beer from the tap. Since they were in the Rocky Mountains, the beer of choice was a glass of Coors from the tap. Fats followed suit, and they drank in silence.

"This next step is critical," Fats said.

"Why don't you explain?"

"We need to remove the body from the back room and into your truck without anyone seeing."

"What's the plan?" Zander was enjoying putting Fats in the hot seat.

"You pull the body and tarp to the back door. I'll go around the front and check to see if anyone is around. Then, I'll go around the building, wait until I think everything is clear, and knock on the door. Then we'll load the body into the pickup and go."

Zander stroked his chin pretending to consider the options.

"Where's the pickup parked?"

"Out back."

"How far is it from the back door?"

"I see your point. I'll need to back it up to the door."

Zander rubbed his chin once more, and he could see the move was starting to irritate Fats. So he did it again.

"That seems to work for me except for one detail."

"What's that?" Fats seemed impatient.

"You will be the one to drag the body from the back room. I'll be the one to check out the surroundings and move the pickup to the back door."

"Why is that?"

"It's your shitstorm. It's my pickup, and I have the keys. You will be doing most of the heavy lifting."

Fats knew it was true, and Zander couldn't blame him for trying. That was just how he rolled.

"Let's go," Fats said, as he moved toward the back room.

Zander let himself out the door and locked it behind him. The street was almost deserted. A were a few cars were parked around the bar down the street, but there was no movement. Zander walked down the block and turned the corner. All the houses were dark. The occupants were in bed or gone. Zander turned into the alley that led to the back of the Branchwater. He got into his pickup and backed it up to the back door.

Fats waited patiently, and when Zander knocked, he opened the door. Together they hoisted the heavy tarp into the bed of the pickup. Fats closed the tailgate, while Zander rolled and secured the cover over the top of the pickup's bed.

"Damn, that woman was solid," Zander said.

"You don't know the half of it. Let's get out of here."

They rode in silence out of Frisco. They headed south to Breckenridge and once they were past the city lights, Fats felt he could breathe once again.

"Almost there, "he said to himself.

Zander ignored the comment.

Fats yelled out.

"Stop. We've got to go back."

"We are not going back. What is with you anyway?"

"I forgot the vegetable oil." Fats' voice was full of panic.

"We are not going back. We'll improvise if needed."

Fats nodded, but Zander could see his hands shaking. Fats had a way of pretending to have this nonchalant personality, but Zander knew he was high-strung.

"Relax. We've got this. It's going to be fine. The worst thing we could do now is panic."

Fats said nothing and peered out into the darkness.

Zander turned off the hard surfaced road and onto gravel. He knew that the entrance to the mine's airshaft was a few miles ahead. He decided to engage Fats in some conversation.

"Tell me more about this woman in the back."

Fats looked at him like he was insane.

"Was she good in bed?"

"No, man. We aren't talking about the dead. What's wrong with you?"

"I'm in my pickup with a dead body of a woman, that you and Fran killed in a bar that I used to own, and you ask what's wrong with me?"

"Point taken. Let's just say the woman was bat-assed crazy, and that's why I'm in this predicament."

"Remind me again why this should be my predicament as well?"

"I always share everything with my friends," Fats said and then smiled at Zander.

Zander realized he was almost back to normal. He was smiling to himself when they reached the gate that led to the mountain path. Zander remembered how hard it had been to climb the steep ruts that served as the road. He stopped and switched the transmission into 4-wheel drive.

"Fats, go open the gate. I'll drive through, and then you close it behind us."

Fats opened the door and struggled to get the rusted gate open enough for the pickup to pass through.

Zander drove through, and Fats closed the gate. It closed much easier than it opened.

"I could have used some of that vegetable oil on the hinges."

Zander ignored the comment.

"Almost there. Hold onto your ass. This is going to be rough."

Fats grabbed onto the handle above the side window of the pickup. He remembered his last ride up this road. This was much better, because he had been in the back of a jeep with The Rooster's body. Fats had killed the guy by sticking the sharp end of a walking stick into his left eye. He hadn't concerned himself with the killing because it had been self-defense. The Rooster was trying to kill him and his friends. The thought made him stop and think about it some more. He had said "friends," but that wasn't quite true. It was his friend Zander but also the bitch Sara Jane. It would have been better if they had thrown two bodies down the airshaft that night. The one they missed was Sara Jane, and she had come back to haunt them again and again.

Zander held onto the wheel as tightly as possible, as they bounced and scraped up the hill.

"If this damages my pickup, you'll be paying," Zander said.

"Bill me," Fats replied.

They reached the outcropping of rocks that hid the airshaft to the mine below. Zander stopped the truck next to the rocks making sure the front of the pickup was pointing downward. There was no need in having the body slide down the hill as they tried to remove it from the pickup's bed.

Together, Zander and Fats opened the cover exposing the body to the night sky. Fats took his flashlight and found his way over to the airshaft. He shined it over the area, and then he picked up a stick and disappeared from view. When he reappeared, he was holding the stick partway from one of the ends.

"What's up, Fats?"

"Took a measurement of the shaft. She's got to clear this much." He showed Zander the measurement.

Zander shook his head.

"You'd better get a move on, then. I don't want to be out here all night."

Fats jumped into the pickup and fumbled around with the stick until he seemed satisfied.

"It's going to be tight. I wish we had some lubricant."

"I've got a quart of 10w40 under the seat. It's got great viscosity." Zander always liked that word.

"Are you insane? We can't put motor oil on her. It would be a desecration of the body."

"I'm confused. What's the difference between vegetable oil and motor oil?"

"Vegetable oil is plant-based,"

Zander didn't have the heart to tell Fats that petroleum was, at one time, plant- based as well. He knew it would be like talking to a wall once his mind was made up.

"Tell me what you want. Do you want this woman's body stuck partway in the mineshaft, or do you want her to join your buddy the Rooster down there?"

Fats went to the front seat to search for the oil. Zander smiled to himself. Sometimes Fats had to weigh all the options before he could move on.

When he returned, Fats had the quart of oil in his hand.

"Let's get this done," he said and dropped the oil next to the body.

Fats and Zander pulled and pushed and did everything they could to get the body over the rocks. When they had Vera in place, Fats took the oil and smeared it over her chest and butt knowing that those two points were the areas of most resistance. When he was finished, he handed the oil to Zander, and started to push the body into the shaft.

"Wait a minute," Zander said.

He shined his flashlight around the entrance and poured the remaining oil on the rocks that served as the opening of the airshaft. He took his hand and rubbed it all over the area then dropped the empty oil container into the hole.

"Now we do this."

They pushed the woman headfirst into the shaft. They stopped when they realized that her arms had to go first. When that task was accomplished, they began to work the body into the shaft. Fats had been correct when he said it would be a tight fit.

Vera's chest was pliable enough and with just a bit of pushing they got her breasts past the point of resistance. Her hips were another matter. She was stuck in the hole at her waist with her legs sticking straight in the air.

"There's one thing to do," Fats said and took the tarp and put it over the exposed part of Vera's body.

Zander watched him with some fascination. He wondered what he was planning.

Fats started pushing on her legs with out any luck. The legs were moving, and he couldn't get a solid grip. Realizing he couldn't get enough weight on the legs to move her, he let the tarp slide down between her legs and placed his foot into her crotch. With one foot on the rocks, he put some weight on the body and tried to force it down into the cavern below. At first there was resistance, but as Fats put more weight on his crotched foot the body began to move.

Once the movement began, it went faster than Fats anticipated. Zander heard a sucking sound as her hips and butt slid through the hole. Fats hadn't shifted his weight back to the foot on the rocks fast enough and lost his balance. His legs went into the hole, and he scrambled to catch a rock before he followed the body into the recesses below.

Zander watched him with fascination. He wondered how many feet it was to the floor of the cavern. He thought it might be a long way, and he had come without rope to throw down if Fats lost his grip.

Fats decided not to move because the rocks were slippery from the oil.

"You had to oil everything, didn't you?" Fats sounded peeved.

"Hey, I didn't know you were going to jump all over her."

"Are you going to help me out of here or just talk me to death?"

"Still considering the options."

Fats tried to reach out a hand, but started to slip further into the hole. Zander knew it was time to stop tormenting him. The tarp hadn't followed Vera into the shaft, and Zander took one end and fed it down to Fats.

"Grab onto the tarp. I'll pull you up."

Fats made a grab with the hand he had tried to give to Zander and caught the tarp. He transferred his other hand onto the tarp and Zander began to pull him up. The canvas was awkward, and Zander was struggling to get it past the rocks.

"Help me out here. You're dead weight. Use your feet and try to get a toe-hold somewhere."

Fats followed direction and, what seemed like an eternity, Zander got him to the top.

"Damn, I thought I was a goner there for a minute."

"You almost were. That wasn't the most intelligent thing you ever did."

"It's right up there with all the other shit I've done. But here I am." Fats started to fold up the tarp.

"What are you doing?" Zander asked.

"I'm taking this thing home. It might be one of my lucky charms."
Zander pulled it from his arms."

"You'll do no such thing. That's evidence. What if someone comes looking for her, and they find this thing with her blood or DNA on it?"

"Hadn't thought about it."

"Seems to be the story of your life."

Fats tossed the tarp into the shaft. It stuck into the mouth of the hole.
"You had to fold it didn't you?"

Fats shrugged and started to put his foot on the tarp to force it down.
"Damn it Fats, stop."

"I don't want to go down that road again" Fats said and pulled back his foot.

Zander took a large rock and threw it down on the tarp with both hands. It served the purpose, and the tarp and rock disappeared from sight. As the rock hit the bottom of the shaft, there was a loud sound. Fats thought it sounded like a bat hitting a softball. He felt sick, when he thought of Vera's body and the rock.

"Let's get out of here," Fats said walking toward the pickup.

Zander thought it was an excellent idea. He was happy to have this behind him. Maybe he could concentrate on what to do about Aubrey. Things couldn't get much worse.

That was before he went back and checked his answering service.

15

Millie awoke with a start. She had been dreaming about the events of the night and wasn't certain it had been a dream at all. She would have liked to explain things away with a dream, but she knew it couldn't be done. Many things needed her attention, and she had to get started.

She decided, that before anything else, she would contact the father. She went to her purse and found the information she got from Jayne's sister. She knew that his name was Sander Van Zee but went by the nickname of Zander.

She had an old, black, rotary Bakelite phone. It was just fine for her needs, and she dialed the number that was listed in her notes. When the answering service operator picked up, Millie left the message that she had a job for the man called Zander. She gave the operator all the other necessary information with the best time to contact her.

Millie needed to speak with Zander. She also realized that if she had shared any more information it might easily scare him off. If she had the time, she would have chartered a plane and talked to him face to face. That wasn't possible, and it was better that she had some time to think about what she would say to this Zander character.

When she returned to the hospital, Jayne was sitting on the bed dressed in her street clothes.

"What do you think you are doing?" Millie asked louder than she had intended.

"I'm going back home with you. I feel helpless just laying here."

"Are you sure you're up to it?" Millie softened her tone.

"We'll find out, won't we?"

"I suppose that's true. Have you been released by the staff?"

Jayne stood and wobbled a bit. Millie reached out to steady her, but Jayne pushed her hand away.

"The doctor told me I could leave if I could navigate out of here on my own. So that's what I'm going to do."

"I can't believe she would say something like that."

Jayne smiled.

"She didn't have much choice. I think she said something to the effect of "like mother, like daughter."

Millie couldn't help but smile herself. She knew there was truth in that statement.

"Well, let's get going." Millie took Jayne's small suitcase from the bed.

"Give me that. I'm supposed to be self-sufficient."

"Not a chance. You don't need anything ripping apart because you were being stupid. I'll take this to the car and pick you up out front. You just take it slow and no steps. Take the elevator."

Jayne moved slowly. It wasn't because she wanted to, but she was weak and still hurting. She had quit taking the painkillers because it made her groggy and then couldn't think straight. She needed all her faculties to get through this latest turn of events.

When she reached the car, Millie got out and opened the passenger door. She was about to help Jayne into the car, when Jayne stopped her.

"I'll do this on my own, if you don't mind."

"Whatever you say." Millie returned to driver's seat.

Jayne lowered herself into the car and shut the door. Millie waited patiently and drove off after Jayne buckled up.

"If that seatbelt is too uncomfortable you don't have to use it. I'm going to drive slowly and avoid all the bumps that I can."

"It's the law, and I'm not sure I trust your driving." Jayne looked out the window.

Millie was amused by her daughter's hard-core approach. She knew that Jayne was hurting, but she also knew she would never admit to it. That would show weakness, and it was a trait they both shared.

There were no other words spoken on the way back to the estate. Millie thought about it and realized that it was now her daughter's estate also. It would be her granddaughter's place as soon as they got her back. It was some comfort she could hold onto until the baby would be returned. Millie knew that she would be returned.

They drove up the driveway, still in silence. Millie got out and retrieved Jayne's bag from the rear seat. Jayne opened the car door but remained in the seat.

"I believe I could use some help getting out of this seat," Jayne said grudgingly.

"I thought you wanted to do this on your own." Millie was enjoying seeing Jayne struggle to ask for help.

"That was at the hospital. We're home now, and nobody can see me."

"Should I be concerned that you're not ready to be home?"

"You should not concern yourself with any thoughts of that nature. I'm able to take care of myself."

"We'll see." Millie opened the door and set the bag inside. "Well, are you coming inside or are you just going to sit there?"

Jayne looked straight ahead, fuming. She knew what she had to do, and it made her angry. She had never asked for help from anyone for anything. It galled her to do it now.

"Could you please help me out of this car?" Jayne asked without looking at Millie.

"I would be happy to help you," Millie said.

She helped Jayne out of the seat and put her arms around her.

"We are a family now. It is not beneath either of us to ask for help."

"It's easy for you to say, you didn't just lose your daughter."

The minute the words came out of Jayne's mouth she was sorry. Millie had lost her daughter for many years, and she knew what Jayne was feeling.

"I know you didn't mean that," Millie said, and helped Jayne to the door.

There were no steps, and both women were thankful for that small piece of luck.

"I'm sorry. I just don't know why I say things like that."

"It's a family trait. We don't have a filter between our thoughts and tongue. It's something I have to work on."

"It appears I need work as well. Will you forgive me?"

"Not another word about it. It's forgotten already."

Millie helped Jayne into the house. She saw Rosita hurrying toward the house waving her hand.

"What is it Rosita? What's wrong?"

"Hector found this stuck in the gate a little bit after you left this morning," she said, trying to catch her breath.

"Come inside. Let's see what this is all about," Millie said.

She knew what it was before she opened the envelope. The same newsprint with her name was on the front.

"Did Hector see anyone?" Millie asked.

"He went up and down the road hoping to see someone leaving, but he saw nothing."

"Thank you, Rosita. If I need you for anything, I'll come and get you," Millie said, as she ushered Rosita out of the door.

"You were a bit short with her, don't you think?" Jayne asked.

"It was by design. I'm sure this is the ransom note, and the fewer people involved the better. We'll have time to enlist help from Hector and Rosita later."

Jayne was standing, and Millie realized she needed to sit down. They walked into the living room, and both sat on a couch. Jayne needed to see what was in the letter, but Millie put it down on the coffee table. She got up and moved toward the kitchen.

"Don't touch that letter. I'm going to get some rubber gloves. The envelope is worthless because everyone touched it. We might be able to get some prints from the actual letter, however."

Jayne was impressed. She hadn't given any thought about fingerprints.

16

Zander and Fats rode back to Frisco in silence. Zander was thinking about his next move in regard to Aubrey's disappearance. Fats had other things on his mind. It was hard for him to comprehend what Fran was going through. Killing Vera had been the right thing to do, but shooting someone always took a toll on the person who had to do the deed. He knew all about it, and he was opposed to any type of killing unless it was necessary. This had been necessary, but no easier. Fats wished he had pulled the trigger.

"Let's forget about going back to bar. I need to check on Fran." Fats sounded concerned.

Zander realized he hadn't made any plans concerning where he would be staying.

"I can drop you off. I'll need to check into a hotel."

"What are talking about? You'll stay at your place."

"I don't want to get in the way. You and Fran have things to work out."

Fats looked at Zander like he had lost his mind. Then he realized that he hadn't told him about the change in their housing. Zander had graciously allowed them to stay at cabin when he left for Florida. Fats knew it was temporary, however. At least he was hoping that's how it would be.

They had found a cabin within a stone's throw from Zander's. Fran had worked non-stop to make it into a homey little place. It was all the two of them would need. The cabin's walls were made from large logs and served to keep the place cool in the summer and warm in the winters. It was a true Rocky Mountain cabin and mirrored Zander's place.

After Fats explained the situation, Zander felt some comfort in the fact he could stay in his place. He tried to put the memory that he had shared it with Sara Jane for a brief time out of his mind.

"What are the plans for tomorrow?"

"Business as usual," Fats said.

"Maybe you ought to rethink that idea. Fran may need you. You've both had a quite a scare, and I don't think you've been using the best judgment. Take the time you need, and let me take care of the Branchwater until you both recover."

"Thanks, Zander. You're a real friend," Fats said.

They were traveling south of Breckenridge and heading back to the cabins north of Frisco. Zander hit the brakes hard and swerved to the shoulder. He put the pickup into park and turned to Fats.

"What the hell?" Fats asked.

"This Vera woman. Was she alone when she came into the bar?"

"Well, yeah. I think I told you that."

"But was she traveling alone?"

Fats realized what Zander was asking. He knew there was always a chance that there could be a witness. Fats seemed pretty sure that was not the case.

"She was pretty much a loner. Hell, I'm sure she ended up killing whatever friends she had. I don't think we need to worry about any witnesses."

"Then we have another problem."

"What would that be?"

"How did she get to Frisco?"

The comment made Fats think. He rubbed the bridge of his nose feeling a headache coming.

"I see the conundrum. Why do you feel you always need to rain on my parade?"

"Because your parades are always short term, and you've never provided a staging area."

Fats knew Zander was checking into his hippie lingo and decided not to play along.

"What now?"

"Didn't you say she came from South Dakota?"

"That's right."

"We need to go back to Frisco and look for a vehicle with South Dakota plates."

"Then what?" Fats decided to let Zander explain whatever idea he might have. He could take time for argument later, if needed.

"We find the car and then decide what to do with it. Think about it, while we head to Frisco." Zander put the pickup in gear and headed back north.

When they reached Main Street, Zander drove west looking for South Dakota cars. They reached the street's end and headed back east until they were within a block of the Branchwater. Fats had been using his flashlight to check out the plates from the open window.

There it was.

"That's it. Pull over."

Zander parked right next to the car, but they both stayed in the pickup. Fats looked at Zander and could see the concern on his face.

"What?"

"That's a Bentley."

"And?"

"It's going to be a problem. We can't leave it here. It is bound to draw all kinds of attention."

"It is a good looking vehicle," Fats said, as he shined his flashlight on the car.

He couldn't put a name to the actual color, but it seemed to be close to copper. He could see the interior, and it was like butter. It was indeed a beautiful vehicle, and Fats appreciated beautiful automobiles.

Zander had been thinking, while Fats scrutinized the car.

"What should we do with it?"

"Let's sink it in the Dillon reservoir. Nobody will ever find it there. It's too deep."

"Not a good idea."

"Why not? That baby's deep."

"It is right now. But you've seen it when we don't have a large snowfall. It shrinks to half its size. Besides, how would we get it to the deepest spot? Put it on a barge? Don't you think that might draw some attention?"

"Is this a test? Why don't you just tell me what you're thinking?" Fats seemed irritated.

His tone of voice made Zander smile. He couldn't help paying Fats back with his own type of irritating behavior.

"This vehicle cost somewhere around five hundred thousand. Someone will be wondering what happened to it."

Fats nodded in agreement. He wanted to say that he would take it, get it re-painted, and add it to his collection. He knew Zander wouldn't agree because of the body in the bottom of the mine. He waited for Zander to continue.

"We need to get it out of Frisco to some other area, where it won't draw attention to you or the bar."

"Where are you thinking?"

"A ski area. Someplace where it might set for quite a while before anyone notices."

"How about Vail?"

"Vail is too far away, and we need to ditch this right now. I think that Copper Mountain is a better choice. We could park it in one of the hotel lots and lock it up. First, we'll need to get into the car. Can you hot wire this thing?"

Fats said nothing but got out of the truck and went over to the driver's door. He shined his flashlight into the car. Before he could open the door, Zander threw him the gloves he had been wearing when they got rid of the body.

"Don't touch anything until you put on the gloves. We don't want to be leaving any prints." Zander checked around him and was happy it was late. He saw no action on the streets.

Fats fitted the gloves and opened the door. It wasn't locked. Sitting in the driver's seat, he thought about Vera driving the Bentley naked. It made him smile. One could always the hope the keys would be in the ignition, but no one could be that lucky. Looking under the seat produced nothing. Then he had a thought. He had seen Vera put her keys in the visor once, when she stopped at her business. He checked, and it was the first stroke of luck Fats had in a very long time.

He put the keys into the ignition and started the Bentley. He had to admit that it was a fine vehicle, and he would be somewhat sad to leave it behind. It was purring like a kitten when he climbed back into the pickup.

"How did you know the keys would be there?" Zander asked.

"She was naked. Where else could she put them?"

"Do you want to drive the pickup?" Zander asked.

"What do you think?" Fats got back into the Bentley. "You follow me."

"Fine. Don't do anything stupid. Stay under the speed limit," Zander said leaning over to pull the passenger door shut.

It was a short drive between Frisco and Copper Mountain, but it was also a world apart. Frisco had the working Colorado citizens, while Copper Mountain boasted the vacationing transplants with all their money to spend. It would be the perfect place to lose the Bentley.

Fats behaved himself and found a parking lot. He enjoyed the drive in the luxury automobile, but he also knew that he was vulnerable in it. He parked the car next to a row of others. It would stick out like a wedding prick, but there was no other option.

Fats turned off the ignition and exited the car with the keys in hand. He hit the lock button and watched the locks on the four doors go down. He put the keys in his pocket and climbed back into the pickup.

"That was a fine night's work. Now I think it's time to make our departure before our fortune of felicitude forsakes us."

Zander rolled his eyes. He liked it better when Fats was concerned and dropped the vocabulary dump.

"Anything else?"

"No, I believe this should do. Home, James."

Zander drove out of the ski area. By the time he reached the interstate, Fats had fallen asleep.

When they reached Zander's cabin, Zander had the notion to park the pickup in the driveway and let Fats sleep. It wouldn't have been fair to Fran. She had enough on her plate without worrying about Fats.

Zander drove down the road, until he came to what he thought was Fats place. He stopped the truck at the house.

"Wake up, you derelict. You're home."

Fats stirred and sat up. He looked around, trying to get his bearings.

"This isn't mine. It's the next one." Fats pointed ahead.

"Just get out and walk. You could use the air to clear your head," Zander said.

Fats opened the door and slipped out.

"See you in the a.m."

"Remember what I told you. Take care of Fran. Don't come back until you know she's okay."

"Oh, right."

Zander knew he would be seeing Fats the next day regardless of what he told him. He put the pickup into gear and turned around. When he reached his cabin, he turned into the drive, and turned off the ignition. He stared at the cabin in the moonlight. Many memories were exploding in his mind. Most of them were bad.

He decided he needed to confront those feelings, and there was no time like the present. When he opened the door, he felt the wall for the light switch. He paused as the lights came on, and he adjusted his eyes.

The place was as he had left it. He found some comfort in that, and yet he had hoped that things had changed. He thought there would be fewer memories to deal with if things looked different.

The repair he had done on the cupboard from the bullet from the Rooster's gun almost perfect. If someone was unaware what happened, Zander was sure no one would even notice.

He walked around and checked out the cabin and then went back out to the pickup and got his things. He put his bag into the bedroom and came back out and sat on the couch. He wanted to get everything straight in his mind making sure he left nothing to chance. The smallest detail sometimes was enough to bring down a perfect plan. Fats could do without any more trouble, and so could he. Try as he might to find fault with what they did. He couldn't find anything wrong.

Zander relaxed and decided to check out the fridge. He figured there wouldn't be anything in it, but there might be a chance Fats would have left a beer or two.

Zander was surprised when he opened the refrigerator's door. Twelve bottles of Coors beer were staring him in the face, and that was all that was in there. It made Zander smile. He could always rely on Fats.

He was drinking his second beer when he decided to call his answering service. The operator had left a recorded message from someone from Florida with a return phone number. Zander was tired and knew it was two hours later on the East Coast. He decided to wait and deal with it later.

How important could it be anyway? He was quite sure it had nothing to do with Aubrey anyway. She needed all his concentration. Everything else could wait.

17

Harris and Holly drove back from the hospital in silence. When they got to the road that led to the compound, Holly could see that changes had been made to the entrance. A rope had been stretched between two posts to keep out unwanted traffic in the past. Now there was a big gate with a chain and padlock blocking the entrance.

Harris got out and fooled with the combination on the lock until it opened. He swung open the gate, got back into the car, and drove through the opening.

He turned to Holly.

"Get out. Close and lock the gate."

Holly said nothing. She was seething inside but would never give Harris the satisfaction of seeing her angry. She would do as she was told until she wouldn't.

After locking the gate, she got back into the car.

"What's with the extra security?"

"We just kidnapped a baby. Don't you think it would be better to make it harder to get to us?"

"Well, we aren't staying here, so I think it is unnecessary." Holly's comment seemed harmless to her.

Harris, on the other hand, did not share that assessment. He backhanded her across the front of her face. Holly's nose started to bleed. Harris smiled and put the car into gear. He drove to their trailer and turned off the ignition.

"I won't have you back talk me. Next time your punishment will be more severe. Do you understand?"

Holly said nothing but nodded once. She put her head back, holding her nose to try and stop the bleeding. Harris seemed satisfied. He went into the trailer. It was late, and he went to bed. Holly stayed in the car until her nose stopped bleeding. She left the car and sat on the steps. She was close to tears, but she promised herself that she wouldn't cry. She wouldn't give Harris the satisfaction.

Looking around, she noticed a light on in Papa Henry's trailer. She decided to check it out and walked over to the window. Holly stayed a few steps back so no one would see her looking in. Helen was sitting in a rocker, and the baby was in her arms. It appeared that they were both asleep. Holly stared and wondered what was going on. She knew that things were not going to work out as she had planned.

Holly got closer to the window to get a better look. Just as she approached the window, her left foot stepped on something hidden in the weeds and she turned her ankle. Her weight shifted, and before she could get back her balance she hit the trailer with her shoulder. When she got back on her feet, she peeked into the trailer to make sure Helen hadn't heard anything. She was disappointed. Helen was looking at her, and after a few moments motioned her inside. Holly was nervous that she might have disturbed Papa Henry, but she climbed into the trailer anyway. Helen motioned her to sit in the chair closest to the rocker.

"What are you doing?" Helen asked, in not much more than a whisper.

"Just checking to see if the baby is okay."

"She's fine. Healthy little thing. Likes to eat." Helen motioned to the kitchen counter with a number of empty bottles. "I had to dig these out of storage. Haven't used any baby bottles in quite some time."

Holly smiled and nodded. She was happy the little one was doing so well. She had been sitting sideways, hoping Helen hadn't noticed her bruised and bloody face.

"What happened to you?" Helen asked.

"Your son hit me. Apparently, I ask too many questions. I just wanted to know what was going on."

Helen shook her head in disgust.

"I think I need to repeat my advice. If I were you, I would leave this place and never look back."

"You keep saying that but you never explain why."

"Something terrible is going to happen because of this child. I can feel it in my bones."

"Harris and I are leaving tomorrow with Sandra. We're going far away where no one can find us. We'll raise this child with love and kindness. She'll have everything I never had."

"Don't be stupid."

"I don't understand what you're saying."

"You and Harris are never going to get this child for your own. It's been decided to hold her for ransom. She'll bring more money than this family has ever seen at one time."

"What if Miss DePont won't pay?"

"Then Papa Henry will sell her. He knows of a place up in Georgia. Regardless, he won't let you keep this child. It would be too much of a risk."

"I won't let that happen. None of it."

Helen's face fell. She looked at Holly.

"Then this family will kill you."

Holly was stunned. She had no words to respond.

"I never had a daughter. I always wanted a little girl to spoil. I'd like to think she would have become someone like you, but it was never meant to be. Now I have this little girl in my arms, and those same feeling come rushing back."

Holly was surprised by the comment. It was hard to believe that Helen had feelings for her. Her dislike of the women simply melted away.

"Let's take the baby and leave. It would just be the two of us. We could make a good life for her somewhere else."

Helen sat and rocked for some time before she spoke.

"It's too late for me. I'm stuck here, and that's just a fact of life. I've accepted it. Besides, Henry would have no qualms about killing us both if we fouled up his plans. It's not too late for you. Get out of here tonight before all this blows up."

They heard a voice from the bedroom.

"Who are you talking to?" It was Papa Henry.

Helen pointed to the door and waved her hand signaling Holly to get out. Holly quietly opened the door and was almost out when she heard Helen respond.

"Just talking to the baby."

"Don't get attached to that kid. One way or another, she's got to go. The sooner the better."

Holly turned to close the door when she saw Helen look at her. She mouthed the word "go." Holly knew that everything Helen told her was true. She just needed to figure out how to handle it. She was still turning all the ideas over in her head, when she reached their trailer. Holly wanted to be nowhere near Harris and decided to sleep in the backseat of her car. She fell asleep around five. At seven she awoke because someone was pounding on the back window. It was Harris.

"Get up. You need to go to work, and I need some breakfast."

Holy felt terrible. Her face ached where Harris had hit her. She hoped she wouldn't get a black eye on top of everything else. She got out of the back of the car and went inside. She could find very little to eat in the trailer and started to panic. She decided to take the offensive.

"There's nothing to eat here. I haven't had time to pick up anything at the store. Did you?"

"That's not my job. That's women's work."

"Well, if you want something to eat, you'd better go out and find some eggs."

Holly knew he wouldn't do it.

"Never mind. I'll just go have breakfast with my parents."

"You do that," Holly said, and went into the bathroom to take a shower.

She heard the door slam as Harris left the trailer. The sound gave her a bit of comfort.

Holly undressed and checked herself out in the bathroom mirror. It looked like neither of her eyes was affected by the slap. Her nose was a bit swollen but not so bad as to draw much attention. It was even better when she washed away the dried blood. She thought that she would put some ice on her nose when she got to work.

Living off the grid with the Harris family meant that the things most people took for granted were unavailable to this family. The idea made Holly laugh out loud. This wasn't any kind of family. Helen's advice had been right on the mark. She would need to leave and never come back.

Holly's sense of right and wrong wouldn't allow her to do that, until she knew the child would be reunited with her mother. If she had to go to Miss Millie and confess, that's what she would do. It would be a last resort, because it would put her in jeopardy with the Harris family. She could hardly afford that.

Holly's shift started at noon, but she got herself ready for work anyway. Just as she was ready to leave the trailer, Harris came back.

"Where you going?"

"I thought I'd go to work early and see what was going on. It's better if I'm seen at the hospital as much as possible."

Harris looked at her, trying to decide if she was telling the truth. Satisfied, he took her keys.

"I'll drive you."

"I can drive myself." Holly tried not to sound angry.

"No, I'll drive. You can't get out of here without the combination to the lock."

Holly hadn't thought about the new gate.

"Why don't to give it to me?"

"You don't need it. I'll drop you off and pick you up until this thing with the baby is settled."

"Are you going to tell me what's going on?" Holly was careful not let on the she knew anything. It wouldn't help Helen if Harris figured out where she had heard about their plan.

"You don't need to concern yourself with anything right now. When the time is right, Papa Henry will let you know."

When they got to the gate, Harris opened it. Holly tried to see the combination, but she was too far away to see the numbers. It made her panic when she realized that she no longer had control of her own car. If she wanted to leave right now, there was no way she could do it without transportation.

Holly looked out the window as they drove to the hospital. She tried to think of ways she could leave the compound with her vehicle. Ramming the gate would damage the car, and she couldn't go far in a disabled vehicle. Her best plan would be to go to the market to get supplies. It would be interesting to know if Harris would allow her to drive there alone, but she knew he hated to get groceries. It was more of what he called "women's work." It was worth a shot.

"We need groceries. Since you have the car, why don't you stop on your way home?"

For a moment, Holly thought he was going to hit her again. But then he stopped himself.

"I'll think about it."

"If you don't want to do it. I can do it after work. You would just need to let me out of the gate."

Harris laughed.

"Better yet, I'll drive you over after work and stay in the car."

Holly's heart sank. She started to think of something else. This entire part of her life was circling the bowl and was about to be flushed away. She couldn't let it happen.

When they drove into the employee parking lot, Holly could see one police car. It made her a bit nervous. She knew she would face questioning about the events of the previous night.

Holly opened the door and was turning to get out when Harris spoke.

"Aren't you going to give your husband a goodbye kiss?"

"My face hurts too much where you hit me."

She left the car and slammed the door. That was the moment she got some of her power back.

18

Zander woke with the sun shining in his face. He looked at the clock thinking it was early. It was after nine. The mountains had a way of confusing sunrises and sunsets. He rubbed his eyes and realized he could smell coffee. He got out of bed walked into the kitchen to find Fats reading the Denver paper.

"Well, look at this. Sleeping Beauty lives. It's nice you get to face the day while it is still in the a.m."

"What the hell are you doing here?"

"Fran kicked me out. She said I was hovering. What does that mean anyway?"

"It means she's feeling better and wants you out of her hair."

"Well, at least that's some good news."

"So, my original question was what are you doing here?"

"It's too early to go to the bar, and I had no other place to frequent. Therefore, you get the pleasure of my company. Coffee is brewed and ready for consumption."

"Thanks. I don't suppose you made breakfast?"

"Not in my bailiwick. I might suggest toast and cheese this fine morning."

"Great. I'll have Cheerios."

"Suit yourself. Cheese has a way of binding you up. It is the prefect companion to coffee since that elixir is nature's laxative. Cereal, on the other hand, just adds to the properties of the coffee. "Loose as a Goose" comes to mind."

"Enough. I've lost my appetite. I'll just have the coffee."

Zander poured himself a mug and took a sip. He spit it into the sink.

"What's the matter with you?" Fats asked.

"It's cold and tastes terrible."

"I suppose that may be true, since I made it an hour-and-a-half in the past."

Zander dumped the remainder of the coffee into the sink and made a new pot.

"You could have warned me."

"What would be the fun in that?"

"Anything of interest in the paper?"

"It seems to be the same old drivel. Looks like a good line-up for Red Rocks this year. They have a number of oldies groups that might be of interest to you."

"I think I'm getting a bit too long of tooth to attend rock concerts. I can't stand the aggravation of dealing with the crowds."

"I hear you, man, but you've got to fight against the dying of the light."

"What does that mean?'

"Don't know. I read it in some poem and thought it was way cool. I think it means you need to live while you're living."

"I don't believe it means that I have to attend rock concerts if they piss me off."

"Can't argue with that. The aggravation might be detrimental to your longevity."

Zander poured more coffee and sat down at the table with Fats.

"Hey you could pour me another cup."

"I could, but then I would miss the opportunity to tell you to get it yourself."

"Such an annoying behavior. Is this your way of chastising me for my inability to warn you about the cold coffee?"

"Of course. Paybacks are always desirable," Zander said, as he picked up the paper.

Fats went to the coffee maker and filled his cup.

"Hey, do you want to talk about last night?"

"I don't want to hear anything about last night ever again."

"But I have questions that need some answers."

Zander stared at Fats for a long time. It was long enough to make Fats squirm.

"We discussed everything we needed last night. This chapter in your life is closed. It is for me, anyway. It would be best for both of us if you no longer thought or spoke about it. Nothing good would ever come of speaking to anyone of the events of last night or anything that led up to those events. Am I making this clear?" Zander was speaking more forcefully than he had wanted.

Fats nodded and looked down.

"It's just that I need to talk things through before I can let them go."

"Consider everything talked through," Zander said. "Finish your coffee, and lets go down to the Branchwater. It's time to get ready to open up for the day."

Fats stood.

"Can't attend with you, my sage. Fran and I need to go to the market and pick up a few things for the bar. We shall see you when that task has been completed."

"Wait. Are you telling me Fran is going to work today?"

"That would be an affirmative, O Great Seer."

"Don't you think it's a bit soon?"

"Of course I do and told her in words similar. Fran has complete control of her own destiny if you hadn't noticed. She punctuated her response with some fiery words and a wicked left hook that missed the old proboscis by mere centimeters."

Zander laughed and shook his head. Those two were a pair just made for each other. He was still smiling, when he and Fats went their own way.

Zander wanted to get to the bar and make a few phone calls. One would be to the number his answering service had listed. The other would be to Max Kuhn in Key West. Max was a friend he had met in his reconnection with Sara Jane. Zander wanted to enlist his help to find information concerning Aubrey's whereabouts. Max had a past that gave him access to things that Zander could only wonder about.

Zander hated not taking care of things. He had put these two things off the night before. He wanted them taken care of before any more time had passed because it drove him nuts. The answering service call would be a job that Herbie thought Zander could do for someone he met. Zander wasn't sure he wanted to take on anything until his situation with Aubrey was settled. He would make that call first and turn down whatever that job might entail. That idea would be preempted by a whole new set of problems, however.

Zander drove to the Branchwater and parked in the back. It was little before 10:00, and they wouldn't open the door until 11:00. He would have some uninterrupted time to make his calls.

The bar was dark, and Zander decided not to turn on any lights. It would to discourage some passer-by from knocking on the door wanting to get in early. He went behind the bar and put on a fresh pot of coffee before sitting down next to the telephone. He reached into his back pocket for his wallet and went through it until he found the number he had scribbled down the previous night. It was a Florida prefix, and he knew the area code was somewhere in the northern part of the state. He knew the number for both Herbie and Fran and it belonged to neither.

He dialed the number realizing that it was two hours later on the east coast. It would almost be lunchtime, and maybe he would be lucky getting in contact with whoever made the call. He could hear the phone ringing. It rang six times, and he was about to hang up, when he heard someone breathlessly answer.

"Hello."

Zander thought the person on the other end sounded irritated. He decided to try and turn on his charm.

"My goodness. You seem out of breath. I hope this call didn't interrupt anything too important."

"Who is this?" Millie said, not masking any of her aggravation.

"You called my answering service and left a number to call you back. That's what I'm doing right now."

It took Millie a moment to realize who was speaking to her. She tried to remember his name and came up with it after a few moments.

"You are Zander then?"

"Correct. Once again I apologize for any interruption I may have caused."

"I was expecting your call yesterday." Millie didn't try to be friendly.

"Sorry, I was indisposed." Zander was starting to resent this woman. It wasn't a good way to start any kind of business relationship. He was close to ending the call when the woman spoke again. This time her tone softened a bit.

"My name is Amelia DePont. People call me Millie."

"I see. How did you get my number?"

"I assume you are familiar with Sara Jane De Graff?"

Zander's face fell. He was happy no one could see it.

"Yes. I know that name. I used to know her quite well. That relationship has outlived it usefulness. I am no longer in contact with the woman."

"I know all the background. For years she thought I was her aunt, but I'm her mother." Millie waited for a response, but there wasn't one. "Hello. Are you there?"

"I'm here. I'm also confused," Zander said.

"It doesn't matter. Time enough to explain later. You need to come to Perry, Florida."

"Why in the world would I want to even consider doing that? This sounds like something Sara Jane cooked up, and I will never trust her again." It was Zander's turn to be hot.

"Ratchet it down, boy. You need to listen to what I have to tell you."

"You've got about two minutes before I hang up."

"Feisty young man. I like that. I see now why you and Sara Jane are at odds. Too much alike." Millie was amused.

Her amusement was lost on Zander.

"Time's running out."

"Keep your pants on. That's something you should have considered when you were in Key West."

Zander felt like this was heading south.

"I'm sure I don't know what you are talking about."

"Of course you do. Sara Jane came to me pregnant. It's your child."

Zander almost fell to the floor.

"That's not even possible."

"You know it is. She told me all about your last encounter. She had a girl in case you are wondering."

Zander hadn't even thought that far ahead. He was in shock.

"A girl? What's her name?"

"Sandra."

The name was almost too much for Zander to even fathom. He couldn't respond.

"Pretty much cements the whole deal. Don't you think? Sandra is pretty close to Sander. Too close not to believe that she's named after you."

There was no argument from Zander. In the back of his mind he knew everything she said was true. It was his kind of luck. He was quiet for a time trying to organize his thoughts into something coherent.

"Is the baby all right? Is there something wrong? Is that why you want me to come to Perry?"

"Of course there's something wrong. Why else would I call you? You need to come to Perry."

Zander had seen Perry on the map and knew it wasn't that far away from Cedar Key where Herbie and Gail lived. He would be calling his friend as soon as this conversation ended.

"I'll need time to get things arranged. I just can't walk away from things around here. I have other problems of my own."

"Other problems? You have no idea about the problems you have right here." This time Millie was hot.

"Are you going to tell me what's wrong?" Zander asked.

"Well, I wasn't going to tell you on the phone, but you are so damn bull-headed I suppose I have no choice."

That comment made Zander smile.

"Now you are getting the real me."

"I wouldn't be proud of that if I were you, Sonny. Your daughter has been kidnapped."

"What the hell? Who would want to kidnap a baby?'

"Don't be naïve. All kinds of people for all kinds of reasons kidnap children every day. This particular reason has to do with my wealth and the ransom these criminals believe they can extort from me."

"I need to speak to Sara Jane."

She's resting and can't come to the phone. It was a rough delivery. She doesn't know that I called you, either."

"What the hell does that mean?"

"It means she's just like you and doesn't want to be reminded of what happened between the two of you."

"I suppose I'll need to come to you then."

"Now you've got the idea. One other thing, she doesn't go by Sara Jane any longer."

"What's her name this time?"

If Zander's comment surprised Millie, she never let on.

"She calls herself Jayne Grafton now."

"Oh, that's an oldie but goody."

"Perhaps. It isn't germane to the issue now is it?"

"You are right. I apologize. It's just that this is quite of bit of drama you have unloaded on me today."

"I'm sorry for that as well. Perhaps when you get here, we can start on some stronger footing."

"I'll do my best."

"Of course you will. I've done due diligence on you and found that you have an outstanding character minus the few flaws we have already discussed. I will make the arrangements for you to fly from the Denver airport to the airport in Tampa. When you reach Florida, I'll have someone pick you up at the airport. All this will be of no cost to you." Millie was firm.

"I suppose I'll be working for you then?"

"Yes. You'll be working for me but mostly for yourself. Sandra is your daughter after all. We will discuss your fee when you get here."

Zander wanted to say there would be no fee, but bit his tongue before he could say the words. It was hard to know if any of this was on the up-and-up or if it was just another one of Sara Jane's tricks.

"Please give me a number where I can call you to share the information when I've secured your transportation."

Zander gave Millie the bar's phone number. He realized he needed to go to Wall-Mart and get another cell phone before he left for Florida.

"When do you think you'll make the flight arrangements?"

"I want you here by tomorrow. I will make that happen. So anything you need to do, you'd better get completed today. I will arrange for you to be here, and rest assured, you will be."

Millie hung up abruptly giving Zander no time to ask any further questions. He hung up the bar phone and his head started spinning again.

19

When Fran and Fats entered the bar thirty minutes later, Zander's head was laying on the bar. Fats thought he was sleeping.

"Wake up, my good man. It is almost bewitching time at the Branchwater. The doors need to be opened."

Zander said nothing and never move his head an inch.

Fats' level of concern was instant.

"Zander, what's wrong? Are you okay?" he turned to Fran, "Is he even breathing?"

Fran walked behind the bar and put her hand on Zander's shoulder.

"What's wrong, Zander?"

Zander raised his head and put his hand on Fran's hand.

"There doesn't seem to be anything right. I just found out that Sara Jane has a child and it's mine."

Neither Fran nor Fats reacted. Zander noticed.

"You knew? Why not? Why shouldn't I be the last person to find out?"

"In all fairness, I was the one who told Fats not to tell you."

"Why would you do that?" Zander's voice held no anger but just a deep feeling of helplessness.

"Think about it. It wasn't any of our business. This had to be between you two. Besides, you have seen what happens when Fats gets involved in your life," Fran said trying to lighten Zander's load.

"Who else knows? Herbie?"

They both nodded.

"He's the one who told me about it. He saw her in some shop trying on maternity clothes. Gail wouldn't let him tell you either. So, he just told me," Fats said.

"Co-conspirators. This just keeps getting worse and worse." Zander felt very tired.

"How did you find out about all of this?" Fats asked.

"Someone named Amelia DePont called my answering service, and I just got finished talking to her."

Zander decided to share the other bad news concerning his newly discovered offspring. He kept the news short and to the point. Neither Fran nor Fats gave away much facially during the explanation. Zander wondered if they had known about kidnapping as well.

"Now what happens?" Fats tried to seem contrite.

"She's making arrangements for me to fly to Florida tomorrow."

"I'll take you to the airport. What time?"

"She will be calling the Branchwater later with the information. If I'm not here, one of you two will need to take it down."

"I'll be here all day. I'll take care of it. That way you'll know the information is correct." Fran looked at Fats.

"Hey, I think that was a shot," Fats said, frowning.

"You are quicker than I give you credit," Zander said, with just a hint of a smile.

"Another shot. Do I have a target on my forehead?"

Zander decided to ignore his comment.

"I've got a few things to take care of before I leave tomorrow. I need to pack, and it looks like I'm going to need another cell phone."

"Want me to make a Wal-Mart run while you go home and pack?"

"I was just going to suggest that."

"Great minds."

"There's no plural there."

"Another shot. I'm so full of holes there will be nothing left of me. I'd better leave before I disappear all together." Fats bolted for the back door.

Fran and Zander watched him leave.

"Please don't be too hard on him, Zander. He does have your best interest at heart even if it comes out convoluted."

"Did you know about the kidnapping?"

Fran frowned.

"Of course not. That would have been a game changer. We're not totally without compassion."

Zander regretted his comment. He had forgotten the trauma that Fran had experienced just twenty-four hours earlier.

"I am so sorry, Fran. You've had your own things to deal with, and here I am feeling sorry for myself. That has got to change. I need to take control. I'll see you later." Zander followed the same path out the door that Fats had taken earlier.

"We'll be waiting. You have friends you can lean on."

Fran watched him leave and wondered how he was going to handle being a father. Then she remembered he was also dealing with his loss of Aubrey. A lot of things had happened in the bar over the last few days, and none of them were good.

Zander went home and threw a few things into his canvas bag. When he was finished, he thought about calling Max and asking him to look into Aubrey's disappearance. Max had contacts with government people and also with some people in Cuba. This would be a huge favor and one he couldn't treat lightly. He remembered he no longer had a working landline at his cabin. He would have to wait for the cell phone Fats decided to pick up for him. Everyone would need to have his number. He made a mental note to call Herbie as well. He had decided that he wouldn't be taking any DePont transportation from the airport. Herbie would be picking him up, and he would be staying with them until he could work things out.

Zander was back at the Branchwater in less than an hour. Fran was serving some regulars at the tables, and Fats was behind the bar unwrapping Zander's new cell phone.

"I don't know why they have to put all this plastic around these things. It's almost impossible to unravel." Fat said, talking to himself.

"It's so the customers don't steal them from the stores," Zander said, as he entered the bar area.

Fats jumped and almost slid off his stool.

"Damn, man. Announce yourself before you enter."

Just as Zander was about to reply, the phone rang. Fats reached under the bar. Zander waved him off thinking it might be DePont with his flight information. He went around the bar and answered on the fourth ring.

"I was almost beginning to think no one worked there." Millie was short.

Zander could tell from her tone that she was someone who demanded what she wanted when she wanted it. It reminded him of Sara Jane, and he was surprised that he failed to have stronger negative feelings.

Millie gave Zander his flight information. He wrote it down on a bar check and slipped it into his pocket. He would be flying into Tampa on a direct flight.

"I'll have my man Hector pick you up. Look for a sign with your name on it," Millie said.

"You can keep your man at home. I won't need his services," Zander said, with resolve in his voice.

"What's your plan?"

"I'll rent a car. I have a friend in the area and plan to stay there."

"Why?" Millie's response was clipped.

"Do you think these kidnappers know where you live?"

"Obviously. They left the notes on my gate. What's your point?"

"You need to realize that they are watching your every move. They aren't going to want to see that you've enlisted anyone else to help you. The child's life may depend on that."

"Your child."

"Yes, my child. That makes it all that much more important. I have your number, and I'll call when I arrive."

"We need to meet here. Jayne will need to be involved in whatever we decide."

"I agree. It will have to be a late night meeting. Have your people keep watch for any strangers hanging around."

"I'll give you directions."

"That's not necessary. I'll find it. Sounds like everyone knows about your whereabouts."

"When can I expect your call?"

"In a day or two. I want to check out the area and maybe talk to a few of the locals. I need to get a feel for the place."

"Very well. The clock's ticking."

"Do you have an actual ransom demand?"

"Not yet."

"Then we have time. Not a whole lot we can do until then. I may be able to stumble on something if I take it slow."

"Fine." Millie hung up.

Zander liked how the conversation had progressed. He hadn't let Millie take control, which he knew would be important down the line. Emotion was something that couldn't enter this situation or there would be some serious mistakes made.

Fats had been listening but said nothing. He handed Zander the cell phone he had been able to unwrap. Zander pulled out his billfold and began entering numbers into the phone from a folded piece of paper hidden among his bills.

"Call my number," Fats said.

"What for?"

"I can capture your number in my contacts."

Zander called the number. Fats answered his cell.

"Who's calling please?"

"Shut up." Zander hung up.

"Call my number, too," Fran said, returning to the bar area.

Zander called Fran's number and when she answered, he hung up.

"I'm going to the back and make two other phone calls."

"Who are you calling? Fats asked.

"Herbie for one. I'm going to be staying with him because I may need his help somewhere down the line."

"And?"

"Someone you don't know. He may be able to help with Aubrey. That's all I'm going to tell you."

"Don't you think I should be involved with all aspects of your adventures? Just in case?"

"Just in case of what?"

"Well, maybe you'll need my help with something. It would be easier to help if I know all aspects of what your travels entail."

"That worked out so well the last time I went to Florida didn't it? In fact, if your meddling hadn't surfaced, I wouldn't be in this predicament, would I?"

Fats thought about it.

"Let me get this straight in my mind. You are blaming me for getting that bitch pregnant? I'm not even that good. The lack of keeping it in your pants was all your doing."

"Let's try to ratchet back all this testosterone, boys. Seems to be enough blame to go around, but blame never solves anything." Fran went back to waiting tables.

Zander and Fats watched her leave.

"Isn't she something? Nailed it. We've got to stop getting in each other's way and work together."

"As long as you stay here, and stop trying to steer everything yourself, I'll keep you in the loop."

"That's fair." Fats stuck out his hand, and Zander grabbed it.

"I'm going to need a ride to the airport. This Millie woman has got me booked on the red-eye this evening."

"Make your calls. I'll let Fran know."

Zander went to the back room and sat on an empty beer keg. He called Herbie's number first. Herbie picked up. Zander was surprised because the phone had seemed to offer no ringing.

"Hello."

"Herbie, it's Zander."

"Zander, I didn't recognize your number." Zander thought he could hear concern in Herbie's voice.

"It's a new phone. I had to get rid of the other one when Aubrey and I left your place. Remember?"

"I do. How is she?"

"She's gone Herbie. They found her and took her right under my damn nose."

"What are you going to do?"

"I'm calling Max after this phone call to you."

"Good. If anyone can help you, he can."

"Before I can deal with that problem, I need to deal with another one."

"What's that?"

"I think you know. You decided to keep secret the fact that Sara Jane was pregnant."

It was quiet on Herbie's end so some time.

"Gail wouldn't let me. She said I needed to keep my nose out of your business, and if Sara Jane wanted you to know she would tell you." Herbie was contrite.

"I'm not here to bust your balls, Herbie. A new wrinkle has been added to this already contentious situation."

"Now what?" Herbie asked.

"The baby has been kidnapped. It seems that this person called Amelia DePont is some relation to Sara Jane. She must be wealthy, and someone wants to extort money in exchange for the baby."

"Could things get any worse?" Herbie asked.

"I don't know, I hope not. That's why I will be coming to Florida and plan staying with you until we get this figured out."

"When are you coming?"

"I'll be there later tonight. You'd better tell Gail so it isn't a total surprise."

"I'll call her later. I'm just finishing up my route and should be home for dinner. Will you be joining us?"

"No. Don't plan on me until late. I have a late flight to Tampa. I'll rent a car and come up to Cedar Key. I'll need to bounce off some thoughts, and I could use both your and Gail's ears."

"We will wait up for you. Call us when your leave the Tampa airport."

"Thanks Herbie. I appreciate it."

"I have been feeling terrible not having told you about the pregnancy. Whatever help you need, I'll be here for you. So will Gail."

Zander hung up and placed his next call to Max in Key West.

20

Zander boarded the American Airlines flight at 7:00 p.m. It was already 9:00 in Florida, and he knew it would be late when he reached Herbie and Fran in Cedar Key. Just before takeoff, Zander took out his phone, and called Herbie to tell him he wouldn't be arriving until late the next morning. He decided to get a hotel near the Tampa airport to avoid putting everyone out.

After the call, Zander settled in and fell asleep. No one was seated next to him, so he wouldn't be bothered by any small talk. The flight attendants overlooked him for their usual soft drink peddling. A little over three hours later, he awoke when the captain announced that everyone needed to prepare for final approach to the Tampa airport. It was the best-uninterrupted sleep he had experienced recently.

While he waited at the car rental desk for the paperwork to be completed, he saw a kiosk with a number of hotels. A phone on the kiosk was hooked to a hotel when a button was pushed adjacent to the advertisement. Zander chose a middle-of-the-road chain that was less than a mile from the airport. He grudgingly gave up his credit card number to hold the room. He hated to leave a trail and always paid cash when he could.

There was a car waiting for him in the lot. It was gray in color and mirrored a thousand other models on the road. Zander hated it, but he knew it wouldn't draw much attention, and attention was the last thing he needed on this trip. He knew that anonymity would be his greatest weapon.

The hotel was acceptable. When he was able to sit on the bed to relax, it was after 1:00. Zander was afraid he wouldn't be able to sleep. He was wrong. He hadn't even undressed but fell asleep on top of the bed. He never moved until 8:00 the next morning. He got off the bed and undressed. The shower felt good, and he turned it as hot as he could stand. The bathroom was full of steam, and he couldn't see anything in the mirror. It was no matter. Looking at himself was not a priority.

The hotel boasted a great free breakfast. Zander looked it over and decided against the waffle and settled for sausages and scrambled eggs. The food was passable, but the coffee was suburb. He had three large cups, before he decided to get himself on the road.

He took 19/98 north out of Tampa. It was toll road and had little traffic. Zander was thankful for that. Florida had too many people for his taste, and he enjoyed the slower pace of old northern Florida. He was anxious to see Cedar Key and Herbie and Gail again. The highway 24 turnoff almost caught Zander daydreaming. He was able to hit the brakes and make the turn without hitting anything. Someone in a passing car honked. Zander ignored it and in 21 miles he was parking next to Herbie and Gail's home. Herbie's truck was parked in the driveway. Zander was happy about that. He wanted to share what he knew and get on his way. He could have shared everything he knew with Gail, but he just wasn't comfortable doing that. Fats told him he had trust issues with women. Zander thought he might be right and knew it stemmed from his tumultuous relationship with Sara Jane.

Zander knocked on the door, and Herbie came bounding out. He put his arms around Zander and squeezed. Zander realized that the three cups of coffee had kicked in, and he needed to go.

"I've got to use your bathroom, or I'll be letting it go on your floor."

Herbie let him go.

"You know where it is."

Zander opened the door and trotted toward the bathroom.

"Hi, Zander," Gail said, as Zander raised his hand in a half-assed wave.

Zander came back to the kitchen when he was finished.

"Sorry, Gail. I had too much coffee this morning."

"I'd imagine you'll need it again soon. Coffee is nature's way of cleaning the kidneys but it also is a great natural laxative." Gail was enjoying making Zander uncomfortable.

"Did you have to even mention that?" Zander turned around and returned to the bathroom. He remembered this same conversation coming out of Fats the day before.

"There's air freshener on the counter. After all, Herbie lives here." Gail called after Zander.

Herbie shook his head and smiled.

"You like to torment him, don't you?"

"He gets embarrassed so easily. I find that endearing. You used to be like that."

"I know. I guess I got used to you." Herbie put his arms around Gail.

Zander finished his bathroom crusade and came out sheepishly.

"Did you flush?" Gail asked.

Zander just looked at Gail.

"Did you wash your hands?" Gail was unrelenting.

Zander's face flushed.

"She's just messing with you," Herbie said, trying to put Zander at ease.

"I know. I'm sorry for my rude behavior."

Both Gail and Herbie laughed. Gail went over and put her arms around Zander and gave him a huge kiss on the cheek.

"You are the comic relief around here. I don't know what we would do without your visits. They just need to become more frequent."

"I wish this was just a friendly visit, Gail. I'm afraid I have other issues to deal with right now."

"Are you talking about being a father?"

Zander was shocked, until he remembered that Herbie had told him that Gail wouldn't let him spill the news about the pregnancy.

"Well, that's just the tip of everything. I don't know how I'm going to handle the rest of it."

"I'm making lunch right now. Why don't you and Herbie go out and have a beer while I finish up. Don't talk about anything until I'm able to hear it."

Herbie nodded and took out two Yuenglings from the refrigerator.

"Let's go out on the deck and look at the muck. The tide is out. It's such a beautiful sight," Herbie said, joking.

Zander followed Herbie out to the screened porch area.

"I like what you've done here," Zander said, looking around.

"It's a finely woven screen and keeps out most of the no-seeums. It's the way we can be out here at dusk. Sit." Herbie handed a beer to Zander, and they both found a chair.

The two friends took their sips of beer and gazed out at the low tide. Nothing was said between the two, and nothing needed to be said. Sometimes you just needed two friends sitting together.

Soon enough, Gail came out and joined them. She had a glass of Chardonnay in her hands.

"Zander, you now may share the real reason for your visit."

Zander nodded and for the next fifteen minutes explained the twists and turns his life had taken after he had left Cedar Key the last time. Neither Gail nor Herbie spoke during his explanation.

Zander shared what he had learned over the past twenty-four hours. When he finished, he took down a good three quarters of his beer. Talking always made him thirsty.

"I can't even fathom how many dramas your life has seen. How do you cope with it all?" Gail asked.

"I don't know anything different. My entire life has been like this."

"Are you happy?" Gail always went right for the truth.

Zander sat and thought for a while. Herbie was uncomfortable with Gail's directness.

"Gail, that's just rude."

"It's okay, Herbie. I should be able to answer a question like that. I hadn't ever thought about happiness until I met Aubrey. The time I spent with her made me realize that I was indeed happy and maybe for the first time in my life. Then she was taken. That made it even worse. Not knowing true happiness was bad enough, but having it taken away once you realized what it was, ushered in a feeling of total helplessness. Depression started to set in until I got the call. Things started moving so fast that I just haven't had time to consider my happiness."

"But it has to be a nagging factor somewhere," Gail said.

"I suppose, but I've got the kidnapping to solve," Zander said and stopped. "I guess I have two kidnappings. I hadn't considered that Aubrey was kidnapped, but she was."

"You have someone to lean on with that issue." Herbie said.

"I do. If Max can't help, then nothing can be done."

"What do you plan to do from this point on?" Gail asked.

"I need to go and speak with this Millie DePont character. I'll need to wait until it gets dark. I don't want anyone to know I'm here and helping. Maybe you can help me locate the woman's home. I'm not familiar with the Perry area."

"I'll do one better than that. I'm going to go with you and show you where she lives," Herbie said.

"I don't want to involve either of you in any of my problems." Zander was firm.

"We've talked about this before you arrived. Herbie and I agree that you need help with this. Besides, you haven't always made very good decisions when it comes to the mother of your child," Gail said.

Zander gave no argument. Involving his friends made him nervous. Herbie was smiling, as he watched Zander's mind turn over what Gail had said.

"You need someone to share your ideas before you go off half-cocked." Herbie thought that maybe the half-cocked line went a little overboard.

"That would be a true statement, and since there isn't anyone else around, you'll have to do."

"You are such a funny guy," Herbie said with a twinkle in his eye.

"How long will it take to get there?"

"We can make the DePont estate in a little over an hour."

"Estate?"

"Amelia DePont has more money than any of us will ever see in our lifetime. Maybe that's why Sara Jane ended up there."

Zander knew what Herbie was saying. Sara Jane had ulterior motives with almost everything she did. It would make sense for her to line herself up with someone of wealth and means. He was surprised that after he heard the news about the kidnapping his feelings about Sara Jane had somewhat softened. It puzzled him, and he struggled to make some sense of it.

"We should leave so we arrive after dark," Zander said.

Herbie like it when he heard Zander say "we." He hadn't been sure that Zander wanted anyone tagging along.

"That shouldn't be a problem. What's the plan?"

"I'll call this Millie woman and tell her when we will be arriving."

"Why all the cloak and dagger stuff?" Herbie asked.

"I believe that the kidnappers will be watching the place. They have passed some communication about not involving the police or anyone from the outside."

"You'd better tell her to open the gate so we don't have to wait when we get there."

"That's a good idea. I'll call her when we get close."

"I still have a hard time seeing you circumnavigate a cell phone," Herbie said, shaking his head.

"I can do it, but I don't have to like it. You'll do the driving. I need to keep my eyes open and my phone ready to go."

"Gail, we will have to use your car. I can't be driving the truck. It's too conspicuous," Herbie said looking at Gail.

"No. You'll be driving my rental. I don't want anything being traced back to either of you. We just don't know what we are dealing with here."

"But what about the insurance?" Herbie asked. "What if we have an accident?"

"You let me worry about that. You're going to drive my rental, or stay home."

Herbie knew Zander had made up his mind, and it would do no good to try and change it. Gail broke the impasse by telling her two boys that it was lunchtime.

The afternoon was filled with pleasant reminiscing conversation. Zander enjoyed his friends, and he realized it could very well be the last time he would have a conflict-free afternoon for quite some time.

21

When Herbie told Zander they were getting close to the DePont estate, Zander made the call to Millie. Zander told her to give them ten minutes and open the gate. At first Millie seemed to be perturbed at hearing the word "we."

Zander ignored her questions and told her to do what he asked and that he would fill her in later. He was looking around when Herbie told him that the driveway was about a mile away.

"Let's go past the gate for at least a mile," Zander replied.

"Why would we do that?" Herbie asked.

"We need to know if anyone is watching the place."

Herbie complied and drove past the entrance to the DePont estate. They proceeded north and saw a flatbed truck in a small access road that led into some woods. Zander looked closely at the vehicle when they went by and saw the glow of a cigarette from someone sitting inside.

"Bingo. Herbie drive on until we are out of sight. I'll tell you when to stop."

Herbie drove on without speaking. He figured Zander would tell him when he wanted anything more. It never took that long.

"Okay, stop here and turn around," Zander said. "When you get to the front of the truck, stop so he can't pull out."

"Then what?" Herbie asked.

"I've got an idea that might help allow me to be seen around here without jeopardizing the safety of my daughter."

Herbie was confused by this apparent change in tactics but decided to keep his mouth shut. When he returned to the access road, he pulled in front of the truck as was instructed. Zander bounced out of the car and was knocking on the door of the truck before Herbie had the car shifted into park.

After a few minutes of pointing and talking, Zander returned to the car.

"It's okay to drive into the DePont's drive."

"What in the world did you say to the guy?"

"I told him I was the father of the kidnapped child and was trying to find out where the DePont estate was located."

"I don't understand why you would give yourself away," Herbie argued.

"Think about it. Wouldn't it be logical for the father to be involved with a kidnapped child? This way, that's all they think I am. I'll be able to move around while they watch and won't be sending any red flags other than being a frustrated father."

"What about me? Who does he think I am?"

"He didn't see you, and you'll be dropping me off and leaving. I want you to take the rental and go back to Cedar Key."

"I'm confused," Herbie said, as he turned into the DePont estate.

"These people will think that you were just my driver. You'll need to let him see you leave. If I need you down the line, I'll call."

"What about transportation? Isn't there some better option?"

"Herbie, don't you think that this Amelia has resources I can tap into? Besides, she called me. So, she's going to have to step up and provide me whatever I need."

Herbie thought Zander sounded a little cold especially when there was his child's life to consider. He nothing good to say about Sara Jane, but this situation went way beyond personal grievances.

The outside lights were on when Herbie drove up and found a woman standing with her arms folded. Herbie thought she looked formidable and was happy he wouldn't be staying. Zander turned to Herbie when he stopped the car.

"Thanks for everything, Herbie. Sorry that I'm changing up the plans, and they aren't going to involve you."

"There was never much of a plan now was there? You've been flying by the seat of your pants since you arrived. I hope everything turns out in the best interest of the child." Herbie had heard that line on some show on television.

"That's the goal, but I would be lying if I told you that I wasn't deeply concerned. The longer this drags out the less likely we'll find the child alive."

"Then you'd better get your ass in gear, my friend."

Zander opened the door and got out. He turned back to Herbie and leaned into the car.

"When you leave, stop at the end of the driveway near the gate, and make sure the guy in the truck sees you."

"Will do. You'd better stop talking to me and meet this woman," Herbie gestured at Millie, "She looks perturbed."

"Not looking forward to any of this," Zander said, and slammed the door.

Herbie jerked the car into gear and headed down the driveway before Zander even took a step. He got to the gate and stopped like he was instructed. He noticed another vehicle next to the truck. He it was hard to make out and wanted to avoid drawing any more attention. He turned south and took off down the road. He noticed the second vehicle following him after a few minutes. He kept his speed down and made sure whoever was following kept sight of the rental car he was driving. The vehicle followed him after he had turned onto highway 19/98 for five miles or so. Herbie saw the car turn around and head back up the highway, after he went through a bump in the road called Tenille. When the taillights disappeared, Herbie stepped on the accelerator. He wanted to get home and share what had happened with Gail before he forgot any details.

Zander walked up the drive to the waiting woman. Zander could see she was no one to trifle with, and the way she had her arms crossed in front of her body told him that she wasn't happy. He decided not to give her any satisfaction and be preemptive.

"Amelia DePont I presume. I'm Sander Van Zee. You can call me Zander." He smiled and put out his hand.

Millie kept her pose and looked at Zander, not offering to take his hand. Zander withdrew his offer to shake.

"Who was that person dropping you off? I thought I told you that no one else needed to be involved." Millie's voice was even, but Zander knew she was angry.

"Nice to meet you. I'm afraid you have more going on then you realize. I had to make some adjustments," Zander said.

Millie was interested in what this Zander character had to say. She would never admit to it, but she liked the way he handled himself. Not many people had the nerve to stand up to Millie, so she generally took notice of those that did.

"Let's not stand out here flexing our muscles at each other. You need to tell me what is going on," Millie said, as she moved to open the door.

Zander took her hand before she could turn the door handle. It shocked Millie and she pulled away.

"Sorry, I didn't mean to startle you. I just need to have you bring me up to speed before we involve Sara Jane," Zander said, as he let go of her hand.

"She goes by Jayne these days. I wouldn't call her Sara Jane if I were you."

Zander nodded, deciding not to make any negative comments before he could size up Millie.

"Is there someplace we could go without disturbing Jayne? We need to talk about things before all the other baggage gets opened. We don't have time for drama if we're going to save my daughter."

Millie was impressed. This was something she would have suggested herself.

"Jayne is upstairs in her room trying to recuperate. The delivery was an awful experience for her. It was so bad that she won't be having children in the future."

Zander thought about saying she shouldn't have had this one either but caught himself just in time and buried that notion. He wanted to find out what details Millie knew so he could begin working on the problem.

"Do you have someplace private we can discuss the events that led to all this? I don't want to even talk to Jayne until we are up to speed."

"I agree. Let's take a ride. I'll let my driver know, and he can bring around my car."

"I'll drive. I want the two of us discussing everything without other ears involved. We don't know where any of this conspiracy starts and ends," Zander said.

At first Millie thought she would be getting angry at the comment. She had complete trust in her staff and had never had a moment's doubt about anyone's loyalty.

The comment surprised her, however. This Zander character was correct in his assumptions. Until they knew what was happening, they would need to keep their trust in a very small circle. After all, people had done far less for money. Mille would never believe that anyone close to her sold her out. She just couldn't take any chances when family was involved.

Hector brought the car around, and Millie dismissed him. He seemed confused as he left. Zander got behind the wheel, and Millie sat in the passenger's seat. Hector had been driving Millie around for a long time, and she had never sat in the front. He wondered who the new Anglo thought he was, driving around his employer. It was not like Millie not to share her thoughts with him, and it irritated him. He would go and talk it over with Rosita. He needed a female's perspective before letting his feelings get hurt unnecessarily.

Zander drove the Caddy to the front gate and stopped. He pointed at the flatbed truck before he turned to go past the truck.

"You are being watched. It made me change my plan to remain anonymous." Zander explained what he had done.

"Someone needs to follow the truck when he leaves here." Millie was firm.

"We need to be careful before we start showing our hand," Zander said.

As if on cue, Zander's cell phone rang. He pulled it out of his pocket and saw it was Herbie. After a short conversation, Zander thanked Herbie for the call.

"It was my friend, Herbie, who dropped me off previously. He said that someone in another vehicle followed him. It seems they are working in pairs. I'll need to have all your information, and you need to have mine before we try to force these people into any corners."

Millie agreed, and they drove around the streets of Perry for over an hour while they shared information. When Zander was satisfied that he knew everything Mille knew, he suggested they return to the estate.

"No, let's go to one of my properties and have a drink. You need to know a few other things before we get ourselves embroiled too much further."

Zander took her direction and drove to the little bar/restaurant that she had introduced to Sara Jane and Sheila. This whole thing was complicated, and she felt Zander had the right to know the entire truth. Millie always liked all the cards on the table.

The place was buzzing with people and their children. Someone found a table away from the hubbub in the corner for Millie and Zander. They ordered a drink. Zander opted for a Yuengling, while Millie asked for a glass of Chardonnay. Zander took the time to look around, while they waited for their drinks. He couldn't help be reminded of the Branchwater back in Frisco. Little hometown places were always the best, and he would always be attracted to them.

"I like this place," Zander said to Millie.

"So do I. It fits me so much better than all those fancy highfalutin' places all up and down Florida."

Zander smiled. He hadn't heard anyone use the word "highfalutin' " for a very long time. It was an old word, but it fit. The drinks came, and they had the corner to themselves.

"Please tell me your history with Jayne and try not to leave anything out. Everything you can tell me is important," Millie demanded.

The comment confused Zander. He wondered why their history was important, but he wouldn't escape telling this woman what she wanted. He turned things over in his mind, until he realized he would have to start from the beginning. It would take some time to tell everything, and he would need more than one beer.

22

It took Zander two more Yuenglings to finish his history with Sara Jane. Millie was quiet until she had time to process everything. Zander realized it was quite a bit to take in and hadn't a clue why all of the details were so important.

It was getting late, and the bar had lost most of its patrons. Millie looked around and decided to finish her glass of wine.

"I think we should be getting back."

"I haven't heard the story about your relationship with Jayne," Zander said, and sat back expecting Millie's story.

"There's not enough noise in the place to tell you everything without others overhearing. I'll tell you on the way back." Millie trusted the people in the bar, but there were some things just too private.

Millie was quiet for a few miles, until she turned to Zander and began her story.

"This is something I've told to Jayne and Sheila, so I expect it to be between us. No one else ever needs to know these details."

"I'll agree to those stipulations. I just wonder why Jayne's sister is involved. I thought they were estranged," Zander said, knowing Sheila knew more about Sara Jane than she had ever told him.

"First of all, Sheila is not Jayne's sister."

The shock of the statement made Zander shut up. Millie began her story and left nothing out. She was still talking when they reached the gate to her property. Zander stopped the car and shut off the engine. He needed to know everything before confronting Jayne and trying to endure a battle.

Millie finished her story with what she knew had happened between Jayne and Zander in Key West. If Zander was surprised by Millie's candid explanation, he never let her know. He started the car and drove up to the house. Hector was waiting at the door and got into the car when the two exited. He drove the car to the carriage house.

"You have your own private Valet parking. Not a bad perk."

"Money talks. You can have most everything you ever wanted."

"In your case, that's not always true, is it?"

Millie knew what he meant and decided to ignore the comment.

"Let me show you to your room. It's late, and I think we'll need to get up early and figure out how to proceed. I have a bedroom made up for you in the pool house. It will be far enough away from Jayne, so she won't run into you before I've had the opportunity to smooth things over."

Millie's plans were shattered when she open the huge front door. Jayne was sitting in a wingback chair in the great room staring at the two as they entered. Millie jumped when she noticed her.

"Jayne, you startled me. Why aren't you in bed?"

"I heard you drive up. I wondered what you were doing out all alone at this late hour. Then I see you aren't alone at all. Who gave you permission to involve him?" There was no doubt how Jayne felt about Zander.

Zander thought there couldn't have been any more disdain in her voice. It made him smile.

"Hello, Sara Jane. I guess I should say Jayne. It's hard to keep track of all your aliases these days."

Jayne made no response to Zander but looked at her mother. If she thought she could intimidate Millie, she was badly mistaken.

"I called Zander to help. He's the father and should know what happened. We need to move now, and the more people with a stake in the outcome, the better the result."

"This isn't some business transaction. It's my daughter we are talking about," Jayne shouted.

"Speak up. Maybe someone in the county hasn't heard you. It's his daughter as well."

Zander was enjoying the repartee between mother and daughter. He remained quiet to see where it would lead.

"You know our history. Why would you involve him without first consulting me?" Jayne hadn't lost her edge.

"I think that maybe you've had a long day," Millie said, softening her tone. "Why don't you go to your room and get some sleep? We will try to deal with this in the morning."

"I am not going to be dismissed." Jayne was hot.

"On the contrary, you are dismissed to go to your room." Millie put her hands on her hips, and there was no doubt how the scene was going to end.

Jayne tried to get up out of her chair, but she was still sore and limped out of the room.

"It's good to know that some things will always remain the same." Zander broke his silence

"I'm afraid I've given her my strong will," Millie said.

"It has served her well over the years."

"It just hasn't served you very well, has it?"

"I'm still trying to find some closure. No one else in my life has had that kind of effect on me."

Millie was surprised by Zander's confession. It was something she hadn't expected. It made her like this young man even more.

"Why don't you follow me? I'll show you where you'll stay. My housekeeper has left for home. If you need anything, there will be a light on in the kitchen all night. Everything else you'll need should be available in the pool house."

Zander remembered he had left his bag in the trunk of his rental car. The car was now resting comfortably at Herbie's in Cedar Key. Millie could see that something was bothering him.

"What's wrong?"

"I'm afraid I've left my things in the rental car. I have no change of clothes."

"Write down your sizes and the items you'll need. I'll have them delivered here before you wake up. Put your list under the magnet on the refrigerator in the kitchen before you turn in."

"I am impressed," Zander said.

"What did I tell you about what money does? Any other questions?"

"They can wait until tomorrow."

"Good, see you then. Shall we say no later than 7:30?"

"Agreed," Zander said, and began writing down his list.

• • •

Zander slept restlessly. His dreams had him reliving his past relationships with Sara Jane. He would wake up with a start, and then go right back to dreaming. It wasn't dreaming in Zander's estimation. It was a nightmare. A future together for them could never exist. Of course, the addition of Sandra had changed everything. Zander knew he would have to temper much of his anger if he would expect to have any influence in his daughter's life. He knew working with Millie was crucial to their future.

Zander was up before 6:00, and he felt like he hadn't slept at all. He found a bag with the stuff he had written down the night before. He was amazed and wondered how Millie had pulled off getting clothes before any store had opened. He realized that her sphere of influence was much greater than he could ever have imagined.

He found a pair of cargo shorts that fit. He was hoping for some longer pants so he could wear his boots. He would feel naked without his stun gun and switchblade. He knew wearing his jeans in Florida would make him stick out. No need for any part of that. After finding a shirt he liked, Zander fooled around with the cargo pant's pockets and found they housed both his knife and stun gun without much notice. He wasn't all that enamored with the sandals Millie had left him, but he had no other choice.

He showered and took care of the rest of his business and by 7:00 he was ready to face what the day would bring. He walked out of the pool house and was surprised to see both Millie and Jayne sitting at a table near the pool. He walked over and took a seat opposite Jayne without being asked. She stared at him.

"Breakfast will be served at 7:30. I'm happy you are early. We need to put a few things past us," Millie said.

Zander nodded and looked over at Jayne. She dropped her eyes. It appeared she wasn't as temper-driven as the night before.

"How do you wish to proceed?" Zander asked.

"I was hoping you might have some ideas, but first we must clear the air. I can feel the tension just oozing from you both." Millie smiled.

Zander was surprised. He thought he had masked his feelings quite well.

"We all know the history here. It may be something that can never be resolved, I just don't know. For the sake of the child, however, we have to put all that aside and come together on this." Zander sat back.

"That is the right thing to say," Millie said.

Jayne's eyes never caught Zander's, but he could see she shot a look at Millie that would have killed the weak of heart. Zander decided to take the lead.

"Sara Jane. I'm sorry, I guess it's Jayne now."

Jayne lifted her head. Zander smiled at her.

"We go back a long way. I think about that fact often. I'm sure much of our past would be better forgotten by both of us, but we had some wonderful times together as well. I think I will always have feelings for you. Try as I might, I just can't shake off what we had together. The time for blaming is over. We will never be able to be together as a couple. I know that now, and I will stop trying to resurrect something that can never exist between us. But you are the mother of my child, and we need to work together to get our daughter back."

Zander's statement caught Jayne by surprise. Zander thought he could see some tears forming in the corner of her eyes. Jayne turned away for a few moments and then faced Zander again.

"I'm sorry," Jayne said, so softly that Zander wasn't sure he heard it.

"Well, we're all sorry, and I'm sorry to have to break up this little love fest but breakfast is ready," Millie said, as her cook rolled out a cart with breakfast for the three.

Zander ignored Millie's comment. He pulled his chair around and sat next to Jayne. He put his arm around her.

"I'm sorry, too."

Jayne put her arms around Zander and began sobbing. Zander glanced over at Millie looking to her for guidance. She shrugged her shoulders and began helping pass out the plates of breakfast. She knew this was working out far better than she had planned.

When Jayne stopped sobbing, she took Zander's face in her hands.

"Help me Zander. I know I don't deserve it, but do it for Sandra. Do it for our child."

Now it was Zander's turn to be surprised.

"We both seem to be paying for our sins. I'll get our daughter back. You can be sure of that. The thing I ask is that you don't shut me out. I want to be part of Sandra's life."

"She needs a father even if we can't be together. You are right about that. I am damaged and would eventually screw everything up. But I can be strong for Sandra, and so can you, even if it's not together."

"It's quite nice you two can have this conversation. Maybe it's too late, maybe it isn't. Time will tell. Now, let's have breakfast and talk about what comes next," Millie said.

The three ate in silence, and when they finished, Millie refilled their coffee.

"What is our next move?" Millie asked, as she put down the coffee pot.

"I need to go to the hospital and look things over. Something is bothering me."

"You think it was an inside job?" Millie asked.

"I think it's a place to start."

"But the police have been checking into it and haven't found anything," Jayne said.

"I'm not sure they were looking in all the rights spots. That's going to be my job. Now that I've planted the seed that I'm the father trying to find my child, I don't think I'll draw much attention from the kidnappers."

Jayne was confused.

"They are watching us," Millie said.

"How do you know?"

"Zander and his friend caught them yesterday. They're just down the road."

"Do you know who it is?"

"I'm afraid not. I know most people around here, so I sent Hector on a little reconnaissance mission. He watched for a long time and had no idea. If Hector doesn't know who it is, then I'm afraid we are all in the dark."

Jayne stopped talking and drank her coffee. Zander could see she was trying to process everything, and that was good.

"If you can remember anything that seemed unusual while you were in the hospital, it might be helpful," Zander said.

Jayne nodded.

"Jayne dear, are you up for a little trip to the hospital? Maybe it will jar something lose in your memory." Millie was already buying into Zander's idea.

"No. This is a trip I have to make for myself. I need to see things with a fresh pair of eyes, and right now you might influence me with your perspective. I need to make my own assessment before involving you."

At first Zander thought Millie was going to fight him on his idea.

"I don't believe I like sitting on the sidelines like this."

"Zander's right. This is what he does. Let's let him do it," Jayne said.

The comment surprised both Millie and Zander.

23

Zander took Millie's Caddy. He wanted to be sure the watchers watched him. He knew they couldn't miss him in that car.

On the way to the hospital, he called Herbie to meet him. He wanted the bag he left in the trunk of the rental, but he wanted to bounce a few things off his friend as well. It was a disappointment to find that Herbie was on the job somewhere around Sarasota.

"Herbie, I need my stuff, and I wanted to talk to you." Zander's voice couldn't hide his disappointment.

"Hey, it's not a problem, good buddy. I'll have Gail run it up to you. Talk to her. She's a good listener. She can relay your words to me, and if I have any words of wisdom I can call you."

"I suppose that would work minus that wisdom part."

"Still trying to be the comic, I see. When do you think you might see some success in that arena?"

"Just have her meet me in Chiefland. I saw a Dunkin' Doughnuts there. Tell her to be there at 1:00."

"Zander, she could just drive up to Perry and save you a trip."

"No, I don't want anyone else involved for the moment. These people might spook if they think someone else is in the mix. I just can't risk that, there's too much at stake."

"Understood. I'll call her right now. Zander?"

"Yes, Herbie."

"Be careful," Herbie said, and the line went dead.

Zander took a direct route to the Perry hospital. When he arrived he found the parking lot and noticed a flatbed truck similar to the one parked near Millie's gate. It ignited his inner alarm. He always knew when it happened, because the hairs on the back of his neck stood up.

There was someone sitting in the truck. Whoever it was seemed to take interest in Millie's vehicle, because he sat up straight when Zander parked the Caddy. Zander thought it might be interesting to initiate confrontation. He walked over to the flatbed and knocked on the window. The man in the truck did his best to ignore the intrusion, but it was difficult with Zander staring at him. He rolled down the window.

"Yeah?"

"I wonder if you could help me?"

"Probably not."

"I'm just wondering if this is the only hospital in the Perry area."

"Yeah."

"Did you hear about a kidnapping of a child that happened here?"

"Everybody has."

"Well, I'm the father, and I wonder if you could give me any details about the abduction?"

"Go inside and ask them. I'm just waiting for a friend. I don't get involved with things that involve the law."

Zander took a step back and smiled.

"That doesn't surprise me one bit." Zander turned and walked toward the door.

The man in the truck watched as Zander entered the hospital. When he was out of sight, he started the truck and left the parking lot a little faster than he had entered. It was apparent he had somewhere to be or someone he needed to talk to.

Zander watched him leave from inside the entrance.

"Mission completed," he said to himself.

It would have been nice to have someone following the follower, but there was too much legwork to do before Zander could enlist the help of others. He walked into the reception area and spied a little old lady at the information desk. He walked over to her and smiled.

"I wonder if you could direct me to the newborn and nursery area?"

"Oh my, I'm afraid that visiting hours don't start until this afternoon."

"It's okay. I just found out I'm a father, and I've never been here before."

"I'm not sure I should do this, but you seem like a nice young man. Take the elevator to the second floor and take a left. Everything is located at the end of the hall."

"Is there a staircase I could use? I'm not one for elevators."

"Certainly. Just go down the end of this hallway. It is clearly marked. It will take you right to where you want to be."

Zander thanked her and told her she was a real asset to the hospital. She waved off his comment but smiled as she pointed to the staircase.

Zander could see that the hospital would have been an easy place to plan an abduction. People were all too trusting. His elevator comment was just an excuse to look around and get a feel for the hospital's layout.

When he reached the staircase, he noticed an exit door to the left. He opened the door and could see a parking area. It was an employee lot. Taking Sandra would have been far too easy. The exit had no alarm, and it appeared people used it frequently.

As he climbed the stairs, he realized that the hospital lacked security. Zander found it odd that with what had just happened, there wouldn't have been new protocols added. It pissed him off. Anyone could wander into the place just as he had done without so much as a question from any staff member.

Zander found the nurses' station and waited while a nurse finished with a phone call.

"Can I help you?" she asked.

"I hope you could give me some information."

"How can I help?"

Zander thought she seemed friendly enough.

"I'm the father of the child who was abducted. I was wondering if you could tell me who was on duty that evening so I could talk to them?"

The nurse's friendly demeanor turned sour.

"I'm afraid I can't help you. This is a police matter, and all questions need to be directed to them."

Zander bristled at the sudden loss of her personality.

"Look, I'm here to help find my child. I'm family, so I believe I have the right to talk to people who might give me some vital information."

The nurse snorted. It pissed off Zander even more.

"You can talk to me right now and do what I ask, or I can call Amelia DePont and you can deal with her."

Zander thought he could see just a little hint of concern creep over her face.

"I think I should call the administrator. He might give you permission to talk to some of the staff."

"You do that, but just in case, I'll call Millie and let her know how I'm being treated." Zander started to dial his cell phone.

"Oh, please don't do that. I don't want to lose my job over this."

Zander decided to back off.

"Why don't you take me to the administrator. I'll deal with him, and that should get you off the hook."

"Thank you." The nurse was contrite.

Zander knew that Millie carried clout in the area, but he hadn't realized what effect just dropping her name might have.

The administrator's office was a mess. Papers were stacked all over the desk, the floor, and some shelving located in the corner of the room. Both guest chairs had files stacked above the backs. The remaining chair was for the fat-assed administrator. He filled his office chair with ripples of fat that was quite noticeable through his oversized suit. Zander thought he might have to shop at the local tent and awning. At the very least, he was repulsive. What was worse, the entire office smelled of his sweat.

Zander wanted out of the sweatbox as soon as possible. He cut right to the chase.

"I'm here to talk to your employees who were on duty when my daughter was kidnapped from your hospital."

The administrator opened his mouth, but before any words came out, Zander pulled out his phone and pointed it at him.

"Before you say anything, why don't I call Amelia DePont and you can speak to her."

The fat man was defeated. He glared at the nurse who had brought Zander to the office.

"Give him a list of the people on duty that night. He can speak to anyone on the list." He turned and tried to look out of the window that was blocked by paper and files stacked almost to the ceiling.

Zander smiled and followed the woman back to the nurse's station. The young woman pulled out a file of some sort and began writing down a list of names. Zander looked around and decided to focus on what the nurse was doing.

"That guy was gross. How can you work for someone like that?"

The nurse said nothing, but Zander could see a small upward turn at the corners of her mouth. When she finished, she handed Zander the list.

"Most of the people from that evening are here today. You can find them in the nursery." She pointed toward the door.

Zander thanked her for her help and then had another idea.

"Were you here that night?"

"Yes I was. I was right here at the nurses' station."

"Did you see anything out of the ordinary?"

"I've thought a lot about that night. I didn't see anything unusual. In fact it was very quiet, and I was here at the desk all evening. I would have noticed any strangers or something unusual. It's my job."

Zander was quiet while he considered what she had said. It confirmed what he had expected. This had to be an inside job. No other plausible explanation could exist. He decided not to share his deduction with the nurse. No one needed to be forewarned.

"Thanks for your help. I do appreciate it." He turned toward the nursery door.

"Could I have your name for my records?"

"You can call me Zander. If you need more than that, you can call Amelia DePont, and she can fill in any missing information that she feels is necessary."

The nurse understood.

"By the way, he seldom leaves his office. When he does, we spray it down with disinfectant." She lifted the phone to let the nursery know that Zander would have full permission to interview the people on his list.

It was Zander's turn to smile. The nurse was answering his off-the-cuff question from before. He thought if things were different, he would like this young woman. He knew she was just trying to do her job and be a professional about it. Zander had no time for any of that shit. Every institution had layers of bureaucracy, and he was determined not to let any of it get in his way. It made him think of Aubrey, and sadly he knew that would be a whole other level of bullshit. But it would have to be one problem at a time, and he needed to focus on the present.

When Zander entered the nursery, he noticed one child in the area behind the glass. The baby appeared to be sleeping. All the employees were huddled around the main counter. They straightened up when they saw him.

"My name is Zander. I have a list of people I need to speak to. He handed it to the one of the nurses that looked like she might be in charge.

"We were warned."

"Look, I'm not here trying to get anyone in trouble. I just need to know anything that might help me find my child."

"Your child?" the nurse asked.

"I'm the father," Zander said, feeling very tired.

The icy feeling in the room disappeared. Zander could feel it.

"Let's go to the lounge. You can speak to us there, and we won't be bothered."

"Thank you, that would be fine. But I want to speak to each one of you separate. Something one of you remembers might come up when you aren't listening to another person's account."

"That would be fine. Who would you like to interview first?"

"If you are on the list, I would think you should be first."

"I am, and I'm ready." She turned and walked toward the nurses' lounge.

Zander turned to follow when he noticed a young woman watching him as she pretended to mop the floor. He made a mental note to ask about her.

24

Before the nurse could take a seat, Zander brought her back to the window.

"Who is that?" he asked, pointing to the young woman with the mop.

"She's a nurse wannabe. Nice enough person but not a lot going upstairs, if you know what I mean.

Zander thought he did, but something seemed off about her.

"What's her name?"

"It's Holly," the nurse said, and thought a moment, "Her last name is Perry. It should be on the list."

Zander looked and noticed a Holly on the list but with a different last name.

"I see a Holly Harris but no Perry."

"That's right. She was married recently."

"Was she here the night of the kidnapping?"

"Yes, she was on duty," the nurse said as she checked her list. "She clocked out before all nasty stuff began, as I recall."

Zander made a mental note to speak with her last. Something about her was nagging at him. Zander obtained as much information from the managing nurse as he thought was useful. After that, he went down the list. The rest of the staff had little to add. Their stories all followed each other, and Zander felt he might be wasting his time. Two people who were currently on duty weren't scheduled to work that day. There would be little to gain by interviewing them. He was more interested in the Holly character.

The managing nurse was back out at the nurses' station, and Zander handed her the list.

"I guess the last person I need to talk to is Holly."

The nurse went on the PA and called for Holly to report to the nurses' station. They both waited for over ten minutes until Zander started getting restless.

"Do you suppose she left?"

"Let me check. Everyone knew they were supposed to visit with you," the nurse said, as she checked the time clock.

Zander watched as she screwed up her face.

"She left?"

"Clocked out fifteen minutes ago," the nurse said, clearly frustrated.

Zander was frustrated as well.

"I suppose I could go see her at home," he said, thinking out loud.

"We don't have a current address."

"That seems strange to me," Zander replied.

"Me, too. Wait. She gets picked up by her husband out front of the hospital. He's often late, so she may still be waiting for him on the bench by the parking lot."

Zander said nothing but made quick work of getting himself to the hospital entrance. The nurse watched him go wondering what he was thinking. She was trying to imagine what she would do if one of her four children was abducted. Since it was beyond her comprehension, she went back to the work at hand.

Zander realized he needed to slow down his movements when he exited the hospital. It would avoid alerting this Holly woman if she was still hanging around. After stopping at the hospital entrance, Zander looked around like he was taking in the view. He stopped when he located the bench near the parking lot. A woman was obviously waiting for a ride.

Holly saw him coming and appeared to cower on the bench. It was another one of those bells that went off in Zander's head. He walked to her and sat down.

"Hello. My name is Zander. Yours is Holly, I believe. I think you've been told that I'm the father of the child that was abducted."

"Yes."

"I think you were also told that I needed to interview all of the people on duty that night."

"My shift ended, and I needed to get out here so I didn't miss my ride."

"Looks like you had plenty of time. If I didn't know better, I would think you were trying to avoid talking to me."

Holly looked down. Zander sat back and appeared to stare out toward the road.

"Who is picking you up?"

"My husband."

"What's his name?"

"Harris."

"I mean what's his first name?"

"Harris."

Zander snorted in amusement.

"Interesting. Harris Harris. Were his parents afraid he wouldn't remember his full name?"

Holly smiled.

"You don't know the half of it. The whole family is weird." Holly shut up, realizing she might have said too much.

"I think there's something you're not telling me. I think you want to, however."

Holly was searching for something to say, when Harris drove up in her car. He pulled right up to the bench and rolled down his window.

"Come on let's go. I've got things to do," he yelled at Holly.

Zander looked him over.

"What you lookin' at?" Harris snarled.

"Trying to decide if you are an asshole or just an everyday prick."

"Usually, I would get out and kick your ass, but I just don't have time for dickheads today."

"You should treat your wife with the respect she deserves."

"My wife is none of your business."

"It's been my experience that you should always be careful with people who have access to your toothbrush."

Harris was confused by Zander's words. So he turned, rolled up the window and gave Zander his middle finger.

Zander laughed out loud and turned toward Holly.

"We need to talk."

"Come back to the hospital tomorrow. I start work at 7:00 a.m."

"What time does this asshole drop you off?"

"Between six and six-thirty."

"I'll be here before six. I'll meet you right here."

"No. I don't want Harris to see me speaking with you. He never comes into the hospital, so I'll meet you in the nurses' lounge."

"I feel like you know much more than you're saying. You need to give me some hope here."

Holly rose and turned her back to the car and grabbed Zander's hand.

"Your child is safe. I'll explain tomorrow." Holly dropped Zander's hand, went around the car to the passenger's side, and got in.

Zander watched her go turning over what she had just told him. He felt a weight lifting from his shoulders. He had been right. Holly Harris knew something, and she would be sharing it with Zander.

25

Holly was quiet on her ride home with her husband. She thought about what she had always dreamed home would be like. This wasn't anything close. Harris glanced at her a few times before he spoke.

"What are you thinking about?"

Holly was quiet and failed to answer him. She was considering what to do next. Her meeting with the father of the baby was to take place the next morning, and she had no idea how to proceed.

"Answer me," Harris said.

Holly still kept quiet. She had nothing to say. If someone saw her they would have thought she was calmly sitting in the car. It could not have been further from the truth. Her stomach was rolling, and she thought she was going to be sick. She just wanted everything to go away. That was especially true of the Harris family. Just as she was about to turn to speak to Harris, she felt a blow just above her left eyebrow. It was difficult to see anything but darkness. She was unconscious for a few seconds. Just as she started to regain the light, Harris grabbed her throat with his left hand. In doing so, the steering wheel turned, and the Pontiac left the road.

Holly had no idea what was happening. Harris tried to overcorrect and bring the car back onto the road. He succeeded in bringing the car into a hundred and eighty degree skid. When the tires reached the edge of the shoulder, the car had nowhere to go but over. It was a beautiful flip. It was the kind you might see in a movie, flipping around and landing on all four tires with very little damage to the vehicle.

Holly always wore her seat belt, not so with Harris. He had been thrown from side to side, falling right into Holly's lap on the first flip. Then he fell onto the roof and ended up in the back seat. Harris lay unconscious alone in the back.

The injuries Holly received were from the beating Harris had inflicted, but they had been enough. The side of her face was already bruising where he had clipped her. Her throat had finger marks all over it, and it felt like her windpipe was crushed. She was sure she couldn't talk.

Holly sat trying to clear her head. She realized that this might be the one chance to get out from under the Harris family.

Holly unbuckled her seatbelt and went around to the driver's side of the car. She saw a few dents and crumples where the car had hit the ground on the rollover, but the door opened without any trouble. She turned over the ignition, and the car started. It was an instant relief. Holly drove through the ditch until she came to an access drive that led into a field. She drove the car up the bank and back onto the highway. They were a few miles from the entrance to the compound, so she stopped and put the car into neutral. Holly had no idea what to do next. She needed to think. Everything was so screwed up. The thing she knew for sure was that she wasn't going back to the compound. Harris wasn't stirring in the back, and she thanked the stars for small favors. The problem still existed of what to do with him. Somehow she had to get rid of him. She had never killed anyone, but the thought crossed her mind. She knew in her heart she would never do it.

She put the car back into drive and made a U-turn heading south. She hoped that Harris would remain unconscious until she reached her destination. One place she would be safe was Miss Amelia DePont's estate. Maybe when she told her what the Harris family was plotting, Miss Amelia would be able to help. Thinking of what would happen if Harris woke up and figured out what she was doing scared her. She knew she would be dead.

It was dark and there was no moon, so Holly slowed down trying to be sure not to miss the road that led to the estate. She saw a light that marked the entrance to the estate. She pulled into the drive and pushed the call button on the pillar next to the gate.

"Please state your name and reason why you seem to think it's all right to bother me."

Holly knew it was Amelia DePont. She had heard her speak countless times at the hospital. She cleared her throat.

"Miss Amelia, this is Holly Perry from the hospital," Holly said, but her voice was just a series of squeaks because of what Harris had done to her throat.

Millie heard her say "hospital" and decided that she needed to speak to this person. She pushed the button and the gate opened. By the time Holly drove up to the door, there was a contingency of people out front to meet her. Holly recognized Zander but most of the other people were unfamiliar.

Zander recognized Holly's vehicle. He went to the driver's side and opened the door before Holly even had a chance to turn off the ignition. He did it for her and pulled the keys.

"What are you doing here?" Zander asked. "Our meeting was supposed to take place tomorrow morning."

"Things have changed, I think." Holly seemed confused.

Zander dialed down his rhetoric and helped Holly out of the car. The outdoor lighting shined enough for Zander to see the number someone had caused to her face.

"What happened to you?"

Holly pointed to the back seat and explained what happened earlier that evening.

"We've got to do something with Harris. When he wakes up he'll want to kill me," Holly said.

Millie went around the car and took Holly into the house. Zander opened the back door and checked on Harris. He felt for a pulse unsuccessfully. Millie came back out of the house. She looked at Zander.

"He's dead," Zander said without emotion.

"Good. Come in the house," Millie said to Zander. She turned to Hector. "Get rid of him. You know what to do."

Hector nodded and got into the car. Zander threw him the keys.

"I'll clean everything up and put the car in the carriage house when I'm finished," he said as he drove away.

"Rosita? It appears that it could very well be a long night. Come in and make some coffee." Millie demanded.

Everyone went into the house. Zander knew this was going to be a serious affair. Everyone was seated at the huge dining room table and not the pool house area where many of the previous conversations had taken place before.

The first thing Zander noticed was a small handgun on the table in front of Jayne. He walked over and picked it up.

"There will be no need for firearms. Holly has come to us on her own free will. It would make sense to hear her out before we try to intimidate anyone." Zander shot a glance at Jayne. She returned his glance with a stare that would have killed a lesser man. Zander smiled at her, which did nothing to calm the volatile environment.

Zander took his place at the table and engaged Holly immediately. "Why don't you tell us why you decided to come here tonight? Don't leave anything out."

Holly started at the beginning. The beginning wasn't something the people at the table wanted to hear, but they listened anyway as Holly told about her life. Just as Jayne was about to explode, Holly told how the Harris family decided to kidnap little Sandra. She was careful not to disclose her original idea of taking the child to call her own. In her mind, she realized it had been a stupid idea right from the beginning. Nothing bad should happen to Sandra, but her self-preservation was working. Her goal was now to help this family and make her escape from the Harris family.

When Holly finished her life story, Zander and Millie sat back in their chairs thinking about the next step. Jayne wasn't convinced that Holly was telling them the actual truth.

"I don't believe you. When are they going to ask for the ransom?"

"I don't know. They don't tell me anything."

"You are a lying bitch."

Holly began to weep softly into her hands. It just served to incense Jayne even more.

"Your tears won't work here. You need to start being truthful. You are a part of this, and this is just another ploy to get more money from us."

Holly had no idea what Jayne was talking about, and it just made her more upset. More tears were running down her cheeks, and she was confused. Just when she thought she would tell them about her own plans for the baby, Rosita came in with the coffee. Millie spoke.

"Rosita, please take our guest to one of the spare rooms and get her settled." She turned to Holly. "Pull yourself together, and when you feel ready, come back down. We will need to talk to you some more after we decide how to proceed."

Jayne stood up to protest, but Millie whirled around toward her.

"You will sit. Your anger is doing nothing to help the situation."

Jayne opened her mouth to answer, but Millie's response was instantaneous.

"I told you to sit," Millie said, with some venom in her voice.

At any other time, Zander would have enjoyed the heck out of seeing these two trying for a knockout. Time was now more important because of Holly's entrance into their problem. He decided to try and take control and get the two women back on point.

"You two can put on the gloves at some later time. Right now, we've got to decide how we're going to solve this problem. Things have changed and we need to act before the Harris family discovers their son's death and Holly's defection."

Jayne knew what Zander was saying, and she sat back in her chair and lost the attitude.

"What do we do now? You seem to be in charge," Jayne said, still not on board.

"The first thing I need to do is make a few phone calls. I think we're going to need more hands," Zander said.

"Why do you think you need to bring in strangers? I've got a number of good men who would be willing to help us," Millie said.

Zander thought about what she had said. He had thought about calling Herbie but realized that using Millie's men was a better idea. Besides, how much help Herbie would have been was always a big question. He had to make one call regardless.

"I think that would be a good idea. Can you get the ball rolling and get them here tonight?" Zander asked.

"Of course, I'll do it right now." Amelia DePont stood. "What are you planning?"

"I need to make one call and get some advice from someone I trust," Zander said.

Millie nodded.

"Jayne, you can help me read the phone numbers," Millie said, and helped Jayne get up from her chair.

"I'm going to the pool house and make the call. I'll be right back," Zander said.

As he walked over to his quarters, Zander wasn't feeling all that good about how the evening had turned out. They were forced into being reactive, and now there were two issues that needed his attention. He hated not being in charge. The element of surprise was always the better choice.

His call to Max Kuhn in Key West was answered on the second ring.

26

"Sander Van Zee. I presume this isn't a social call, since you've never called me socially." Max tried to sound terse, but Zander knew he was just playing him.

Zander was confused about how Max knew who was calling. He had a new cell phone, and he hadn't shared the number.

"How did you know it was me?" Zander asked.

"Herbie called and told me you might need my help."

"What else did he tell you?"

"He was quite guarded. I could tell he wanted to say more, but he was conflicted. I didn't press him any further."

Zander smiled to himself. He wished Fats had some of Herbie's good sense.

"I've got two major issues that I'm dealing with, and I need some advice and maybe some help if it would work for you."

"Quite frankly, I've been missing the action. I think Mona may need a break from me as well," Max laughed.

Zander wasted no time telling Max about his situation with Jayne and Sandra. He tried to keep it as brief as possible, but there were so many angles to consider. His explanation took longer than he wanted.

Max wasted no time when he finished.

"You've got to act. I would like to come up and help, but that would delay what you should be doing right now."

"Then help me plan our next move. I'm at a loss right now."

"Understandably so, you've got too much skin in the game. You can take that literally."

Zander knew what he was saying but kept his mouth shut and waited for Max to give him what he needed.

Max talked for another ten minutes asking Zander questions and filling in what he thought should be done. When he finished, he paused.

"What was the other issue?"

"Maybe I've already asked too much of you. This could wait until the problem is solved."

"Nonsense. You wouldn't have mentioned another problem if it wasn't pressing. Remember who you are speaking to."

Zander knew he was right and gave his abbreviated history with Aubrey. The explanation took longer than he wanted as well. Everything was making him jumpy because of his lack of action.

Max tried to calm him down.

"This is something I can help you with. I still have contacts in Cuba and I can get the intel we need and help you with an action plan. And Zander?"

"Yes?" Zander asked dreading what might come next.

"You need to act on your first problem. You also need to involve the young woman. You need her eyes and her understanding of the layout to help with your element of surprise."

Zander hadn't thought much about Holly but knew Max was right.

"I'll call you when I know more," Max said and hung up.

Zander thought about what Max had told him. He wanted to talk more strategy but knew he was right. They had to act.

Zander walked briskly back to the dining room. His call had taken longer than he anticipated. The table had three men seated that Zander had never seen before. Just as he was about to sit down, Hector entered wiping his hands on a towel. Hector nodded to Millie, and Zander realized he had completed the task she had asked him to do. Zander would need to know nothing more about it. He had enough to think about without obsessing where Hector had buried the body.

"We are all here and waiting," Millie said, with an edge to her voice.

Zander knew it was a rebuke for keeping everyone waiting. Millie never waited for anyone. He ignored her comment.

"We need to have Holly here. Someone needs to go get her," Zander said.

"I don't think that would be in our best interest," Jayne mumbled.

Millie saw that Zander had something in mind and knew she needed to rely on his judgment.

"Rosita, please go upstairs and get Holly," Millie called out to the kitchen.

Zander heard her footsteps climbing the stairs. When Amelia DePont spoke, everyone listened.

Zander felt all eyes resting on him, as he took his place at the table. He looked over at Millie. She caught the question in his eyes.

"These men work for me, and I have their complete trust."

"I don't doubt it for a moment. This could very well get very nasty and people may get hurt. It might mean you might have to take a life. Are you ready for something like that?"

No one spoke but all four men looked over at Millie. She spoke for them.

"I told you they have my complete trust. These men have been with me for many years and have done many things I'd rather not even mention. They are without reproach, and you can trust your life to them."

"That's good to know. Welcome aboard, gentlemen," Zander said, and he could see the men relax.

"I don't know why you need to involve this woman who stole our child." Jayne was still angry.

"She may be the best chance we have of getting into the Harris compound without detection."

"So, what are you going to do with her?"

"The first thing we need to do is tell her the truth about her husband."

"Do you think that's wise? She might shut down," Millie asked.

"Maybe, but she was being honest with us, so we need to return the trust. Frankly, I don't think it will have an adverse affect, and if I have read her right, I would expect quite the opposite."

"Mr. Zander, what can we do to help you right now?" Hector asked.

"The first thing we need is to find out if that flatbed truck is still out there watching the gate. I'm hoping that Holly's unannounced arrival went undetected. If so, I want you to secure the vehicle and bring it back here."

"We can do that. What about the driver?"

"I'm sure he's part of the Harris clan. We can't risk him going back and warning the family. If you have a secure place you can keep him without interference from the outside, go ahead and lock him up. We can decide what to do with him later." Zander said, and looked away.

Whoever was in the truck was no longer important, but he wasn't about to order his death either.

The men stood, and Millie ushered them out of the main entrance. She was saying something to Hector that Zander couldn't make out. He decided the less he knew the better.

As Millie came back into the room, Rosita and Holly entered from the kitchen area.

"Here she is Miss Amelia," Rosita said, and made an exit.

"Sit down please," Millie said to Holly.

Holly looked fearful, and Zander thought it might work to their advantage.

"We are going to be asking you for your help in recovering our daughter," Zander said, and motioned toward Jayne.

"I'm afraid of what the family will do to me. I'm afraid my husband will beat me and maybe even kill me." Holly's voice was quivering as she spoke.

"It surprises me that this is the first you've spoken about your husband," Zander said.

Holly dropped her eyes. The longer she was out of Harris' control the less frightened she felt. Maybe it had been a mistake not to ask about him. She could see now that it was an error. She hoped she could correct it.

"Is he okay? No one said anything, so I thought someone brought him to the hospital to get checked?"

"He's dead, you idiot," Jayne blurted out."

Zander almost came out of his chair. He would deal with Jayne later, but right now he had to calm the waters.

"Always the tactician. Isn't that right, Jayne?"

He turned to Holly.

"I'm afraid Harris didn't make it. His neck was broken."

Zander saw some of the tension leave Holly's rigid frame. She said nothing.

"He won't be hurting you ever again, dear," Millie said, trying her best to console.

Holly nodded, and then she got a panicked look in her eyes.

"The family will kill me."

"No, they won't. We will be moving on them first. Our goal is to take them by surprise. That's where you come in."

What Holly was hearing made her nervous. All she wanted to do was to run as far away from this place as possible. Being in the mix to get back the child wasn't something she had been anticipating. She could play along, however.

"What do you want me to do?"

"We'll know more when Millie's men return, but right now we need information."

"Like what?" Holly had no idea what Zander needed.

"We need to know the family schedule."

Holly thought for a few moments.

"Well, most days the men leave by 6:30."

"Where do they go?"

"I don't know. They don't share that with me. I think they go to steal things. Harris told me they have a bootlegging business somewhere north in the hills. They are gone most of the day."

"Who's got Sandra?" Jayne asked still angry.

"Papa Henry's wife. Her name is Helen. She's not a bad person. She just got caught up with the family like I did. She would never hurt your child."

"So, when the men leave for the day, where are Helen and Sandra?" Zander asked, trying to keep the conversation on point.

"They stay in Papa Henry's trailer. Sometime she takes the baby out for a walk in a little wagon. Mostly they just stay in the trailer." Holly was feeling a bit less nervous.

"We will need you to point out the trailer when the time comes," Zander said.

"But they always lock the gate. We can't get in there without the combination."

Millie stood up and crossed the room to where she had placed her bag earlier. She took out her phone and pressed a number in her contacts. Someone answered on the other end.

"Hector, we need the combination for the lock on the gate of the Harris compound." She paused. "When you have it secured. Call me back."

Zander looked up at Millie.

"What's their status?"

"They are almost ready to rush to truck and driver. It appears he never moved."

"That's at least some good news."

Zander thought for a few moments.

"Once we get the flatbed, we'll have Hector drive it to the compound. The other three men will be hidden under a tarp in the back. Hector will open the gate and drive into the area. Holly and I will be right behind in her car. Hopefully, it will look like she and Harris are returning home. It may give us enough time to surprise Helen and anyone left to get the jump on them."

"You think you can trust her?" Jayne asked.

Zander reached into his pocket and pulled out the switchblade. He opened it for effect.

"I think when Holly realizes all the alternatives, she will be more than happy to help us."

Holly's eyes were wide. If she had thought at all about some kind of betrayal, it was all but lost. She nodded in complete agreement.

Millie heard it first. It was the sound of a vehicle coming up the drive. It was very loud and Zander knew it was the flatbed truck. It sounded like a straight pipe coming right out of the manifold. He shouldn't have been surprised that there wasn't a muffler. He was concerned about the noise at first, but realized he might be able to use to his advantage. That sound would be familiar and the people in the compound would be at ease when they rolled into view.

Hector came into the foyer and waited for instructions. The other three waited outside for their instructions to come later. Zander approached Hector.

"Did the man communicate the combination to the gate?"

"I'm afraid there was no communication. But we found these numbers taped to the dash. It appears to be the combination. I think maybe this boy couldn't remember it, so he wrote it down." Hector handed the slip of paper to Zander.

Zander knew what this meant, and he did not like what he was hearing. Millie and Jayne had entered the room with an armload of rifles.

"What the hell is this? We want to do this without any bloodshed." Zander was insistent.

"Too late for that. Two of the Harris boys have been eliminated. How do you think the rest of the family is going to react? I want you there with more than just your little pecker in your hand." She looked over at Jayne. "It appears you've done enough damage with that little thing already."

Zander was about to ask her why she thought it was little, but he checked that thought. Millie passed out the rifles to Hector and the three men outside. She was about to give one to Zander, but he declined.

Millie went back out of the room and soon returned with two handguns. She put them on the table near the door.

"Look at them. Which one do you want?"

"I don't need a handgun."

"Yes you do. That little knife won't do you much good with all the testosterone flying around with all these Harris assholes. I want you to bring back my granddaughter alive, and if that means you have to kill everyone of them sonsabitches, then that's what you will do."

It was the first time all evening that Jayne cracked a smile. She knew about Zander's aversion to firearms, and she also knew he had never taken a human life. Maybe it was about time he faced who he was. It made her happy to see him uncomfortable.

Zander looked at both pistols. One was a semi-automatic .45 caliber and he had no idea how to even fire it. The other was a .38 revolver. He had shot a similar handgun when he was young. It was a .22 rim fire, and he and some friends had used it to fire at rats in the town dump at night with headlights from a car. He picked up the .38.

"I'll take this one, but I'm not going to use it."

"You'll use it if you have to. Remember what's at stake here. It's loaded, so be careful. Don't cock it unless you are ready to shoot."

Zander felt no need to argue, and he stuck the revolver into his waistband. He motioned to the others to follow him outside. Millie's men got into the truck. Hector was driving. Zander helped cover the remaining three with the tarp. Hector put the guns on the cab floor.

Millie brought Holly out of the house, while Zander walked to the carriage house to get the Pontiac. Holly seemed reluctant to get into the car, when Zander drove up.

"Get in the damn car unless you want to end up like your husband," Jayne said, and gave her a push.

Holly got into the car.

27

Zander led the way with the help of Holly's direction. Trusting Holly was not at the same level of concern as Jayne was experiencing. He knew she was a survivor, and she would look for the best way to come out on top. Zander hoped she understood that this was by far her best option. Had she been telling them the entire truth? He doubted it very much, but it didn't matter. Things had come too far, and whether they liked it or not, everything had been put into motion.

At first Zander had been upset by Holly's unannounced appearance at the DePont estate. After careful consideration, he knew that it was the catalyst they needed. Time was running out, and the longer they prolonged the inevitable, the tougher it would become to keep Sandra safe. Zander never liked making plans on the run, but he had no other options. He decided to make this work.

"How much farther?"

Holly shrugged.

"Maybe five or six miles. I don't know. I just know when it's time to turn."

Zander wanted to go over what they would be doing when they got into the compound. Since it was almost 6:30 and the darkness was morphing into gray, he decided to wait until they identified the entrance. He would decide what to do after that. He wanted to wait until he was sure the men had left for the day. It would not be advantageous to been seen by the family in their own vehicles. The goal would be to find Sandra and remove her without firing a single bullet.

It was hard to know if that would even be possible, but it was a lofty goal.

"The gate is just up ahead after the curve," Holly said.

Zander slowed down and drove past the gate. Hector and the men followed, and the group kept driving until they came to a secondary road. Zander turned off and went up the road for almost a mile before he stopped. Zander had no idea where the road led, but there was swamp on both sides of the road. The dirt track had no shoulder on either side. Zander realized they needed to turn around or they would land in some nasty muck. He pulled the keys from the ignition, in case he had misjudged Holly's intentions.

"Let's get turned around," he yelled at Hector before the truck came to a stop.

Hector was no novice at driving trucks. He had driven logging trucks most of his life. Before Zander got the keys back into the ignition, Hector had the truck turned around and was waiting for Zander to follow suit.

Hector was smiling when Zander approached the truck.

"What now, Mr. Zander?" Hector asked.

Zander liked this man and was happy he and the others had his back.

"Why don't you tell the others to get out from under that tarp and stretch their legs for a while. I want to see what's going on. I'll take the car up to the main road to do some recon. I may go on foot and see if I can confirm that the Harris men have left."

"I know of this Henry Harris fellow. I think there is one way to settle this." Hector pointed to his rifle. "People like this never go away."

It was hard to hear, but Zander knew Hector was right. He had met a handful of people with similar traits. He helped get rid of two of those bodies.

"Let's try my way first."

"Okay. What do you want us to do?"

"Just stay here. Do you have your phone?"

Hector showed his phone.

"Good. Give me the number."

They exchanged numbers, and Zander was proud of himself for being able to enter Hector's number without any help. He returned to the Pontiac and helped Holly out of the car.

"You stay with Hector until I call for you."

Holly's eyes registered panic.

"Don't worry. These men with treat you with respect. They work for Amelia DePont. What would happen if she learned they failed do as she had instructed?"

Holly dropped her head and nodded. Zander led Holly over to the truck.

"Watch Holly," he said to Hector. "I'm taking the Pontiac and try to get some indication of what's happening. Stay put, and I'll get back to you as soon as I can."

Zander got back into the Pontiac and headed to the spot where they turned off the highway. He paused and looked down toward the entrance to the compound. He knew he would have to drive down the road to get a better look. It made him nervous to be driving a vehicle they would recognize. He hadn't planned that part very well.

There was no other choice. Zander took to the road and drove at a reasonable speed right past the compound entrance. Nothing was visible at first glance. He drove past and turned around. Zander knew what he had to do and drove back.

"Hector, give me one of your men. He needs to drive me to the entrance and drop me off."

Hector spoke to one of the three men, and Zander took his place in the passenger seat. The two sped off, and soon Zander told him to slow down.

"Don't stop the car, just slow enough for me to jump out just before the entrance. Then you turn around down the road and return to the others."

Hector's man nodded and slowed to a crawl so Zander could jump out. Zander's feet hit the pavement, and he almost turned an ankle. He was able to regain his footing at the last moment, but it scared him. He wouldn't be any good to anyone with a sprained ankle or worse. He waved to the driver to show he was okay and ducked into the woods.

Zander's plan was to follow the lane by staying just off the path that served as the driveway. Enough cover for him to duck down and hide if a vehicle appeared.

What he hadn't seen from the road was that the lane had been built up, and both sides were wet and swampy. Zander was walking through water and muck up over his calves. It was rough going, and he was almost thankful when he heard motor noise coming from the compound. He flattened out behind a small thicket of long needle pines hoping that he would be out of the muck. No such luck, and Zander found himself wet from head to foot. He hated getting his boxer briefs wet. Nothing was worse than a wet crouch in his estimation.

A flatbed truck came lumbering down the lane. Zander tried to look as they went past, but the trees blocked his view. He saw there were men in the cab and some on back, but he there was no a head count. When they passed him, he was able to sit up and watch from behind the little thicket without being seen. The truck stopped at the gate, and someone jumped out. The truck drove ahead after a moment, and they unlocked and locked the gate. The truck took a left and went down the road. Soon, it was out of earshot.

Zander stood and worked out the kinks from his screwball position from behind the trees. He felt for his left front pocket. It was as wet as everything else clinging to his body. He reached into his pocket looking for the piece of paper with the combination to the lock on the gate. He pulled it out trying to make sure not to shred the wet paper. It looked like a huge spit wad. He unraveled it. It was written with an ink pen, and the ink had smeared and all the numbers had disappeared. All that was left was an indigo smear.

Zander sat down on the lane. He wondered if anything else could go wrong. He was starting to feel sorry for himself when reality hit him. He had to make a move no matter what the consequences. All this planning was going nowhere. He picked up the phone. He had a panic attack, when he pulled it out of his right front pocket. It was wet like everything else.

Zander looked at the phone wondering if he would have to walk back the two miles to where the car and truck were waiting. He pressed the call button. The phone had powered on. It was working. Zander made the call.

"Hector, bring the car and the truck to the gate. You wouldn't have made a copy of the combination to the lock by chance."

"No mister Zander. I gave that to you. Did you lose it?"

"Something on that order. I'll explain later."

"We are on our way." Hector hung up.

Zander's phone made a strange squealing noise, and then the light from the keyboard went dark. Zander didn't bother thinking about the luck he just experienced having the phone work for even a short time. He just wondered how many damn phones he would have to buy in his lifetime. He hated them, and they obviously hated him as well.

He walked toward the entrance and kept out of sight, until Hector drove into the area in front of the gate.

"What happened to you, Mr. Zander?" Hector tried not to smile.

"I didn't realize that this place was mostly swamp and muck."

"You do now."

"You are a funny man, Hector. We don't have time for this. Obviously, I don't have the lock combination any longer but I might try and remember it if you would like."

"There were four sets of numbers, do you remember them?"

"I said I could try."

"We don't have time. Take the truck and ram the gate. We need to knock it down and get in there and out as fast as we can."

Hector screwed up his face.

"That's a big gate. I will need some speed."

"How much?"

"At least 50 miles per hour, I think."

"That's going to create a lot of noise don't you think?'

"Can't be helped. We've got no tools or no bolt cutter to get through the chain."

"Just do it, and do it fast."

Hector backed up the truck and looked both ways to get the best path to hit the gate. He decided to go south because there wouldn't as much of an angle. He could hit the gate without worrying about skidding out or rolling the truck. Hector drove a half-mile before he turned around. He hoped the old truck would make fifty before it shook him to death. He had driven a worse piece of shit in the past, but it was hard to remember when.

Zander heard him barreling up the road and made sure the Pontiac was out of the way before Hector hit the gate. He had no idea if this would work, or if they would have a twisted piece of steel blocking the driveway when it was over.

Zander saw Hector make the curve in the road and head straight for the gate. He thought he saw a smile on his face. Apparently, Hector was enjoying this little demolition derby.

The truck hit the gate just under 59 miles an hour. Zander heard the crash as the gate's hinges gave way and it flew to the left, still being held by the chain and the lock. The post cracked at ground level and flew along with the gate into the muck on the left of the driveway.

Hector hit the brakes and skidded to a stop with his right wheel almost off the lane. The three men who had been watching with the weapons in their arms cheered and ran toward the truck. Hector got out and gave Zander thumbs up.

Zander walked over to the truck.

"Do you suppose you could have made just a little more noise so they could hear you in Tallahassee?"

"Mission accomplished, Mr. Zander."

"Not quite yet. Load up, and let's roll. You'd better back up and let us go before you. I'll have Holly tell me how we should enter the compound. If there are any surprises still left, we'll want to make use of them."

As Hector backed up the truck, the other men took their places. Zander looked at the front end and saw little damage from ramming the gate. No one made trucks like that anymore.

Zander got into the Pontiac and asked Holly how to proceed.

"I think you should come with the others in the truck. Give me a few minutes to talk to Helen before you come in with any guns. I think I can reason with her."

Zander considered her comment.

"I'm going to trust you with this. You need to know, however, if you try to do something to endanger Sandra, your life will end here today."

Holly looked at Zander.

"I would never do anything to hurt the baby."

"But you could do something that might screw things up. Like you might want to take the child for your own."

Holly's mouth dropped open.

"I don't think you are a killer."

"I'm not, but I can't speak for the others." Zander pointed back toward the truck.

"I have never meant any harm. I won't be the cause of any harm now. You can trust me." Holly wondered how Zander knew her secret.

"Holly, I know you've been through much and lost much in your life. I can't blame you for trying to take a few pieces back for yourself. Just realize that it won't be with Sandra. You can make everything right, and you can do it now." Zander jumped on the back of the truck with the two other men.

Holly sat thinking about what Zander had said. She got out the passenger door and moved to the driver's side. She turned over the engine and started the Pontiac. Soon she was driving down the lane for the last time.

28

Zander and the others would follow Holly but stop before they entered the compound. They would wait until she gave the all-clear signal. Zander would give Holly ten full minutes, and then they would go in and try to salvage the situation.

Holly drove to the trailer she shared with Harris. He was gone now. She felt nothing. All the hope and promise she held so close had evaporated. Now there was contempt, and she included herself in that contempt. How could she have let this go so far? It was a question she couldn't answer.

She turned off the ignition. The trailer blocked her view of Papa Henry and Helen's place. She was certain that Helen would have heard her drive in, but she stopped herself from going up to see her. Holly wanted Helen to come to her. She went into the trailer's bedroom. Her bag was in the closet, and soon she was throwing everything she owned into it. It wasn't much. When she was almost finished, there was a knock on the door. Holly threw the bag in the closet and shut the door.

She walked into the kitchen, and saw Helen sitting at the kitchen table.

"Come in," Holly said, her voice dripping sarcasm.

"Where's Harris?" Helen asked. Her voice sounded tired.

"Which one?" Holly's belligerence surprised even her.

"Try not to talk stupid. It won't serve any purpose."

Holly shrugged and went to the cooler. Her mouth went dry, and she needed something to drink.

"Where's Harris?" Helen asked again.

Holly grabbed a can of Dr. Pepper and opened it. The soda was warm because the ice had melted in the cooler. Holly didn't care. She took a seat opposite Helen and took a swallow. When she finished she looked Helen square in the eyes.

"He's dead." She took another drink.

Helen stood.

"What have you done?"

"I haven't done anything." Holly pointed to her face. "He was beating me while he was driving and lost control. The car rolled over, and he broke his neck."

Helen sat back down. Holly waited for her to speak. She had no malice in her heart, and wondered why she had lived like this all these years without some kind of "Come to Jesus" meeting. Holly's contempt for Helen was fueled by the fact that Zander and the other men were waiting just outside the compound.

Helen spoke.

"Where's the body? The police weren't involved were they?" There was no panic in Helen's voice.

"No. His body is buried somewhere on Miss Amelia's property, I think."

Helen was at a loss for words. No comprehension existed in what Holly was telling her. Holly liked having the upper hand.

"There are some men waiting for my signal. They are here to take back the child. One of them is the father."

Helen stared at Holly, but there was defeat in her face.

"Where is the baby?" Holly asked.

"She's in our trailer, asleep. At least she was a few minutes ago."

"Let's go," Holly said, standing.

"I hope you know what you are doing. The family will never stand for this, and you know what they will do."

"I think we took the wrong child. Amelia DePont has many resources, and we need out of this as soon as possible."

Helen was having a hard time wrapping her head around what had just happened. Her whole world had just come crashing down, such as it was. She knew she had to switch into some kind of defense mode. It was nothing she could muster at the moment. She stood and walked out the door with Holly trailing her.

When they got into the open, Holly waved to the truck, and Hector started the engine and followed the two to Helen's trailer. When Helen saw the truck she gasped.

"Harvey was driving that truck. Where is he?"

Zander jumped off the truck and heard what Helen asked.

"Where do you think he is? You've lost two sons today. It seems like it is up to you whether or not you lose any more." Zander walked right up to Helen and took her hand. "We are not here to hurt you. I want my daughter back, but I'm prepared to do whatever it takes to accomplish it."

Helen understood the gravity of the situation. The Harris family was in danger of extinction if plans went as this man had planned. She knew she was caught between what her husband would want and doing what was right. She decided to do what was right. Maybe something still could be salvaged from this huge debacle.

"The baby is in that trailer." She pointed.

"Let's go. We'll take Sandra and leave you to explain the situation to the Harris boys. You may wish to emphasize how important it would be for them not to seek some kind of retribution. It would end badly for everyone."

Helen, Holly, and Zander entered the trailer and went right to the bedroom. Sandra was fast asleep, and Zander thought that was a good sign. She looked healthy and seemed to be thriving.

"You've taken good care of her. I thank you for that," Zander said, turning to Helen.

"She was the daughter I never had," Helen said without emotion.

"I think I can understand, but I don't understand how you could possible think it would be acceptable to raise a child in an environment like this."

"We were going to leave and find a place away from all of this. We would have raised her proper," Holly said, coming to Helen's defense.

Helen smiled ruefully.

"That was never going to happen. It was just a pipe dream."

The door opened, and Hector yelled.

"There's a truck coming. I think it just turned into the lane."

"Papa Henry is back. You've got to get out of here," Helen almost yelled.

"We're armed, so it wouldn't be in their best interest to start anything," Zander said.

"So are they, and they will shoot first."

Zander took Sandra and ran out of the trailer with Holly following. With any luck, they would wait until the truck drove into the compound and make their escape when the Harris boys got out of the truck.

Unfortunately, that wouldn't be happening.

• • •

When Papa Henry had driven out of the compound at about 6:30 that morning, he had turned left and headed toward the second flatbed truck stationed down the road from Amelia DePont's gate.

His son Howard would be taking Harvey's place on watch. He wasn't worried that Harvey wouldn't be able to pull his weight. He knew that he had slept the night away in the truck. He would remember to be extra hard on him today. The thought made him smile.

He lost that smile when he realized the truck wasn't where it supposed to be. Some ass kicking would be happening if Harvey left his post. Henry turned into the access road and stopped the truck. Everyone piled out and off the flatbed.

"Look around. See if you can find anything," Papa Henry said, as he lit a cigarette he had rolled himself.

The boys fanned out, and it wasn't long before Hunter shouted.

"Papa Henry over here. We see a body."

Henry showed little movement as he leaned against the truck.

"Well, don't just stand there. Check it out."

"I don't want to. I think he's dead." Hunter stood his ground.

"Harold, get over there and find out what is going on. Tell your little pussy brother to come back here."

When Hunter came back to the truck, Henry put his cigarette on the fender and caught Hunter with a right hook, and he fell to the ground.

"When I tell you to do something, you will do it." Henry picked his cigarette back up.

Hunter's nose was gushing blood, and it was at bit off center. It appeared to be broken. He said nothing.

Harold was walking toward to the truck.

"What did you find?" Papa Henry asked.

"It's Harvey. He's dead."

Henry showed no emotion. He took another drag from his smoke and then flipped the butt onto the road.

"Load up boys. We're going back home. Something ain't right. Load up them rifles too."

"What about Harvey?"

"He's dead. He ain't going nowhere. Now do as you're told."

The boys got back into the truck, and Papa Henry made sure each had a rifle and ammunition.

"Double check them guns. I'm a thinking we're about to have a war on our hands. Let's go home and start from there."

By the time the truck reached the compound road, the boys had loaded all the guns. Papa Henry never used a rifle. He had a .44 magnum in a hidden holster inside his pants. His massive girth was the perfect hiding place. If it was uncomfortable, no one ever knew.

Papa Henry turned the truck into the lane and stopped to unlock the gate, but he saw it wouldn't be necessary.

"God damn it all. Get ready to shoot. If there is someone in there, they aren't going to be leaving. You kill everyone that ain't family."

He revved up the truck's engine and dropped it into gear.

That's when Hector heard them coming.

• • •

Papa Henry drove the truck into the compound and headed for his trailer. He knew whoever had broken the gate would be after the child. The truck came to a sliding stop, and the boys all jumped out and stood with their rifles raised. Henry headed into the trailer.

Zander and the men knew they had no time to get into the car. He gave Holly the baby and got down on his knees and looked over to where the truck had stopped. He knew Helen would have no choice but to tell Henry where they were. Luckily the vehicles were out of sight, so it gave him a few minutes to decide what to do.

Holly was moving to the trailer's front door. Zander realized she was planning to take the baby inside.

"Holly you can't go in there. If they start shooting it won't be safe in that tin can."

Holly stopped and waited for instruction. She had followed what others had told her to do all of her life. How could she change now?

"Where should I take Sandra?" Holly asked with concern in her voice.

Zander looked around and saw that the Pontiac was parked next to the truck.

"Get behind the front wheel of the truck. That should give you enough cover with the car in front. Lay as flat as possible, and be sure Sandra is sheltered."

Holly knew she would put her body between Sandra and any bullets that might come her way. It was the least she could do, since she was the one who caused this shit storm in the first place.

Zander stood and returned to the other men.

"Hector, take a man and go on the left to the other trailer. Tell the other two boys to go right and keep down. Find some cover. We need these assholes in some crossfire. Let's go. We don't have much time. Wait for my signal, so we can use the cross fire to our best advantage." Zander's men found their places. Zander hid himself at the left side of Holly's trailer, where he could keep an eye on everything.

The movement was not undetected, however. One Harris boy saw Hector run over to the other trailer and yelled out to Henry.

"Papa Henry. I see one of 'em. Come out."

Henry came storming out of his trailer.

"Where is he?"

Harold pointed to the trailer where Hector was hiding.

Papa Henry started to laugh and called out.

"Just remember. It was you who caused this."

He spoke something to his boys. They turned toward Harris and Holly's trailer and began firing their rifles at it.

There were gunshots and gunpowder filling the air. When the rifles were empty they stopped, reloaded, and started shooting again. When they finished, the trailer was riddled with holes. It looked like it was ready to disintegrate.

Zander and the men kept down. Zander could see Holly behind the front wheel of the truck. It looked like she and the baby were unscathed. Holly waved to Zander indicating everything was good.

Papa Henry looked at the trailer before he spoke.

"Looks like nobody is going to come out on top today. If you are still alive, you should come out, and we'll talk. Maybe we'll let you live."

Zander decided it was time to give something back.

29

Zander spoke to Hector and then stood up with his hands raised in the air. He took a step and stopped.

"I'm here. So talk."

"Come closer so we can have a conversation." Papa Henry was trying to sound compassionate.

Zander wasn't buying any of it. He could feel the handgun in his waistband and knew he would be using it. It would not bother him. In fact, he would be happy to put a bullet or two in this huge man's head. He had to get closer to do that. He looked around making sure his men saw him. Then Zander dropped his arms, fell to his knees and rolled, pulling out his handgun.

Right on cue, Hector and the other boys began shooting. The Harris boys were taken off guard. It was enough to catch them in the cross firings. Two of the boys went down. That left the two oldest Harris boys, Harold and Harvey. Harold dropped to the ground and began returning fire at Hector. Harvey followed suit and aimed at the other two men. He never got a shot off. One of Hector's men was a good shot and put a bullet right into his forehead. The top of his head exploded.

Zander knew his handgun was no match for the rifles. He was too far away, and he wanted to save the six shots in the revolver. He watched with a kind of fascination that one might have when a series of things happened that were out of the realm of experience and understanding.

Papa Henry reacted with unusual speed for a huge man. The moment the shooting started he ducked back into the trailer and slammed the door. Harold saw his father had left him alone and decided to make a break for the trailer as well. When he stood and turned toward the front entrance, Hector put a bullet in his back.

Zander looked at the blood and carnage surrounding him. He was surprised the gore hadn't made him sick. The emotion he felt was anger. He stood and yelled out to Hector and his men.

"Is everyone okay?"

Hector stood and Zander could see a gash on his forehead with blood running down into his eyes.

"Someone got a lucky shot but just a graze. I'll be all right.

Zander noticed Holly was starting to stand.

"Holly, stay down. This isn't over." Holly sat back down covering Sandra with her body.

Zander directed his attention to Henry.

"Henry Harris, this is over. You need to come out with your hands in the air."

There was no answer.

"I don't want to start shooting holes in in your trailer, but that's just what we'll do if you don't come out. Think of your wife. She doesn't deserve to be killed for your mistakes."

There was the sound of breaking glass and a shot rang out from the trailer. Zander could feel the air rush by his left ear as the bullet missed the mark just wide. Zander fell to the ground. Hector and his men opened fire putting shots back into the window Henry had used to fire at Zander.

Zander stood up and raised his hand for the men to stop firing.

"This is your last chance. Come out or you will die along with the rest of your family."

A few minutes went by and Zander was about to give the order to commence shooting when a voice rang out.

"Don't shoot. We're coming out." Henry said.

The trailer door opened, and Henry came out shoving Helen in front of him. He had his arm around her neck and was trying to use her as a shield."

The sight almost made Zander laugh out loud. This huge man trying to hide behind the slender woman was ridiculous. Any one of the men could have put a bullet into his massive body with little effort. Zander did notice that Henry had replaced his rifle with a handgun and was holding it to Helen's head.

"Why don't you drop the weapon? This is over. You've lost," Zander said.

"Not unless you want me to kill this woman it ain't."

Zander couldn't believe his ears.

"She's your wife. How could you even say such a thing?" Zander asked.

"I'm a survivor. It don't matter what it takes."

Zander looked at Helen. He saw nothing in her eyes. She had no fear, disgust, or even hatred. It was as if the life had been drained from her. Zander understood what she had lost in such a short time. Her whole family was gone and now even her husband had betrayed her. Zander felt her sadness.

"You men back off. We're going to get into the truck and leave."

"I'm afraid I can't let you do that. You have to pay for your sins today. You can do it alive and with the law, or you can leave this earth with your boys." Zander was firm.

"Not unless you want me to shoot Helen here. Don't think that I won't do it." Henry took the butt of his gun and hit Helen on the side of her face.

Helen almost collapsed but Henry held her up.

"You don't have to hurt her. Just leave her. We'll let you go," Zander said.

Henry laughed.

"Fat chance. How stupid do you think I am?" Henry felt the power had shifted in his favor.

Zander thought about a reply but knew it might set things in motion that would be the end for Helen. Holly had vouched for her and Zander knew she had taken good care of Sandra.

"How far do you think you'll get?" The sheriff will be all over you."

Henry laughed.

"So, where are they? If you were working with them, they would be all over this place."

"It just takes a phone call." Zander reached into his pocket and pulled out his cell.

"Go ahead. I'll be long gone by the time they get here."

Zander knew Henry was trying to force them into a standoff. He realized he had all the cards stacked in his favor and was trying to decide his next move. Helen's arms slumped in front of her. Zander wondered if she was about to collapse. Then he saw her right hand move down to her apron pocket, and Zander could see a small handgun in her palm. It looked like a Derringer. He remembered seeing one on an old western when he was a kid. Some fancy gunslinger with the first name of Yancey used to sport one.

Zander wondered what she was planning to do. He had to get Henry's attention away from her somehow. He took a step.

"Let's put an end to this. You've lost the edge. Just give it up."

Henry moved the pistol from Helen's head and pointed it at Zander.

"One more step, and I'll put a bullet in your smartass mouth."

"My men will cut you down if you try."

"But you'll be just as dead," he trained the gun on Zander.

Helen took the advantage Zander had provided. She raised the Derringer in her right hand and when she had it chest high, she moved and brought it up and shoved it right into Henry's left eye and pulled the trigger.

Henry looked confused. He stood for a second or two before the gun dropped from his hand. He looked down at Helen, with the eye that still had sight, and then toppled over backward.

Zander picked up his revolver and started to move toward Helen. So did Hector and his men.

"Stay where you are and listen to me," Helen commanded.

Zander held up his hand. Everyone froze.

"This isn't your fault. We'll make sure the law knows what happened."

A half-smile crept across Helen's mouth.

"What difference does it make? What do I have left? My family is gone. I had such hopes for Harris and Holly. I thought that if they could get away from this place, I could have some peace of mind. Maybe the chain of evil that came from this place could be broken."

"It's not on you. This is on Henry Harris."

"Who's fooling who? I maybe once even thought something like that, but it was just a lie. I should have done something long ago, but I was weak. I turned a blind eye to everything. I enabled this family to become what they were. At the very least I could have left, but I was too weak to do even that." Helen flipped the button on the derringer and pulled back the hammer.

Zander knew exactly what he was seeing.

"Helen, don't you see? The burden has been lifted. You no longer have to endure the sins of the father."

"It would always be hanging over my head though, wouldn't it? Look at me. I'm all used up. What in the world would I do now? There is just no place left for me."

Zander heard some sirens in the distance. He figured Millie had contacted them as soon as they had left. He wondered why it had taken them so long to get here.

"The sheriff will be here in a moment. Why don't you put the gun down, and we'll sort everything out."

"It's too late for that. Please take care of the child. I guess you're the father. Don't be too hard on Holly. She got caught up in all this, and it wasn't her idea. This whole place is toxic. When you can, burn it to the ground." Helen placed the Derringer under her chin, smiled at Zander and pulled the trigger. She went down in a crumpled heap right next to Henry.

Zander was stunned. It was the first suicide he had ever witnessed. He hoped he would never have to see another. It wasn't a surprise, however. Helen was at the end of her rope. Nothing else was left for her on this earth, and she took the only way out she knew.

Zander had never been without hope. Sure, he had been depressed from time to time but suicide was so final. Things always had a promise to become better. At least in his mind he believed it to be true.

The men had moved up and were checking the bodies of the Harris boys when Zander heard the police cars rumble down the lane. Four cars with two men in each vehicle pulled into the compound clearing. Right behind was Millie's Caddy. Zander could see Millie driving and Jayne in the passenger's seat. Millie drove right up to Zander and stopped the car. Both jumped out.

"Is it over?" Millie asked.

Before Zander could reply, Jayne grabbed his hand.

"Sandra?"

"She's fine. Holly protected her from these assholes. I think without her help she wouldn't have made it." Zander was embellishing somewhat to make Holly seem the hero. "She's over behind the truck."

Jayne ran over and picked up both Holly and Sandra. Jayne hugged both Holly and Sandra together. Zander liked what he saw.

The sheriff walked over to Zander and took out a notebook.

"I think I should get your statement while everything is fresh in your memory. Why don't you come and sit in the vehicle, and we can talk."

Zander nodded and followed him to the cruiser. Millie had gathered Hector and his men and was talking to them. They placed their rifles into Millie's trunk and moved to where they had been stationed explaining to Millie what had happened. The task force had fanned out and was searching each trailer.

No one saw Jayne grab one of the rifles out of the trunk and walk out in front of where the Harris family had fallen. One by one, she approached the bodies and put a single bullet in each man's head.

The sheriff jumped out of his car and was heading toward Jayne when Millie intercepted. She put up her hand and the sheriff stopped in his tracks. Millie leaned over and whispered something in his ear, and he relaxed and watched.

Zander sat alone in the cruiser and was amazed at the power that this woman wielded. He knew what Jayne was doing. It was her way of closing this chapter of her life. Zander hoped she wouldn't include him in her shooting spree. He was content to stay where he was sitting.

Jayne came to Henry's body. She looked at him and then at Helen. No one would ever know what she was thinking. Jayne bent over and put the rifle down resting it on Henry's leg. She grabbed Helen by the arms and moved her away from Henry's body. Jayne had decided that the woman had enough misery in her life. She had no need to be next to it in death.

When Jayne released Helen, she walked back over to where she had rested the rifle. Just as she reached for it, Henry's hand wrapped around her ankle. Henry's other hand clutched the stock of the gun. The fat pig still had some life.

Jayne's eyes got big. She wondered how she could have been that stupid. She should have put a bullet into the man's head before she moved Helen. Henry's grip on her ankle was like a vice. She knew there was no breaking free. She tried kicking his fist with her other foot, but he wouldn't let go. Henry turned his head and looked at her with his one good eye and smiled. That image would stay with Jayne forever. Many people had come and gone in her life, some were good and some were bad. She had never seen someone who was pure evil until now.

Henry was trying to get up. Hector and his men were spellbound. They had no clue as to how this man could still be alive. While everyone stared at the scene, Zander had jumped from the vehicle, and ran toward Jayne. On the way, he pulled out his revolver. Just as Henry rolled to one side, Zander reached him.

He put the gun to his head and pulled the trigger. Henry let go of Jayne's ankle. He rolled back and looked up at Zander. Zander emptied the revolver's remaining five shots into Henry's face. If someone had come on the scene and tried to identify Henry by facial recognition, it would have been impossible.

Zander was still pulling the trigger on empty chambers when the sheriff put his hand on the revolver and took it away.

30

Zander was in shock. The fear of losing Jayne still somehow motivated him, and that was more disbelief than anything. The sheriff put his arm around Zander and held him.

"Henry was dead before you pulled the trigger. It was just a reflex action. I've seen it many times."

Zander wasn't quite so sure. He had been involved in the final demise of the Rooster, but it hadn't been anything he did that caused the death. This felt different. It might be something that could keep him awake at night. He doubted it, however. This man was beyond contempt. Anyone who would use his family the way Henry had, did not deserve to walk the earth with the rest of the human race. That's what he would be telling himself.

Zander could feel Jayne looking at him. He picked up the rifle that was still in Henry's hand and gave it to Jayne. He motioned toward Henry's lifeless body. Jayne understood. Since Henry's face was no longer there, she put the rifle to Henry's chest and put two slugs in his center mass. Then she handed the rifle to the sheriff. With a single nod to Zander, she walked back to where she had left Holly and Sandra. Zander watched her go and realized that Jayne would be fine. Violence was something she wasn't unfamiliar with in her life. He hoped he would be able to follow her lead.

The sheriff took Zander over to his vehicle and began the slow process of disseminating information. Ordinarily, it would have involved many questions about how Zander became involved. Since Millie had given her approval, the sheriff was interested in his story.

Zander answered his questions while keeping his eye on Jayne. He could see her take their child in her arms. He felt a bit of warmth at Jayne's action. What happened next stunned him.

Jayne led Holly to Millie's Caddy and put her inside along with Sandra. Then she went over to Millie, who was speaking to Hector and his men, took her hand and led her to the car. They both got in and drove off. Zander was confused and wanted to follow them. The sheriff had other plans for him.

After over an hour of questions, Zander was free to go. The sheriff's department impounded the Pontiac and the truck, leaving Zander and Hector and his men without transportation. When they protested, they were given rides back to the DePont estate by some of the deputies.

Zander was happy to leave the compound, hoping never to come back. The place had to be eradicated from the face of the earth. He would remember to tell Millie as much.

The ride back was quiet. Zander rode with Hector in one cruiser, and the other three followed in another. When they turned into the driveway that let to the DePont estate, Hector put his hand on Zander's arm.

"You did a good job today. You saved your daughter and Miss Millie's granddaughter. She will be very grateful."

Zander smiled, but he doubted it very much. He doubted Millie displayed much gratefulness ever. She was a difficult nut to crack, and Zander had no idea what made her tick. He realized that it shouldn't be a surprise, since Jayne was a carbon copy.

Zander walked toward the door feeling drained. He just wanted to find a bed and sleep. Hector and his men went for their vehicles. Zander thought they might be going back to work. It would be just another day in the life of being Amelia DePont's employees.

Zander reached for the handle on the front door, and it magically opened. Millie was standing in the door, blocking the entrance. She stepped out and closed the gigantic door with a loud clang.

"We need to get some things straight before you go in with your guns blazing," Millie said and then stopped.

Zander just looked at her.

"Sorry, that wasn't the best metaphor considering what has happened today."

Zander agreed.

"I need you to understand what will happen now that we have your daughter and my granddaughter back." Millie's voice was firm.

"I'm not the enemy here." Zander's voice was just as firm.

"Oh, I realize all that. My concern is what you think you're going to do concerning her future."

Zander realized he hadn't given Sandra's future any thought at all. He was concerned just making sure she had a future.

"I'm not here to cause trouble," Zander said.

"Good. Here's what will happen. Jayne and Sandra will live here with me. We will raise this beautiful child to realize her full potential. I have the means and the desire to give her everything she needs, and it's time Jayne paid attention to her own life. Together, they will have a good life here without wants or needs."

Zander considered what she had just told him.

"So, where does that leave me in the whole scheme of things?"

"Where do you want it to leave you?"

"I hadn't thought much about it, to tell you the truth."

"I thought as much. You and Jayne are more alike than you realize."

The comment caught Zander off-guard, but more importantly it pissed him off. He knew he and Jayne were nothing alike.

"We are complete opposites," Zander said trying to hide his anger.

"Keep telling yourself that. I find it humorous that Jayne says the same thing. Yet here you are almost together again. Everything happens for a reason."

Zander hated the words, but he knew it to be true. He believed the same thing. There were no coincidences.

"What do you think we should do to move ahead, then?"

"Are you sure you want to hear it?" Millie asked.

"Someone has to make some decisions. I suppose you are the most qualified."

Millie smiled. She liked what Zander had just said, and it cemented her feelings for him.

"I would like you to come live with us and help me run the business."

Zander started disagree.

"Just hear me out, Zander. I said that's what I would like. I know it could never happen. You two would end up killing each other, and then I would have to raise Sandra on my own. I'm too old to do that."

Zander knew she was exaggerating, but she was closer to the truth than she might think.

"I'm listening," Zander said.

"You will always be Sandra's father, and you will always be welcome here. Come when you want, and never be afraid to be part of her life. You just can't live here. It wouldn't be good for anyone. I assume you have your own life and plans that you need to realize."

Zander decided not to share his other problem. It served to make him more anxious. One problem solved and another needed his attention. Millie could see his discomfort.

"It looks like I hit a nerve. Care to share?"

"Not right now. If I can work things out, I might tell you sometime in the future. What I will tell you is that there is another issue almost as problematic as the one we just experienced."

"It sounds serious. What are you still doing here?"

Zander wondered how much she knew about what he was going through. He knew her sources were deep, and he wouldn't be surprised if she had all the information.

"I'll be leaving soon. I just need to make some contacts first. Besides, I didn't want to leave until I knew how everything was going to sort out."

"Does our little conversation give at least some peace of mind?"

"Some. I need to talk to Jayne and hold my daughter just to make it all clearer," Zander said and then had another thought. "Have you thought about what will happen to Holly?"

Millie looked at Zander and then smiled.

"I may have judged you too harshly. I think I'll let Jayne explain."

Millie went to the door, opened it and walked inside. Zander followed. He felt like a puppy following its new master. He thought it was strange that the feeling offered little distaste.

Jayne and Holly were in the living room sitting on one of the many couches. Jayne was holding the baby, and it looked as if Holly was giving her some child rearing tips. Zander knew Jayne could use all the tips she could get. He had a hard time visualizing Jayne as a caring and nurturing mother.

"Could I hold Sandra?" Zander asked, walking over to the couch.

Jayne looked at him and then cleared a spot for him on the couch. Zander sat wondering how to pull off holding a child. He could never remember holding a child even once in his life. Being an only child himself precluded having young children around him while growing up.

Jayne handed Sandra over.

"Put your hand under her head and pull her close to your chest."

"She's so little."

"Yes, but she's a fighter. You won't break her by just holding her."

Zander wasn't quite so sure, but he took the job seriously.

"Is this right?" He asked Jayne.

"Sure. Now rock her back and forth just a little. The movement always seems to settle her down after being passed to another person."

Zander liked what he was feeling. He had no idea how to raise an infant, but he was willing to take on some of the responsibility if called upon.

Jayne was looking at him critically, as Zander tried to master his role as parent. Millie decided to push the conversation.

"Holly, would you go out to the kitchen and fix a bottle for Sandra?" Millie asked.

Holly got up and left the room.

"Why don't you tell Zander our plans for Holly?"

Zander was interested and wondered what was going to happen to the young woman.

Jayne looked away and then back into Zander's eyes.

"Millie and I are going to hire Holly to be Sandra's Nanny."

Zander stopped rocking Sandra.

"Do you think that's wise considering her role in the abduction?"

"Let me answer that," Millie said. "I've spoken with her, and I'm at ease having her in this household."

"Are you planning to have some safeguards in place in case she wants the child for her own?" Zander asked, playing the devil's advocate.

"Look at her situation. Where would she go? She needs some kind of home where her worth is appreciated. Trust me, I've taken in all kinds of strays and have a hundred percent success. I'm a good judge of character, and she will fit into this family perfectly."

Zander smiled. He couldn't have suggested a better scenario. He thought he was a good judge of character as well, and he knew Holly had a good heart.

"Are you okay with this?" Zander asked Jayne.

"I'll admit I had my doubts. Millie seems to feel it is for the best, and after I visited with Holly, I have to think she'll be a big help around here."

Zander could hardly believe what he was hearing. Jayne was putting trust into someone other than herself. Stranger things had happened but not in Zander's experience.

Holly came back with the bottle, and Zander happily handed Sandra back to her.

"Why don't you take her up to her room and feed her, dear? When she's finished, put her down for a nap. Holly turned to leave but then spoke to Zander.

"Thank you for what you did today. You saved me."

The comment surprised Zander. He tried to think of something to say.

"Holly, without your help today, things could have gone terribly wrong for Sandra and maybe even the rest of us. It's me who should be thanking you. I'll be in your debt."

Holly said nothing, but Zander could see a smile creep across her face as she left the room.

"Where do we go from here?" Jayne asked.

"I think we should all go over to the pool house and have a drink. We earned it," Millie said.

Zander knew he had other important things to do, but that could wait until tomorrow. Right now he needed a drink, and he wanted to leave on good terms with both Millie and Jayne. Maybe he needed a number of drinks. It was still early, but it had already been a very long day.

31

Holly got up early the next day. The others had spent most of the day drinking and reliving the events. Even Millie had a snootful. Zander had every intention of making his series of expected calls. He failed miserably.

There was a knock at his door in the pool house. When he looked at the clock it read 10:10. Zander jumped out of bed not realizing where he was until a sharp pain hit him in the left eye. Then he remembered the fine bourbon Millie had served the night before.

"Are you alive in there?"

It was Millie's voice. Zander figured he'd better answer, or she might come charging in. He hadn't undressed from the day before and had no desire having Millie finding him like that. He had returned to pass out on the top of the bed. Zander hated drinking to excess. He needed to maintain control and booze had a way of making him lose whatever inhibitions he might normally use to keep himself in check. He wondered what he had said the night before.

"I'll be out shortly. I need to shower."

"That's a good idea. Breakfast has long passed, but my cook will throw together whatever you might want."

The thought of food had a nauseating effect.

"I think I'll pass on the food," Zander said and started undressing.

"You aren't alone. I'll be in the living room. When you are ready, come find me."

Zander wondered what Millie wanted from him. Her tone sounded ominous, and Zander decided not to spend any more time here than necessary. He had Aubrey's well-being to put first now that Sandra was safe.

He hurried his shower and was out of the bedroom in twenty minutes. He found Millie sitting in the living room alone. She was speaking into a phone when Zander entered the room. She motioned him to sit down. Zander looked around at the room and realized he hadn't given his surroundings much consideration. Sandra had taken his entire attention, and he hadn't the time to focus on unnecessary stimuli.

The room was appointed tastefully, but it was far from opulent. Zander liked that. He knew Millie was a pragmatic person. She liked fine things but wasn't overt about it.

Millie hung up the phone.

"What can I get you this morning? You look like shit, by the way."

"Thanks. You're no rosebush yourself."

Millie laughed.

"Touché. Would you like breakfast?"

"No. Maybe just some coffee if it isn't too much trouble."

Millie had cups and a carafe of coffee, and she poured Zander a cup. Zander took his first sip and noticed his hand was shaking just a little.

"Looks like you might need some fresh air," Millie said.

"Must have had some fun last night," Zander replied.

"I wouldn't call it fun necessarily. Maybe we just were relieved and tried to forget how close we came to a real tragedy."

Zander drained his cup and held it out for Millie to refill. She did so right on cue.

"What did you want to talk to me about?" Zander asked.

"Just wondering how you plan to proceed. This relationship with Jayne and Sandra is bound to get complicated. We should decide how to make less so."

"That might be a topic for future debate. Right now, I've got another situation with a woman named Aubrey."

Zander explained the short version of events to Millie. She listened without interruption. When he was finished, she poured more coffee.

"I thought my life was filled with entanglements. I can see that you win that prize, however. What's your next move?"

"I'll need to make some phone calls. I should let a few people know what has happened."

Millie knew what he meant.

"I suppose this Fats fellow does deserve an explanation. Didn't you have a friend who dropped you off before? He could use a call as well, I presume."

Millie's mind was a steel trap. Zander realized she seldom missed much and never forgot anything. He had never mentioned Max to her, and he thought maybe he should keep a few things private.

"I'm planning to get on that," Zander said and drained his coffee cup.

"Before you do, there is something you need to see. I call it closure." Millie got up and motioned for Zander to follow her.

They walked through the door and Millie's Caddy was waiting in the driveway.

"The keys are in the ignition. You drive."

"Where are we going?" Zander realized he may have sounded peeved, but he wanted to move on.

"We're going back to the Harris compound."

Zander was confused. He had no idea why anyone would want to go back to that place. He realized Millie had her reasons.

As they drove Millie did most of the talking. She mostly talked about Jayne and Sandra. Zander could tell she was excited to have her family around her. He still had no idea how he would fit into that equation. He needed more time to think about being a father.

When they reached the lane leading into the compound, Zander could see that there had been some heavy equipment using the road. There were deep ruts leading to the trailers. He wondered what was happening. The drive had cleared his head from the night before, and he noticed his hands had stopped shaking.

Zander expected to see the place crawling with law enforcement. What he saw was heavy equipment working the place over.

"What's going on? Where are the cops?"

"They have lost interest in the entire situation. Since the Harris family never existed, I suppose they thought dealing with all the paperwork was something they didn't need to do." Millie smiled.

Zander knew she somehow had her hand in the whole thing. The earthmovers were making huge trenches next to each trailer. He stopped the car making sure he was out of the way of any machine. He turned to Millie.

"What happened to the bodies?"

She pointed to an area close to where the lane emptied into the compound.

"They each have their own unmarked grave. It's more than they deserve, but I'm not one to desecrate the dead. I might be in the same position one of these days." Millie smiled again and turned to look at the site and the men working the machines.

"What's happening here?" Zander asked.

"We're obliterating this place from the earth, and in doing so, any history that went with it. Just watch."

One of the earthmovers pulled away from the trench and Zander saw a caterpillar move in. It was as huge a Cat as Zander had ever seen. The operator raised the blade and proceeded to destroy the trailer by running right over it. In two passes the trailer was flattened to the point of being unrecognizable. The operator lowered the blade and pushed the entire thing into the trench. Soon he was pushing earth over the entire area. The whole process took less than fifteen minutes.

"That's impressive. Where did all this equipment come from?" Zander asked.

"It's from the business. My logging operation needs the best equipment to function properly. Sometimes I have other uses for it as well."

This time it was Zander's turn to smile.

"What will happen to this place?"

"I did some research this morning, and it belongs to the state. The Harris family just squatted here. They never owned anything. It's mostly swampy ground and not much good other than to grow trees. I'm going to meet with someone and see if we can reclaim the land for forestry. Of course that would be down the road a long way. First, we'll have to plant trees, and it might take many years. I might never see it harvested. Maybe Jayne or Sandra will be around for the harvest." She turned to Zander. "The offer still stands. If you want to get involved in the business, I would be happy to make you a limited partner sometime in the future."

Zander looked and shook his head. He knew it would never work. First of all, he knew nothing about the timber business, and more importantly, he knew that the proximity to Jayne would have them at each other's throat. That would not be good for Sandra.

"I know what you are thinking, and you may be right. I just want you to know that the offer will always be there. I think I could use a good man around for a change."

Zander liked this woman. She knew the right things to say when she wanted. She also knew all the wrongs things when the situation called for them.

"The sheriff is on board with all this?" Zander asked.

"He answers to me. Let's go." Millie sat back.

Zander started the car and moved back onto the lane that led to the road. He had to straddle the ruts to avoid bottoming the car out. On the way back to the DePont estate, both Millie and Zander were quiet. Each seemed to be lost in thought.

Zander had an idea.

"Could you give me a ride to Cedar Key? I want to get my rental and don't want to bother Herbie or his wife."

"It's the least I could do. But I think I'll be sending Hector. I need to start spending some time at the business, and Sandra and Jayne need some of my attention as well."

"I'll get my things from the pool house and say goodbye to Sandra."

"Sandra and Jayne."

Zander knew he screwed up. Jayne was Sandra's mother. Sandra shouldn't be punished for the fact that he and Jayne were dumbasses.

"You're right. I'm sorry. I need to stop just thinking about myself."

"Yes, you do, but so does Jayne. If this is going to work you will both have to amend your thinking and your actions."

"Someone needs to tell that to Jayne," Zander said without any malice.

"That's my job, and it appears I've got my work cut out for me."

The comment made Zander want to smile. He contained it, however.

As they reached the estate, Zander drove to the front door.

"You get your things, I'll find Hector. He may be at the plant, so it could take a half-hour or so. It will give you time to say your goodbyes for the short term. When you get this other thing handled, you'll need to return. Be thinking about how this relationship is going to work if you are a part-time father."

Zander knew there would be no focus on that problem until he dealt with Aubrey's disappearance. It was far too complex, and he had no answers. He had never been in a situation like this in the past, so he had nothing to use for a comparison.

He went to the pool house and threw his things into his bag. He made sure everything looked presentable. He never left things a mess when he was a guest. His mother had taught him that.

Zander threw his bag near the door and went looking for his daughter to say goodbye. He knew she wasn't old enough to appreciate anything like that, but he also knew it was more for him.

He went into the kitchen and Millie was sitting at the table talking to her housekeeper.

"Have you seen Jayne and Sandra?" Zander asked sticking his head in the door.

"Come in," Millie said. "It seems Jayne, Sandra, and Holly went shopping.

"Shopping?"

"I have been remiss in providing things for a child it seems. I've never had a young person in my home, but that's no excuse. It looks like they need clothing, car seats, strollers, and a baby bed. Things like that."

Zander realized he knew nothing about raising a child. He was happy everyone had Holly to guide them through the process.

"Hector was closer than I thought. He's waiting for you in the pickup out front."

"What about Jayne and Sandra? Shouldn't I be saying goodbye or something?"

"We just missed them. They might be gone for some time. It looks like they have a lot of things to purchase. You have a lot on your plate right now. I'll say your goodbyes for you." Zander thought Millie sounded tired.

Zander nodded and left the room. He felt some relief at not having to face Jayne, as he climbed into Hector's pickup. On the way to Cedar Key, he made his phone calls. The first was to Herbie's landline. The second was to his friend, Fats. The third would be to Max in Key West. He was dreading that call the most.

32

Hector was a good travelling companion. He spoke when spoken to. Zander appreciated that. It was nice not being reminded of the last twenty-hours. His first call was to Herbie and Gail. Gail answered the home phone and told Zander that Herbie was on a delivery but would be home soon. Zander was relieved. He wanted to explain things to Herbie in person, and he knew Herbie would want an immediate response.

The second call was to Fats. He picked up on the second ring.

"What's shaken' mine compadre?"

"I just called to tell you what happened, so I want you to listen and keep your mouth shut." Zander was not in the mood for Fat's hippie bullshit.

"Proceed." Fats knew his place when Zander was in a funk.

Zander told him the entire story. He left nothing out. He wondered what Hector was thinking when he gave his opinion of both Millie and Jayne. He glanced over, but Hector remained stoic.

When Zander finished, he waited for Fat's response. Fats had nothing. Zander broke the silence.

"Well?"

"Are you allowing me to speak?"

"Don't be a smartass."

"I just need to know when to speak and when to keep my mouth shut."

Fats enjoyed feeding it back to his friend. Zander decided to play along.

"When have you ever known when to keep your mouth shut?"

"That hurts me right in my soul."

"When did you get one of those?" Zander was relieved and enjoying the banter with his friend.

"Spirituality is my middle name."

"I thought execute was your middle name."

"Below the belt. A least my middle name doesn't involve being a killjoy."

Zander felt bad that he had brought up Fats' annihilations, since all of them had been in self defense and defense of his friends and family.

"Fats, I apologize. My comment was insensitive and out of line."

"Truth is a bitter pill. I've had my share, and so have you. We must make an effort to keep these past atrocities buried in the vast cosmic universe."

"Yadda Yadda Yadda. How you doing?"

"I'm better now that I know everything has been put right on your end of the spectrum."

"How about Fran?"

"She's a trouper, very little residual effect. I believe she will overcome the darkness that comes with the reflection of past unfortunate events. What will be the future events on your path to exoneration?"

"I have no idea what that even means. You are so full of shit sometimes."

"Most of the time, in many other opinions. I am happy to comply if it makes those of little understanding able to come to grips with their own lack of comprehension."

Zander was impressed with Fats' vocabulary. Where came up with his ornate vocabulary drove him crazy. He would never admit to Fats that he enjoyed listening to him.

"I'm heading to Herbie's to pick up my rental. After I talk to him, I'll be heading down to Key West."

"Have you enlisted this Max dude?"

"I've talked to him, and I need to make contact again. I just needed to talk to you and Herbie first."

"I feel like a lottery winner," Fats said sarcastically.

"Don't push your luck. I can hang up and not call you back with all the juicy details."

"You couldn't be that sadistic."

"You know I could. But I won't. I think I may need all the friends I can get."

"If you need me, just send up a smoke signal, and I'll appear."

"I know, and I appreciate your friendship. This may be something I have to do with Max's help. I'm afraid it's going to take a great deal of stealth, and the less people involved the better."

"I hear you, Captain. Just remember that I'm available if the situation arises."

"Thanks Fats. I'll do my best to keep you in the loop."

"Humph," Fats said and hung up.

Apparently, Fats shared the dislike of saying goodbye. Zander felt the same way. Goodbye always seemed so final. It was almost like saying you would never see him again. He was still thinking about it, when Hector turned onto highway 24. They were a half hour from Cedar Key. Zander tried to collect his thoughts to figure out what to say to Gail and Herbie.

Hector was the first to break the silence.

"I hope everything works out for you."

"Thanks Hector. I feel good about leaving my daughter with you to watch over things," Zander said.

"Many of us owe Miss Amelia much. We are always ready to help her no matter what it takes. Does this mean we will be seeing more of you?"

"Not right away. I've got other things on my plate right now."

"So I've gathered.

Zander looked at him.

Hector smiled and looked back.

"It's hard not to overhear what you were saying on the phone. I don't pry into other people's business. I would like you to know that if you need any help, no matter what, all you have to do is ask."

"Thank you Hector. I'm going to try to keep as many people away from this problem as possible."

"You know where I am if you run into problems you can't solve alone."

Zander was still contemplating what Hector had said, when they rolled up to Herbie and Gail's home. Zander grabbed his bag from the back seat and leaned back into the passenger window.

"Hector, thank you for all you have done. It helps me, just knowing that you are there to watch over Sandra." He thought for a moment. "Keep an eye on Jayne as well."

Zander wondered where that comment came from, as he walked up the sidewalk. He thought his feelings for Jayne had long disappeared. Maybe there was still something there. He tried to shake the thought.

Gail opened the door before he a chance to ring the bell. She threw her arms around Zander's neck and gave him a kiss on the lips. The action took Zander's thought away from Jayne, and he was thankful for that small favor.

Zander had never been comfortable receiving kisses from women he wasn't hooked up with. It made him uncomfortable, but he returned a small peck on Gail's cheek.

"Nobody will ever accuse you of sexual exploitation by the opposite sex."

"That's the way I want it."

"All that Dutch guilt. I thought that maybe you would left that back in Hospers."

Zander remembered that Gail had once been a product of the little Dutch community, even though her background was German. It was impossible for people not to have some of the Duchie-ness rub off when you lived among them.

"Let's leave that stone unturned. Where's Herbie?"

"He should be back momentarily. Why don't you put your things in the bedroom? I'll make a drink for you."

"It's a bit early, don't you think?"

"Not for a Bloody Mary. I've some good mix that will knock your socks off."

"Can't turn that down."

Zander went upstairs to find his bedroom. He wasn't planning to stay the night, but he hadn't contacted Max and wondered

He wondered what he would want him to do. He decided to make the call after Gail made his drink. He would enjoy looking at the bay from the deck off the first floor.

Gail was singing in the kitchen when he returned. She had a great voice and was singing an old Carol King song. Zander listened for a moment before he made his entrance. She was singing "So far away, doesn't anybody stay in one place anymore?" Zander agreed. It made him sad somehow, but he had little to explain why.

Gail saw him and stopped singing.

"Sorry, I didn't see you standing there."

"I'm sorry you stopped singing. It was beautiful. You have a great voice."

Gail's faced reddened.

"Thank you. I don't get much chance to sing anymore, so I just open up around here. Sometimes I forget and sing when people are here."

"I would like to sing with you sometime. Do they have any karaoke around here?"

"That would be fun, Zander. I think we could find a place on the weekends."

"Consider it a date. I need to get all my other loose ends tied together first."

"I'm anxious to hear what happened, but I know I'll have to wait for Herbie so you don't have to tell the whole thing over."

"Thanks. And Gail?"

"Yes?"

"The karaoke invitation is for you. Herbie is not invited to sing."

Gail laughed.

"He will be devastated. He always wants to sing."

"Have you heard him? He sounds like a cross between a rhino and an elephant."

"Oh, he's never sounded that good," Gail said.

Herbie walked in at the precise moment that both Gail mentioned sounding good.

"Who sounded good?"

Gail tried to hide her smile as she moved back to the kitchen counter.

"I just made Zander a drink. Do you want one?"

"Of course. Why do I get the feeling that I might be the subject of something at my expense?"

"Because you are. Go out to the deck, and I'll bring the drinks. Just wait for the explanations until I get there. Zander needs to tell his story once."

Zander and Herbie found a chair overlooking the water.

"You have a beautiful place here, Herbie."

"I know. Sometimes I just look out and wonder how I could have ever been this lucky."

"You deserve it. Life wasn't always so good to you growing up. What you are telling me is that all this is wonderful because of Gail."

"What she sees in me is beyond comprehension."

"Don't sell yourself short. You're a good man. Women have a way of seeing that. That becomes more important the older we get. What was important in our youth just melts away."

Herbie just looked at Zander. Zander wondered what he was thinking. He was about to ask when Gail came in with the drinks on a tray. When everyone was situated, she spoke to Zander.

"Now you can tell us what has happened. Don't leave out one little detail."

Zander began his story. He paused in the middle for Gail to go back and refresh their bloodies. He finished the story by their second drink. It was quiet for a time, and the three looked out at the gulf.

"Wow. That's something to try and wrap your head around," Herbie said, breaking the silence.

"I know. I haven't had time to process it. Unfortunately, I don't think I'll be able to give it much thought right now."

"What's happening?" Gail asked.

"I've got to find Aubrey."

"What's the plan, and how can we help?" Herbie chimed right in.

"You can help by doing nothing. I don't need anyone else getting involved in my messes. I need to contact Max. He was going to do some legwork, and when I resolved the kidnapping he wanted me to contact him."

"Have you done so?" Herbie asked with some anticipation.

"I wanted to talk to you and Gail first and explain what has happened. I called Fats as well. You know how he gets when I leave him out of the loop."

"I do. I suppose he wanted to come down and put in his two cents," Herbie said.

"Not unlike you," Gail replied.

"That's not fair. I'm here. Fats is in Colorado. Big difference."

"You two are more alike than you would like to admit," Gail said.

"I can't talk like him."

"Thank God for that. I couldn't stand two friends with that kind of lingo."

The three laughed together.

"I'll stay the night and then I'll be heading for Key West," Zander said.

"What if Max isn't there?"

"He will be eventually. I'm planning to call him momentarily. Besides, I still need to drive down there. How long do you think it will take me?"

Herbie considered his question.

"Nine or ten hours depending on the traffic."

"Damn it all," Zander said, frustrated.

"Florida's a long state, and you are going almost the distance from north to south. People forget how long it is until they have to make the drive," Herbie said.

"Thanks for geography lesson, Herbie."

"No charge, my friend. I could always drive you."

Zander just eyed him until Gail spoke.

"Come on, Herbie. Help me make dinner. We need to give Zander some privacy to make his call."

Herbie and Gail got up and moved toward the door.

"Thanks, you two. I don't know what I would do without you as my friends."

Herbie and Gail smiled and made their exit.

Zander found his phone and held it in his hand. It was a call he dreaded making, but he knew it was necessary if he wanted to see Aubrey again.

Zander dialed Max's number.

33

Max's phone rang a number of times, until Zander heard a pre-recorded voice telling him to leave a message. It wasn't Max's voice and sounded computer-generated. Zander left a message asking Max to get back to him immediately. He let him know that he would be coming to Key West sometime the following day.

Zander put away his phone and joined Herbie and Gail in the kitchen. He sat down at the table, and Gail brought him a bottle of Key West lager.

What, no Yuengling?" Zander asked.

"We thought you needed something that the Key West natives drink," Gail said.

"What's the news from Max?" Herbie asked.

"Voice mail. I left him a message. Hopefully, he'll get back to me soon."

"I suggest you stay here until you hear from him. No sense going down without knowing anything," Herbie said, stirring something in a huge pot.

"That's just not going to happen. I'm shoving off tomorrow early. I can't afford to spend anymore time here. It's a long drive, and I need to be down there when I hear from him."

Herbie was about to reply, but Gail put a finger on his lips effectively stopping him from comment.

"We understand. If you need anything from us, just call."

"I'll do that for sure, but I don't want to involve anyone else."

Herbie was about to speak again, and this time Gail put her whole hand over his mouth. Zander couldn't help but notice and tried to hide a smile.

"We both understand. Just know that we're here for you."

"I know that, and I don't know how I will ever pay you back for all you've done for me."

This time Herbie caught Gail's hand before she could shush him.

"I'll think of something."

Gail glared at Herbie, and he smiled back. Satisfied, at least for the moment, he could get a word or two into the conversation.

"I'm planning to leave by 6:00 tomorrow morning," Zander said.

"It's still dark then. At least wait until sunrise."

"No. My mind is made up. I want to get through Tampa before the rush."

"Makes sense to me," Gail said, as she went about putting dinner on the table.

Herbie was wise enough to realize that the conversation about Zander's plan to leave was over. He helped Gail with the food, and when everything was on the table, he made a toast with the beers in hand.

"Here's to one of the most bull-headed people I know," Herbie said and looked at Zander.

"He's in very good company," Gail said, looking at Herbie.

They raised their bottles and took a swallow.

"I like this stuff. It may be better than Yuengling," Zander said and took another drink.

"We can agree on this one thing," Herbie replied.

"It's a start," Gail said. "Now let's eat before everything gets cold.

Gail had made some comfort food. It was linguini in white sauce and a chicken breast smothered in marinara. Zander had three helpings and realized he hadn't eaten much while he was dealing with Sandra's abduction.

When he finished, Zander slid his plate as far away as possible.

"Did you save room for some cheesecake?" Gail asked.

Zander groaned.

"No matter, I'll wrap some up for your trip tomorrow."

"Don't go to any trouble. I'll just pick something up down the road."

"Nonsense. Why waste time doing something like that? You already said you wanted to get to Key West."

Zander looked at Gail about to protest, when Herbie cut in.

"Don't argue with her. It's useless."

Zander knew it was true and decided to just let Gail have her way.

"You boys go out on the deck and have your nightcap. I'll clean up around here and join you when I'm finished."

Herbie led Zander out to the deck grabbing a bottle of B and B and three small brandy snifters. When they settled back into the Adirondack chairs, Herbie poured them both a generous helping of the amber liquid.

"What, no cigars?" Zander asked.

"I've got some in the truck. You want me to go get a few? They're Cubans from Key West. At least that's what the guy told me."

"Right. You believed that?"

"Do you want one or not?"

"Nah. I don't want to wake up tomorrow and taste the damn thing for the next week. They're kinda gross."

Herbie nodded in agreement.

"That's what Gail tells me. I can't imagine what it tastes like second-hand."

"That's way more information than I needed."

The two sipped their drinks. Zander looked out over the bay. The tide was in and everything looked pristine. Herbie was watching Zander closely. Zander noticed.

"Something on your mind?"

"Just wondering how all this is going to end."

"Positively, I'm hoping."

"No, I'm not talking about that. I'm wondering when you get Aubrey back and everything seems to be getting back to normal, what is normal going to look like?"

Zander hadn't given his relationship with Aubrey, and now his daughter, much thought. He hadn't had the time to consider everything. There was no reason to think about it now.

"I think I'll let things ride until I can involve Aubrey in the decision-making."

"What if she doesn't want anything to do with Sandra?"

Zander looked a Herbie.

"You don't know her like I do. She would never feel that way. She's the most caring person I've ever met. She's got her head screwed on correctly. She's not like us, Herbie."

Herbie stroked his chin in thought.

"I should be insulted by that last remark."

"But you're not, are you?"

"No, I'm not. I can't explain it. I don't know why you have to be right about this. I feel the same way about Gail. How did we get so lucky, and why did they pick us?" Herbie asked.

"A good question. Let's have another shot and ponder the question."

They both took another good pour, and Zander could see they had put a dent in the bottle. The booze was strong, and after a few more sips, both Zander and Herbie could feel a little shine coming on. Zander wanted to be careful. Traveling to Key West with a hangover was not an option.

Gail joined them when they were almost finished with their second glass. She helped herself and put a few more swallows in the boy's glasses.

"That's a pretty short pour," Herbie said.

Gail looked at the bottle.

"Looks like you two might have overindulged just a bit. I don't think Zander needs a big head while driving tomorrow."

The two boys nodded and were content to nurse the their drinks. Small talk took over the evening with Gail making sure it stayed that way. When Herbie would drift the conversation toward Zander's plan, she would change the subject. Zander thought that these two worked well together. When he finished his drink, Gail went inside and brought out water for everyone.

"Drink water before you go to bed. You'll feel much better tomorrow."

"Thanks Gail. You always do take care of me."

"Someone must." Gail winked. "But that's a job I would happily give to someone else. That someone else would be Aubrey. Besides, I have enough problems just watching over Herbert."

Herbie made a face pretending to be hurt. Zander laughed out loud.

"You guys make me feel right at home when I'm here. I'll do my best to make myself worthy of your friendship and trust."

"I know you will," Gail said.

Not wanting to get maudlin, Zander got up and went to bed without even saying goodnight. Too much was going on in his head, and to break down in front of two of his best friends was not acceptable.

The bed felt good, and Zander realized he hadn't been sleeping well. He hoped that at least the change of scenery, and his friends' presence, would change that for him.

Sleep came to him. It was the booze giving him some numbing of the brain. When the booze wore off about three in the morning, he was awake. He got up, used the bathroom and then looked out the window. Cedar Key was asleep. He wished he could. He walked around and then tried to go back to bed. It was no use. Sleep had already passed him by.

Zander got back up and jumped in the shower. He shaved and took care of the rest of his routine. By 3:30 he was descending the steps as quietly as possible hoping not to wake Herbie and Gail.

He walked through the kitchen and noticed a brown paper bag with a note taped to it. Zander took the note over and read it under the light above the sink.

We knew you'd be trying to sneak out before anyone was awake. This is your care package so you won't have to stop and eat. We put a few bottles of water in the bag as well. Keep hydrated, and don't forget to stop every once and a while to stretch. You're not getting any younger. Herbie says you should pee frequently. I don't know what that's got to do with anything, but he wanted me to tell you. Have a good trip, and don't forget to let us know what is happening when you can.

Zander liked the note and tucked it into his front pocket of his cargo shorts. He took the food and slung his bag over his shoulder. He was as quiet as possible opening the door and closing it behind him. He got into his rental car, and as quietly as possible, started the car. He noticed two people looking at him from their bedroom window, as he drove away.

34

By 6:00 a.m. Zander was an hour south of Tampa/St. Pete. He pulled into a rest stop just south of Bradenton to stretch and relieve himself. When he got back into the car, he checked out the sack that Gail had left for him. He felt his stomach growl as he passed Tampa, but he had wanted to get well past there before he stopped to eat something.

Besides the two waters, there were two sandwiches. One looked like peanut butter and jelly, and the other looked to be ham and cheese. Since it was breakfast time, he chose the peanut butter and jelly. It had always been a favorite of his when he was a youth. It was the one thing he could make for himself without screwing up. The sandwich was delicious, and he tried to wash the peanut butter down with the water. He knew he would taste the stuff for the next few hours.

When he pulled back onto I-75, the sun was starting to appear on the horizon to his left. He reached over in the glove box and retrieved a pair of cheap sunglasses. They had brown lenses because seeing through gray or green was almost impossible. He figured it was because of his red/green colorblindness. That was a theory, but he never went to an eye doctor to confirm. The brown lenses had always served him well. He went through sunglasses at an alarming rate. If he failed to lose them, they were always scratched right at eye level. Brown lenses were not always available, so he was constantly on the lookout for any pair that would fit. It wasn't unusual for Zander to have five or six pair in his possession at one time. Right now, he had this single pair, so he had to be careful with them.

Zander had just passed the last Fort Myers exit when he got the call he was expecting. He noticed there was no information on the caller on his cell phone, so he knew who it was instantly.

"This is Zander."

"How far are you?"

"I just passed Ft. Myers."

"Good, that will give me time to get back."

"What did you find out?"

"Not on the phone. I'll talk to you when you get here."

"Where do we meet?"

"The parking garage off Duval. Park your vehicle, and I'll find you."

"Don't you want to know what I'm driving?"

"Not on the phone. I'll find you."

It was all this cloak-and-dagger stuff that made Zander crazy. He knew Max was careful, but he wondered why it was necessary not to share information. Anything he told him would have helped to calm his nerves. Now all he felt was more anxiety. Max was intrinsic, and he knew better than to try and get anything out of him until he was ready to explain. It just made the time go much slower wondering what kind of danger Aubrey was experiencing.

Zander made the turn on Alligator Alley making his way across Florida to the east. It always felt like he was making good time, when he traveled from west to east at Florida's southern tip. He turned south on 997 until he reached Homestead. He pulled off the road at a rest stop just before highway 1.

He dug into the brown bag and found the ham and cheese. It was a nice day so he decided to eat at the picnic area. The sandwich went down with the last bottle of water. He put the trash back into the bag but felt something at the bottom. He pulled out a small paper plate covered with foil and a plastic fork. Gail had packed him a piece of the cheesecake they had passed on the night before. It was cherry, and that was his favorite.

Zander ate trying to savor each bite. It was delicious, and he was a bit sad as he finished the last bite. He tossed the trash in the nearest receptacle and went into the restroom.

As he was washing his hands, Zander heard the door open and a few footsteps. He expected to hear voices but there was nothing. The hairs on the back of his neck stood up as a warning of something irregular. As Zander reached for the paper towels, he felt a presence hovering around him.

Zander wiped his hands and turned to throw the towel in the basket. He noticed three men in a semi-circle standing around him. They weren't men. Zander thought they looked like some punks. He knew he was about to be rolled, and it pissed him off.

"You boys are about to make a very bad decision."

One of the boys with greasy long hair spoke.

"What would that be?"

"You tell me. Looks like you're the ones invading my space."

Someone snorted. Zander hated snorting. He went for his pocket and brought out "Old Sparky" and hit the button. The leader stayed where he was at but the other two backed off a step or two.

"Ninety thousand volts could be yours if that's what you'd like," Zander said.

The leader reached down into his boot and pulled out what appeared to Zander to be a hunting knife. It looked like a good one, and Zander admired it for a second. Then he pulled out his own blue switchblade and pressed the button making the blade spring to attention.

The other two took another step backward. Greasy Hair turned and spoke out of the side of his mouth.

"Stay where you are. It's three against one."

"I don't know, looks to me like the odds are pretty even," Zander said.

"Shut your mouth and empty your pockets. Maybe we won't hurt you."

"You should try and empty them for me," Zander said and smiled.

The smile seemed to have the desired effect. Grease Ball hesitated just long enough for Zander to act. He kicked him square in the crotch and was on him with "Old Sparky" blazing. Zander wondered if the sparks from the stun gun might set his greasy hair on fire. He hoped the two actions would incapacitate him so he wouldn't have to use his knife. The guy was going nowhere for some time.

Zander turned and put his eyes on the other two. They turned and ran out door. Zander turned his attention back on Mr. Greasy, and he heard a car start up and tires squealing. Zander thought they should invest in a muffler. He ran out of the bathroom and caught the license plate. The car looked to be a jacked up 1959 Ford Fairlane two-door. It was a nice looking cream-colored vehicle. Zander liked the older automobiles. They had great lines and distinctive looks unlike the generic cars of the present.

Zander went back into the bathroom and grabbed Greasy by the collar. He tried to find a spot that wouldn't make his hand stink later and pulled him out into the common area. He gave him another shot of the stun gun and decided to place a call.

The 911 operator asked Zander a series of questions, and he responded in kind. She told him to stay put, and there would be someone responding in 20 minutes. Zander told her he would be gone, but they could find the greaser laid out near the men's restroom. She was about to take issue, when Zander hung up. He had no time for this shit. He made sure he gave him another dose of "Old Sparky" for good measure and got back into the rental car.

As he merged onto Highway 1, Zander felt assured that Greasy wasn't going anywhere. The license number he gave the 911 operator would be enough to put a stop to this little crime ring, or maybe not. It was no longer an issue that concerned him. He needed to get to Key West and speak with Max.

If anything, the incident had gotten his juices flowing. It made him feel like he could make the situation come out in his favor. It made him relax just a little. It was good because his trip had become a slow-go. The traffic was unbearable, and Zander wanted to scream. He knew nothing could be done about it, so he forced himself to take note of all the beauty of the keys as he inched along. The trip from Homestead to Key West took almost four hours. It was after six when he crossed the bridge from Stock Island and took Roosevelt to the parking garage. He pulled out his phone and pressed Max's name. Zander let the phone ring until it went to voicemail. He found a parking place and shut off his engine. He looked at his phone wondering what he should do. It rang in his hand, and he almost dropped it on the floor.

"Do you remember the sex shop just off Duval?" It was Max.

"How could I ever forget that?" Zander's mind went right to Sandra and knew that was where she was conceived.

"Good. I'll be sitting on the bench across the street." Zander's phone went dead.

Obviously, Max was in no mood for a lengthy conversation. Zander could relate. He hated long phone conversations almost as much as he hated using a cell phone. He walked out of the parking garage and wondered when life had become so complex.

Max was where he said he would be, and as Zander walked up to him, he got up. He said nothing but motioned for Zander to follow him. They walked in silence until they reached Front Street. Max walked toward the beach, and Zander saw him uncover a two-man kayak.

"Shit," was all Zander said.

Max ignored his comment and shoved the kayak into the water. He handed Zander a paddle and took his place in the back seat. Zander knew that he would have to wade to get into the front seat, which meant getting his feet wet. He hesitated.

Max Laughed.

"Take off your shoes and hand them to me."

Zander removed his sneakers and handed them to Max. Max stowed them in bungee-corded area at the rear of the kayak. Zander waded to the front and made his effort to try and get into the kayak. He wasn't very graceful and after almost tipping Max out of the back, he found his sea legs.

"Graceful," Max said.

"We could have taken a boat."

"The fewer people that know you are here, the better. We've got a lot of work to do, and I don't need any unnecessary distractions."

Zander knew he needed to stop talking and listen. Max would explain everything when he was ready to share. Until then, there would be frustration on his part if he tried to pursue an explanation.

The sun was beginning to set and the shadows danced across the water. The twinkling lights on Sunset Key began to pop on. Zander glanced over his shoulder and saw the same thing happening all over Key West. The nightlife would be revving up and continue until the early morning hours. Zander was past those days. Now all he could think about was finding Aubrey and spending an evening with her alone. Then he realized that wasn't quite right anymore. He knew that Sandra, his daughter, needed to be included in the equation as well. The thought made his heart race. He couldn't begin to fathom where all of this would lead.

His thoughts were broken, when he heard a snort off the port bow. If scared the shit out of him, and he raised his paddle putting it across his lap.

"What the hell was that?"

Max laughed.

"It's Flipper. He's just saying hello."

"I've never been a fan of the ocean at night. Too many creepy things can do you in."

"You don't need the ocean for that. Walk down Duval at three in the morning."

"Or maybe get hijacked to Cuba," Zander said, with just a little irritation in his voice.

"That too," was all Max would say.

35

Just before they pushed onto shore, Max made a call on his cell. Zander felt the bottom with his paddle and jumped out of the kayak a little more gracefully than he did getting in. He was reaching for the front handle to pull the little plastic boat to shore, when he felt two arms wrap around him. It was Mona. Her arms felt good, and Zander just had to hug her back.

"Let's keep the homecoming rituals at bay until after we've secured the boat," Max barked.

Zander turned around and focused back on the kayak.

"That's what you call this thing? I would think a small dingy would be better." Zander regretted what he had just uttered.

If Max recognized the innuendo with the dingy he never let on. Mona, however, had a huge grin on her face.

"Don't say a word," Zander warned.

"Can't say anything until I talk to your latest heartthrob."

Max had found his land legs and was securing the small boat by lifting it onto a rack right on the shore. Zander was impressed that the seventy-plus gentleman could handle the kayak with little effort. He realized Max was in excellent shape for his age. Maybe that's what drew Mona to him. The age difference seemed to matter little to either of them.

Max told them they needed to get off the beach, and they found the sidewalk that led to the home that Mona and Max shared. Zander thought it might have been a lifetime ago that he spent time with them.

So much that had happened, and had this been a social gathering, he would have been happy to reminisce. He needed information from Max and a plan on how to proceed in finding and rescuing Aubrey, however.

"Put your bag in the spare bedroom," Max commanded.

Zander thought he could smell pasta cooking, and realized he was hungry.

"Smells good in here, Mona."

"Dinner will be ready in a hour. You and Max enjoy a cocktail outside. It's a nice evening and we're past the no-seeums attacks."

"Good to know." Zander went into the spare bedroom and checked himself out in the bathroom mirror. He thought he looked haggard, and it was no surprise to him in the least. He splashed some cold water on his face and dried off with the hand towel hanging on a ring next to the sink. When he returned to the living room, Mona pointed to the outside patio door. Max was sitting at the table outside. Zander made his way to join him.

"Sit down," Max said.

There was a glass of bourbon on the rocks in front of an empty chair. It looked pretty good to Zander, and before he sat, he grabbed the glass and took a huge swallow. It was smooth and went down without any roughness.

"Blantons?" Zander wondered.

"You've got a good set of taste buds."

"It's always been my favorite."

"That's because it's hard to get. We always want what seems to be beyond our reach."

Zander hoped he wasn't talking about Aubrey. He sat down next to Max and took another sip of the amber liquid. It was even better going down the second time and something he needed. He set the glass on the table and turned to look at Max.

Max was looking at some paperwork and took out a map and traced over it with his index finger. Zander watched him while trying to be patient. He knew max would share what he had found about Aubrey when he was ready. He also knew enough to keep his mouth shut until that time.

After what seemed like an eternity, Max shoved the paperwork to the center of the table. He took his untouched glass of bourbon and clicked it with Zander's.

"Here's to a successful extraction."

They both drank. Zander was reassured by Max's toast. He needed to hold on to whatever hope there was concerning Aubrey's rescue. He knew she was still alive, and that relaxed him even more.

Max was quiet as he enjoyed his drink. He wanted to share some small talk with Zander, but when he glanced over at him, he could see Zander was in no mood. He put his glass on the table and turned to Zander.

"Aubrey is alive."

"Well, that's good news," Zander said with hope in his voice.

"I don't want to sugarcoat this. It's the only good news."

"What do you mean?" Zander was alarmed.

"Aubrey was arrested for spying. She's in a Cuban prison."

Zander almost lost the bourbon he had been drinking.

"Do we know where?"

"Some place outside of Havana. It's not good. They throw men and women together in there and leave them to rot. Political prisoners are treated far worse than murderers and rapists. She was alive two days ago. We've got to act and get her out of there as soon as possible, or she won't be long for this earth."

"Do you know her condition?"

"It's not good." Max looked down.

"How long has she been in there?"

"Three weeks, my source tells me."

"Who is that?"

Max looked at Zander, and Zander realized he had overstepped. He waved off his own question.

"We've got to act. I'm working on something right now, and if it pans out, I'll discuss it with you in the morning."

For the first time, Zander noticed a SAT phone on the table next to Max.

"What can I do in the meantime?"

"You can sit and have a drink with me. I'm sorry to have to unload all of this on you just as you got here, but bad news should always be received on an empty stomach," Max said.

Zander wasn't hungry any longer. He stared across the bay toward the nightlife beginning to take shape in downtown Key West. He would give anything to be over there with Aubrey at his side. It was the one thing that mattered in his screwed-up life.

The door opened, and Mona came out and draped her arms around Zander. He looked up at her.

"Max has shared everything with me. Everything is going to be just fine. You know how Max always finds the worst scenarios to keep us from expecting positive results. He can't help it. It's who he is, but I'm working on him. Someday I should be able to change his abhorrent behavior. I just hope I can do it before he dies."

"He's a hard case, alright," Zander said, feeling a little better.

Max was smiling at Mona.

"There's a reason I keep you around."

"Dinner's ready. You two come in and wash up."

Zander liked what Mona had just said. It was like he was a kid again and being told what to do. He realized he needed that right at he moment.

Zander regained most of his appetite and enjoyed Mona's pasta. He liked her homemade marinara sauce and told her so. He helped her with the dishes while Max retrieved the SAT phone and sat in the living room waiting for it to ring.

They were halfway finished with the dishes when Max got up.

"I'm going for a walk. I'll be back before you're finished. We'll have a nightcap when I get back."

Zander wondered where he was going. Mona saw the confusion in his face and threw some dishwater at him.

"You know Max. He's got something he needs to do. I'm sure it has to do with rescuing Aubrey. Just keep in mind that he is fully engaged in all of this, and he won't rest until he gets the conclusion you expect."

Zander smiled, but he wasn't as convinced as Mona seemed to be. Max hadn't been so convincing. He knew it was part of his shtick, but it did nothing to keep Zander from obsessing.

"Tell me about this Aubrey," Mona said.

"I'm sorry. I forget that you've never met. What do you want to know?"

"Tell me everything."

Zander did just that. He started from their first meeting in Everglade City to her abduction on I-80. Mona listened intently, not interrupting. When they had finished with the dishes and everything was put away. She spoke.

"Sounds like she might be the one."

"I would have to agree with you. Things just have gotten so out of hand over the past few weeks."

Mono looked at him but said nothing. Zander realized he hadn't mentioned Jayne or Sandra since he had arrived. He had no idea if Mona knew anything of that situation. He decided to broach the subject.

"Did Max tell you anything about what I've been doing recently?"

"Do you mean the Sara Jane situation?"

Zander nodded.

"There's more. She calls herself Jayne now. She found out that her life had been a lie, and she had a mother she never knew about."

"Zander I have to tell you this straight away. I don't give two hoots or a holler about that woman. She tried to kill me. If I saw her again I would think I would kill her myself. You would be better off to never see her again." Mona was hot.

"There's more," he paused. "I have a daughter."

Mona knew that it was a result of his last encounter with this woman she despised.

"Oh, shit."

"Oh shit, is right," Zander said and looked away.

Mona felt bad. The last thing she had wanted to do was add to Zander's burden at the moment.

"I'm sorry. I shouldn't have said that. She's your daughter no matter how I feel about the mother. You have an obligation. Every daughter needs a dad. Have you thought about how you are going to handle all of this?"

"It's been on my mind," Zander said.

"You can't oversimplify the situation. It's huge. Right now you need to concentrate on getting Aubrey back."

"That's what I've been wrestling with since I left northern Florida. It's quite a bit for this little mind to ponder. I have little capacity up here." He pointed to his head.

"Nonsense. This might have driven a lesser man insane." Mona was back to playing with him, and Zander appreciated even a bit of levity.

Just as he about to respond, the door opened and Max entered carrying a large black bag over his shoulder. Zander had seen the bag before. He knew it carried whatever arsenal Max would need to rescue Aubrey from the Cuban nightmare she had stumbled into. Max never stopped but went straight into his bedroom. Zander heard the bag hit the floor, and he knew it was heavy by the thud it made. Max entered the kitchen shortly after and went to the sink and washed his hands.

"Did anyone contact you?" Zander asked.

"No. I'm not expecting anything until midnight or after. My source is in extreme danger and has to be careful or will end up in a similar position as your Aubrey."

The explanation seemed to satisfy Zander for the moment. The three of them were still standing around the island watching Max watch his hands.

"I think there's better things to do that watch an old man wash his hands. Mona, why don't you pour us some drinks?"

"What would you like?"

"You choose. Surprise us," Max said and grabbed a towel.

"I need more information than that." Mona had her hands on her hips.

"Well, something sweeter for a nightcap," Max paused. "I know, let's have some of that Limoncello you bought."

Max threw the towel at Mona, and it wrapped right around her face.

"You are an asshole," Mona said trying to sound angry.

"I know, but I'm your asshole."

"You are." Mona went over to the bar smiling.

Zander looked at them both feeling a pang of resentment. This was how he should be acting around Aubrey, but she wasn't here. He knew he could never be happy until she was.

36

Zander woke up with the sun. After he showered, he could smell breakfast. He packed his bag and placed it next to the door, before he entered the kitchen. Max and Mona were already sitting at the table drinking coffee. Mona stood and motioned for Zander to sit.

"Breakfast is served." Mona began dishing out something.

Zander sat. He looked over at Max who was engrossed in a file folder full of loose pages. No greeting passed between either of them. Meaningless conversation was a waste of time with so many decisions to be made.

Mona brought over a plate of food and a cup of coffee for Zander. It looked like some kind of egg bake. He liked anything that took on the form of a casserole. Zander took a swig of coffee and then attacked the eggs and sausage.

Max was still engaged in the paperwork. Mona set a plate in front of him and filled his coffee cup.

"Eat this before it gets cold." There would be no arguing.

Max flopped his folder down, found his fork, and began to fulfill Mona's instruction. He looked over at Zander and nodded, not wishing to speak with his mouthful.

"Good morning, Max. I assume that material has to do with finding Aubrey."

"She's already been found. Now we need to figure out how to get her out," Max said.

Zander said nothing. The ball was in Max's court, and he would share his ideas when he was ready."

"Did you sleep well?" Mona asked.

"As good as could be expected under the circumstances, I guess," Zander said, then added, "Thanks for asking."

"You'll sleep when all of this is over."

"I hope you're right," Zander said.

He knew Mona was trying to put him at ease. It wasn't working very well. Zander had too many variables to consider. He had no idea what shape Aubrey was in from her detention in a Cuban prison. He wasn't getting a very good vibe from Max. He hoped she was doing better than her nightmare with that jackass, Corey Prescott. Zander wondered how Aubrey could have ever been involved with a psycho like him. His contentious death had put an end to Zander's anger. Getting eaten by an alligator was just the icing.

Max finished his breakfast and placed his dish in the sink. He grabbed the coffee pot and refilled the cups. Zander noticed he always took care of Mona first. Max was old school and put the women in his life on a pedestal. Zander thought he did the same thing with Aubrey. Then he remembered he had another woman in his life. How in the world would he be able work out this new experience of being a father to Sandra? It was all compounded by his contentious relationship with Jayne. He was lost in that thought when Max spoke.

"We'll be leaving here at 9:30."

Zander looked over and waited for him to continue. Max picked up the file folder once again. Zander had enough.

"Why don't we discuss what's going to happen and what my role will be?"

Max noticed his tone.

"Sorry, I'm used to working alone and sharing things when I think necessary."

"Ain't it the truth," Mona said.

The comment made both Max and Zander smile.

"I apologize. I'm still a work in progress," Max said.

Zander wondered if he was apologizing to Mona or him. He thought it was said more to Mona. Zander knew Max was helping him because of Mona. He also knew he could walk away anytime he wanted. That revelation helped Zander curb his impatience. He looked at Max and waited for him to share when he was ready.

"Zander needs some information, Max. You can't keep things from him any longer," Mona said and got up to take care of the dishes.

"She's right of course. I apologize once more. We will be heading toward Cuba on a shrimper later this morning. I've got a boat waiting for us on the beach. We'll board the vessel and take the boat with us." Max began his explanation

"I'm unfamiliar with a shrimper," Zander said.

"It's a shrimp boat. You've seen them. Big nets on poles that swing out from the ship."

Zander had seen the big ships pass the Fort Myers beach area. A number of them were docked in the intercostal waters. He wasn't all that excited thinking about spending time on a trawler that smelled like dead fish.

Max appeared to read his mind.

"We need a cover to get us close to Cuba's mainland. This ship has been seen in the international waters off Cuba on a regular basis. I know the captain. We've worked together before, and I trust him with my life. It will be the safest way to get down there without being detected."

"How are we going to get Aubrey out of prison? We can't get in there. Neither of us look Cuban," Zander said.

"I'm working on that. I have a contact in the prison. I've worked with him previously."

"Do you trust him?"

"No. But he's all we've got."

The comment made Zander uneasy. He needed to put his trust in Max because he had no other options. This whole scenario was beyond his locus of control. He had no previous experiences to draw upon. Political bullshit had never interested him, and he stayed as far away from it as he could.

"How will he be of use to us?" Zander asked.

"He likes money. He likes dollars and will do most anything to put them into his pocket."

"What's this going to cost?" Zander asked alarmed.

"That's still to be determined. I'm working out the details."

"How?"

"He's got a phone. We are in negotiations right now."

"I don't have any money with me. It will take me time to come up with anything."

"You don't have to worry about that right now. I've got funds to take care of this."

"I can't let you do that. This is my problem. I'll make the payment."

"Of course you will. I'm not doing this for my health. You will pay me back for everything I spend. It's just that we don't have time for you to go find the funding right now."

The comment made Zander relax. He would never allow Max to be burdened with his problems financially.

"What's he asking?"

"He always starts high."

"How high?"

"Just under two million."

Max saw the panic in Zander's face.

"Two million? Who's got that kind of money?" Zander's voice was louder than he intended.

"I do. But you won't have to worry about it. It won't even be close to that. We just need to do the dance."

"I don't like it."

"It's our option, Zander. We need Aubrey out before she's no longer able. I'm not going to sugarcoat this. She will be in horrible shape. You'll need to be prepared for the chance she won't make it."

Zander looked away. There was no fathoming his world without Aubrey in it.

"How much of a chance?" Zander asked.

"I'm not in the odds-making business. We will do the best possible job that we can. Time is of the essence."

"What if we can't get your contact to accept our terms?"

"Then we will lie. He will cooperate one way or another."

Zander liked what Max said. Max wasn't someone to be trifled with even at his age. Zander wondered what kind of sinister force he had been in his younger days. He was happy to have him on his side.

Mona left the room and came back with some clothing slung over her arm.

"You need to change into these," she said and threw the pile in front of Zander.

"Take your bag back into the bedroom and change. We're traveling light. You won't be taking anything with you today. With any luck we'll be back here long before the sun rises," Max said, dismissing Zander.

"I have some questions," Zander replied.

"Save them for the ship. Let's get going." Max stood and went into his bedroom.

Mona put her arms around Zander.

"Just listen to him now. This is what he does best."

"I know, it's just that I'm used to being in control. It's hard for me to let things go."

"Go change your clothes. I've got some boots you'll need to use as well. Leave those Beatle things in the bedroom."

Zander went into the bedroom with the clothes Mona had given him. Everything was black even the socks and underwear. Zander never had worn black skivvies. He had a watch cap pulled down over his forehead. The white visible were his cheeks. He supposed that Max would have something to blacken his face when the time came. When he was finished, he looked in the mirror. He liked what he saw. He looked like some kind of tough guy from the movies. He thought the image fit him. His 6'7'' frame made him appear formidable.

When he emerged from the bedroom, Mona handed him black-laced boots. He put them on by leaning against the wall. While he was hopping around pulling up the footwear, Max came in from the front door. Zander hadn't even heard him leave. He was carrying the large rucksack he had brought in from the night before.

He crossed over to Mona and planted a long lingering kiss on her lips.

"Hopefully, we'll be back sometime early tomorrow morning."

"You need to be careful. I want you coming back to me."

"Understood, my dear." He turned to Zander, "You ready to roll?"

Zander was tying his shoelaces. He stood when he finished.

"I want to thank you both for what you are doing. You wouldn't have to do this for me or Aubrey, and I'm sorry if it puts everyone in harm's way."

"Thank us when it's over," Max said.

"I thought I should do it now in case this doesn't turn out like we plan."

Max just looked at him and shook his head.

"Don't jinx this, Zander. Positive thinking from this point on." Max headed for the door, and Zander followed right behind.

They walked down to the beach trying to stay clear of the resort area. Max led him to an area that Zander hadn't noticed before. A few mangroves and rocks lined the beach area. Something was tied to one of the mangroves. It looked like a large rubber raft. Zander had seen one like it in some movie. It had been full of Navy Seals being delivered to some mission.

"What the hell is that?" Zander asked.

"It will be our transportation later. We will need something to fly under the radar when our mission is successful."

Zander walked over and put his hand on the rubber pontoon. It wasn't rubber at all. It almost felt like some kind of hard plastic. The raft was larger than it looked when he got close. It looked like it might be able to hold seven or eight good-sized men and gear.

"How long will it take for us to get back to Key West from Cuba in this thing?"

"Don't let anything fool you. This baby tops out at sixty and virtually unsinkable. Those pontoons are covered with Kevlar. Bullets aren't going to be a problem."

"What about the people inside?"

"I can't vouch for that. We'll just need to keep our heads down if we get into a situation."

"Is that likely? Do you think there will be a shootout?"

Max said nothing as he pushed the raft into the ocean. Zander decided to get in to avoid getting his boots wet.

37

Max rafted around the west side of the island to avoid being noticed. They both ducked down as far as possible. Had someone been on the beach, they would have seen two heads wearing black watch caps and dark sunglasses. Zander was amazed at how smoothly the craft took the ocean waves. When they cleared the island, Max poured the coals to the odd-looking watercraft. They were flying high in the surf without so much as a bump.

Zander sat back up and tried to take note of his surroundings. Key West was getting smaller as they pushed west. Soon enough, a number of bigger ships came into view. They were all anchored together in what looked like a small city on the water. Zander realized that Key West was a tourist spot and most people wanted to avoid seeing these rusted old tubs in sight of the beaches.

Max only slowed down when he reached one of the shrimp boats. They got alongside, and Max reversed the engine, and they glided in effortlessly. Zander never even felt a bump when they made contact with the hull.

"Damn it, Max. You're pretty good at this shit."

"Years of practice, my friend."

Someone threw down a line and followed it with a rope ladder. Max tied off the rubber boat and held the ladder steady. Zander realized it was his cue to climb aboard. He did so with great effort. Rope ladders were apparently quite tricky. By the time he reached the top, he had found his climbing legs. Max followed him with much less an effort. Zander was feeling like a neophyte in Max's world.

Just as soon as their feet hit the deck, someone went back down the ladder they had just climbed. Zander watched with passing interest. Someone else swung a large mechanical arm over the side. The man on the raft fashioned two straps around the front and rear of the boat and hooked it to the cable that extended from the arm. He gave some sort of hand signal, and the boat was lifted out of the water and swung over to a platform on the aft section of the shrimper.

Zander wanted to ask Max some questions, but he was ushered into the captain's wheelhouse. No one was inside, and Max opened a trapdoor. Stairs lead below, and Max disappeared from sight. Zander followed, mildly curious.

When he got to the bottom, Max had him follow a dark hallway that smelled strongly of fish. Zander knew if he could never get used to the putrid smell. When they reached the end of the hallway, Max opened a watertight door. Zander could not believe his eyes. Men were seated at rows of computer stations and what appeared to be some kind of satellite feeds. Zander's mouth fell open. Max noticed his friend's confusion.

"Things aren't always as they seem. Not everyone gets access to see something this top secret. I'm afraid you are going to have to sign some documents making sure it stays that way. I've vouched for you; so don't do anything that I'll regret later. It would go badly for you."

Zander could see that Max was dead serious. He thought that maybe using dead and serious together wasn't the best idea. He had no reason to share any information concerning the shrimp boat, so he signed the documents without hesitation.

Max led Zander into another room that appeared to be part of the crew's quarters. A large room served as the ship's galley and lounge. It was equipped with whatever was needed for long stays at sea. Video games and big screen televisions were hanging on the walls. It was far too much for Zander to take in all at once.

"Our quarters are through this door," Max said.

Zander followed him down another hallway with a series of doors. Near the hallway's end Zander realized he no longer smelled fish. He asked Max about it.

"The smell is part of the cover. It's manufactured. I don't think there's ever been any sea life brought aboard."

"How did they take an old vessel like this and retrofit it for all the technology?" Zander asked.

"They didn't. This ship is brand new. The exterior was made to look old and dilapidated."

It was at that moment that Zander realized that if Max and his connections couldn't make Aubrey's rescue happen, no one could. He would need to follow directions without question. This entire experience was beyond anything he could have imagined.

"I'm afraid we are going to have to share a berth. The good news is that we both have a bed." Max opened the door.

Zander was expecting two bunks, one over the other. What he saw surprised him. Two queen-sized beds with a sitting area that had a table and two chairs.

"Looks like the government sailors travel in style."

Max looked at him, and Zander knew he shouldn't have said anything. He nodded at Max. Max nodded back in agreement.

"The head is behind that door on the left," Max said.

"Thanks. I think I could use one right about now."

"Why don't you make yourself comfortable. I've got a few things to do. We should be moving out momentarily. I'll meet you in the galley, when I can. It's important that you stay below until we are well on our way."

"I wouldn't mind some fresh air," Zander countered.

"We aren't on the ship's roster. We don't exist on this trip, so we don't want to make any problems for the crew until we are away from port. We will be plenty of time for fresh air after that."

Max left their berth. Zander went into the head. It was a full bathroom with a sink, shower and stool. Zander checked the drawers under the sink area and noticed toothbrushes; toothpaste, razors, shaving cream, deodorant, dental picks, floss, and the list went on. In one of the bottom drawers Zander found tampons and sanitary napkins and other assorted women's items. He hadn't thought that woman would have been on the ship at all until he realized what their mission involved. Aubrey would be going back with them on the ship. At least that's what he thought the plan would be.

Zander had nothing to stow. He was wearing the things in his possession on his back. This wasn't going to be an overnight trip. He had remembered to put the switchblade knife and stun gun in his boots.

He failed to see why, because there would be no time to use them. He needed to be prepared, however.

Since there was nothing much to do in the cabin, Zander decided the galley would at least have something to occupy his time. Coffee and soft drinks and some finger food were available. Zander decided on a bottle of water and a small bag of sea salt potato chips. He went over to a recliner situated in front of a flat screen monitor. It was all rigged up for video games. Zander looked at it and decided to move to where some reruns of old TV shows were playing on a loop.

Zander hadn't played video games since his early twenties. He had been hooked on Pac Man and played it on his Atari until he could turn over the score back to zero when he reached a hundred thousand. His hands had hurt, and he played with winter gloves to avoid getting blisters on his fingers. When he reached the goal, he threw the game system into a box, put it into a closet, and never looked at it again. It was hard to believe how much time he had wasted with so very little reward. It made him wonder what had happened to the Atari. It had been lost in one of his many moves. It was out of date, so he could never think anyone would have wanted to steal the thing. Maybe it had even become a classic.

The TV display was showing an episode of "The Love Boat." Zander watched a few minutes of the program and realized it was one of the cheesiest things he had ever seen. It surprised him because he had watched it almost every Friday night growing up. Apparently, he had become more sophisticated over the years. Attesting to that was impossible because he very little time to watch TV.

Zander got back up from the chair and went to throw away his potato chip bag when he felt the ship lurch. They were underway, and he wondered how long it would take to get to Cuban waters.

Max entered the galley after the disembarking. He walked over to the counter and ran himself some coffee in a paper cup. He motioned for Zander to sit at a table away from the entrance, where they could have a bit of privacy.

"I've been in contact with my source."

Zander waited for him to continue.

Max drank some of his coffee and put the cup back on the table.

"There is some reassuring news. It seems they kept Aubrey in solitary and not with the general population."

"That's good news?" Zander asked knowing solitary could have lasting psychological effects that many times were more devastating than physical abuse.

"Yes it is. At least we know she hasn't been raped. That's what my source said, anyway."

Zander hadn't thought about the consequences of being a woman in a prison with mixed sexes sharing the same facility. He hoped Max was right. He knew there was also the possibility of abuse from the guards.

"Do we know her condition?"

Max took another slug of his coffee.

"She's not in very good shape." Max looked at Zander. "In fact, my guy bribed a guard to give her something to knock her out. She appears to be in a coma."

"What the hell?" Zander asked, raising his voice.

"Calm down. I said it appears she's in a coma. She remained in the infirmary the past week. She'll die in a few hours, and her body will be taken away for cremation."

Zander had no idea where the conversation was going. His mind started spinning when Max said she would die. His breathing had become labored, and he was trying to keep from hyperventilating.

"Put your head between your legs and breathe," Max said and pushed his head down.

When Zander had started breathing normally, Max continued.

"There is another woman in the infirmary. Someone will switch their identities, and the other woman will become Aubrey."

Zander looked at Max.

"Is the woman alive?"

"I didn't ask. You shouldn't concern yourself with any of that. If you want Aubrey out of that prison, there will have to be some concessions made."

Zander just stared at Max trying to wrap his head around what he had just told him. This was all too complex for his brain to cypher.

"You told me you wanted to know what was going down with this whole rescue. If you think it's too much to handle, I'll keep it to myself."

"No. I need to know everything."

"Don't concern yourself with the other woman. She was dead the moment she entered the prison. My source has been keeping her alive to finalize this plan. She was beaten and raped continually, and I have been assured she will never regain consciousness.

"Who is this source of yours?"

"That's something I won't tell you. It is for your own benefit. In case this all goes south on us, the less you know about people involved, the better it will be for you. It might even save your life down the road."

Zander was in for the long haul. He had no other choice. He had to get Aubrey back. He was in uncharted waters. His entire future rested with his friend Max's expertise.

Max pulled out a file of papers and spread them on the table.

"You need to know the plan."

Zander knew he was right but the papers were just a blur. His eyes were out of focus.

38

The explanations started to become clearer when Max began to draw on a blank sheet of paper. For fifteen minutes, Max went over the plan and then went over it again. When he finished, he told Zander to review it for him. Zander thought it might have been overkill. He had always been good at rote memorization, and he did so flawlessly to Max's satisfaction. He put away the papers in a file folder and stuck it into a bag he was carrying.

"You'd better get some sleep," Max said.

"Not tired," Zander replied.

"It's not a suggestion. Our mission will commence precisely at 12:35 am. I'll need you to be firing on all pistons if we plan on making this work."

Zander knew he hadn't been sleeping well but going to bed in the middle of the day hardly interested him. Max's stare told him otherwise, and he excused himself and found the bunkroom. He stretched out on top of the bed and looked at the ceiling. He tried to put everything into perspective but couldn't come close. Zander always felt he was good at putting things in order. It helped him to make sense of what would otherwise be chaos. He could find no order this time, however.

At some point he must have fallen asleep. It was fitful. His mind had never stopped turning over, and he sat straight up when he felt a hand on his shoulder.

"Zander, wake up. We're getting close," Max said.

"What time is it?"

"Almost 10:00. Time to go topside and get ready. Meet me in the galley when you're ready."

Zander got up and went to the head. He splashed water on his face and found a toothbrush and removed the wrapper. It felt good to get the preceding day out of his mouth. When he finished, Zander found his way back into the galley. He was surprised to see it was almost full of people. A line of men was snaking toward what appeared to be the food. Max was sitting at the same table they had been at before. He motioned for Zander to get into line. Zander had decided to bypass food, but he knew he needed to follow Max's direction.

When he had filled his plate with potatoes, meatloaf and green beans, He joined Max.

"Eat up. When you're finished we'll be going topside. I've got a checklist for us to go over, and it looks like you could use some air." Max smiled for the first time since they boarded the ship.

It made Zander relax a little. He ate the food without fanfare. He decided to run himself a large paper cup filled with coffee. He turned toward the table and saw Max stand and move toward the door. Zander followed with his coffee.

When they reached the bridge, Zander noticed there was no moon. Everything was black. It was by design. Max always had everything planned out to the nines.

"We're anchored on a reef at the ten mile limit. In one hour we will splash the raft and be on our way."

"We're taking that thing ten miles?" Zander asked.

Max looked at him with a raised eyebrow.

"Yes. What did you think?"

"I thought we might be taking the ship quite a bit closer."

"You need to understand that this ship will begin its shrimping cover at first light. Hopefully, we'll be long gone by then. They are here to provide cover if something goes wrong. Once we have Aubrey, we head back to Key West."

"We're going all the way back to Key West in that?" Zander asked pointing to the back boat.

"It's about 90 miles. We will be flying under the radar, and I need to you to keep Aubrey secure. We'll be traveling back at full speed."

Zander was afraid to ask how fast that would be, so he just nodded. Max picked up his huge canvas bag and began climbing up to the platform that held the raft. Zander followed.

Max unloaded his bag, which seemed to be tactical gear that Zander couldn't identify. He did see a few handguns and two or three long guns. The last thing Max took from the bag was an odd-looking thing.

"What the hell is that, a bazooka?" Zander asked.

Max started laughing.

"I think they used those in World War II. We call them anti-tank guns today. This isn't one of them, however. What you see here is a heat-seeking missile."

"You think we'll need that?" Zander asked with concern in his voice.

"I hope not. But if a vessel is pursuing us, it might mean the difference between capture and escape. Believe me when I tell you, we don't want anything to do with the word capture."

Max stowed everything in a covered locker next to the right rear pontoon. He leaned over and gave someone a hand signal, and the raft began to lift from the pad. Zander settled in the front with his back to the bow. He wanted to see what Max was doing but the moment they hit the water, the lights on the boat went out and they were in complete darkness. Zander wouldn't be seeing much of anything.

Max fooled around with some electronics off to his left side and soon a screen powered up. Zander knew it was kind of navigation system. He understood it wouldn't be anything he had any knowledge about. Max had contacts and access to things Zander would never be able to fathom.

"Get comfortable. We're going in silent and slow," Max said, as he cranked the starter.

The 300-horse Yamaha engine started with little effort. Zander was surprised how quietly it ran. It was some other government secret stealth technology Zander speculated.

The raft moved out of its tether without the benefit of any running lights. The ocean was calm, and the waves were less than a foot. The trip would be relatively smooth, and it gave Zander time to think about the events of the past few weeks. He had never had what people might call a traditional life. Most people his age were settled down with a job and family. They were buying a house and going to their kids' baseball games. The thing Zander had in common with those folks was that he was now a father. It was far from a traditional parenting situation. He thought that Aubrey would understand when he explained what had happened, but he wasn't sure. He wasn't sure about anything.

Almost an hour went by, and Zander thought they were barely moving. Everything was quiet. No moon or stars were visible, and the thing Zander noticed was a greenish outline of Max's face as he watched the navigation screen. Zander turned his head. Max's face took on a ghoulish countenance that served to unnerve him.

Zander's thoughts were shattered, when Max stopped the boat. He rummaged through a storage locker and pulled out something. Zander could see it was a SAT phone when Max activated the keypad. He pushed a number of buttons and sat back down. Zander watched him, as he held the phone to his ear. Nothing was said on Max's end. Soon, he shut the phone down. Zander waited for an explanation.

"Everything is in place. We're early, but they are ready for the transfer or at least they will be in about twenty minutes."

"How's this going to work?"

"We'll proceed to a spot that we've agreed upon. The tide is out, so I'll beach the boat out on the sandbar and wade through the tide pool to the beach. My contact will be waiting at a spot near a large palm tree hanging out over the water. It's a good place that we've used numerous times in the past."

"I'll be going with you. You'll need help with Aubrey if she's in bad shape."

"You'll be staying with the boat," Max said and reached back into the locker. He brought out a long gun with some type of scope attached. "You'll need to be ready to give us cover. This rifle has a night scope that you'll be able to use to follow our movements. If anyone pursues us on our way back, you will need to make sure they don't stop us. Is that clear?"

It was perfectly clear. Max was telling Zander that he had to take out the pursuers. It wouldn't be a series of warning shots he would be firing.

Max turned off the navigation system, and the boat once again fell into darkness. He started the engine, and they went forward until Zander felt the raft scrape the bottom. He could tell it wasn't rocks but sand beneath. Max showed Zander how the rifle worked and turned on the scope. When he finished, he slipped over the side and began to make his way toward the beach.

Zander wanted to say something, but he knew that sound traveled over the water on a quiet night. He watched Max make his way toward a large overhanging palm. Lights from a vehicle flashed twice, blinding

Zander. When he brought his eye back to the scope, he could see movement on the beach but couldn't make out what was happening.

There was a flash and the sound of a gunshot reached Zander. He tried to focus in on the commotion, and then realized he needed to find Max and watch his back. It wasn't long before he saw someone running toward the raft. It was Max with something slung over his shoulder. Someone else was running next to him. Zander could tell it wasn't a pursuit by the second man, but he could see others behind them that were following with guns.

Max had a good lead, but the others were moving fast. The entire scene was confusing. He couldn't tell if the accompanying runner was Aubrey or if she was the load on Max's back. He did realize that he needed to act if he wanted to see anyone alive again.

Zander focused the eyepiece, as best as he could, and pulled the trigger. The shot went wide and failed to slow up either man. His second shot was a little better. He hit one of the two men in the shoulder. He heard a yelp, but the guy never went down. Zander knew the worst thing he could do at this point was panic. He let his breath out and drew it back in. When he felt he was calm enough, he fired the third shot. He had been aiming at the chest area on the second man, because he knew it was the biggest body mass and the best chance of hitting a moving target.

The shot hit the man right below the throat and he went down. The man with the shoulder wound slowed up a little to see what happened to his friend. When he realized what had happened, he turned back and raised his weapon. Zander thought it looked a lot like an Uzi. He decided not to wait for a report from the weapon. He put two shots into the guy before he could pull his trigger. The first entered his chest dead center. The second hit him just below the navel on his way down. He was dead before he hit the water. The fact that Zander had just killed his first human being hadn't yet registered. He was doing what Max had told him, but more importantly, he was making sure Aubrey had a chance to get back to him alive.

39

Zander dropped the weapon and slipped over the side. He pushed himself through the water, but it felt like he was walking through mud. By the time he reached the tide-pool, Max and the other runner had appeared. He could see it was a man and not Aubrey as he had hoped.

"Good shooting," Max said. "You just saved our lives."

"Aubrey?" Zander asked, with panic rising in him.

"She's out. Help me get her in the boat."

Zander got back into the boat, and Max removed the package he had been carrying on his shoulder. Zander could see that she was wrapped in a thermal blanket. It was silver and crinkled when Max passed her over to him. He placed her in the bottom of the boat as gently as possible. He pulled the covering from her face to get a look at her to make sure she was going to be fine. What he saw made him want to throw up.

Aubrey's face was swollen to the point of being unrecognizable. She had been beaten. He pulled the blanket back up around her face making sure she could breath. He kept the rest of her body covered not wanting to see what the rest of her looked like. He was pissed and stood up in the boat waiting for Max to give him an explanation.

Max was in an animated conversation with the man who had accompanied him. After a few minutes, Max got into the boat and helped the other man into the seat between them.

Max powered up the radar unit, and Zander could see his face light up in the familiar green.

"What happened? I heard a shot."

"Carlos here hasn't enlisted the best of help. It seems his trust was lost to greed on part of his right-hand man. His name was Benedict. Quite fitting for someone who wanted to betray us."

Zander decided not to ask what had happened to him. He figured he knew.

"Pleased to meet you, Mr. Zander," Carlos said.

Zander disliked his tone. It almost sounded like he was mocking.

"What's happening now? I thought it would just be the three of us." Zander's voice mirrored his displeasure.

"Things have changed. Carlos no longer has a cover. He'll need to accompany us, until I can figure out what to do with him."

"I don't like it," Zander grumbled.

"Neither do we. We'll speak of it later. Right now we need to leave this place. The gunfire will have attracted attention, I'm afraid."

Max started the engine, told Zander to sit, and this time cranked the throttle wide open. In ten minutes, they could see the shrimp boat anchored where they had left it. Lights were on all over the ship. They were just out looking for shrimp. Zander assumed they would be stopping before they took off for Key West. He was wrong.

Max flashed a mag light a few times at the ship and got a return signal. Zander could see men rushing around the deck and soon the anchor was being pulled up.

They had passed the ten-mile limit without incident, and Max had placed his heading into the electronics. Zander was holding Aubrey in his lap trying to make sure the ride would be as smooth as he could make it. He looked back toward the shrimper and saw all the lights extinguish. He thought it was strange and looked over at Max.

"The lights just went out on the shrimper."

Max turned around to catch a look.

"That's not good. Something's wrong." Without warning, he cut the throttle. Zander almost lost his hold on Aubrey. Carlos slipped off the seat.

Max reached into the side locker and pulled out what Zander had mistakenly thought was a bazooka earlier. He placed it beside him on his seat.

"What's happening?" Zander asked louder than he had planned.

Carlos was still on the floor in front of the seat he had slipped off. He moved to stand.

"Stay down," Max growled.

Carlos appeared to be reaching for something, when Max kicked him squarely in the face with his size twelve boots. He fell back down. Max was on him. When he got back to his seat, he had something in his hand.

"Looks like we've been betrayed by both Benedict and Carlos. I found this tracking device. We're in trouble. Keep your eyes peeled and take this. If Carlos moves, kill him." Max handed Zander a pistol.

It was too dark to tell what it was, but it had weight. Zander thought it might be a 9mm or a .45. It wouldn't matter; at this short range anything would have been lethal.

Zander looked around and saw lights to his left.

"I see lights on my left," Zander said to Max.

"There are lights coming at us from the North also," Max said.

Carlos started to stir, and Max cracked him over the head with butt of the missile launcher. He took the tracking device and placed it into one of Carlos' pockets. Then he threw him over the side. Before Zander heard the splash, the boat was moving and Max had it up to speed.

"Are you going to leave him in the water?"

"Good point," Max said and turned the boat back around.

Zander saw Carlos floating face down when the raft approached. Max stood and leaned over toward Zander.

"Give me the pistol."

Zander handed it over, and Max leaned over the side firing one shot into Carlos' head. He never moved.

"I think he might have already been dead," Max said, as he handed back the pistol.

The action had been a total surprise. Zander wasn't sure how he felt. Then he realized he felt nothing. This man had almost cost them their lives. He decided he no longer would concern himself over his death.

"No one will find him in the dark."

"Remember the tracker he was carrying? One, or both, of those boats will be homing in on him."

"Will that give us enough time?" Zander asked.

"No, it won't. This boat is fast, but I'm sure there are faster boats pursuing us. Some people call them cigar boats. I like to call them penis boats. Seems like anyone with a little penis drives shit like that." Max laughed.

His laughter served no purpose and failed to put either of them at ease.

"We've got to get going. Aubrey needs to get to a hospital."

"No hospitals. We can't take the risk of exposing her now that's she's officially dead."

Zander hadn't thought about it. Now he realized that if he and Aubrey would ever get to be together, she had to be free of all these governmental entanglements.

"Do you have a plan, then?"

"I do. But right now we have other fish to fry." Max had made a swooping right hand turn.

Zander thought, that on that course, they would miss Key West and land somewhere in the Bahamas.

"Where are we going? Aubrey needs help now."

"I'm aware, but if we don't take care of the situation at hand, we won't have to worry about anything else. These people will blow us out of the water given the chance.

That news made Zander understand the seriousness of their situation. He still needed to know how they were going to handle it.

"We have one missile launcher but there two targets. How will we handle that?"

"We're concerned with the boat ahead of us. The other boat has no doubt found Carlos and realize they can no longer track us through him."

"Won't they have radar on board?" Zander asked.

"This is Cuba we're talking about. They don't have many resources. My best guess is that the rear boat had Carlos to rely on. The boat to our north will be the one with the electronics."

"Is that why you made the turn?"

"Yes. If they mirror our movement, we'll know they are tracking us."

There was no reason to ask the next question, because he saw the lights from the boat turn toward their position.

Max cut the engine and shut down the computer. It was dark in the rubber raft.

"How is Aubrey doing?" Max asked.

"I can't tell. She's breathing but not moving."

"That's good. Whatever they gave her was strong, and let's hope she remains out until all this is over."

Zander liked the idea. If they were going to die out here, it would be much better if Aubrey never regained consciousness.

"Get down as low as possible. I don't know what arms they have on that boat, but the Kevlar on the pontoons should keep us safe enough from gunfire. I don't think they'll have anything big mounted on those fast boats. I'm sure they are in communication with the boat to the south, but that's not a problem."

Zander wanted to understand and continue, but he knew he had already exhausted his amount of acceptable questioning. He saw the keyboard of the SAT phone light up. Max had turned away from Zander and was speaking into the receiver. Zander couldn't hear anything.

Max turned off the phone. Zander heard some sounds coming from his seat, and it sounded like Max was loading the missal launcher. He couldn't see anything, but he felt the movements. He had heard that people who lost eyesight might have their other senses heightened. It might be true, but he wasn't feeling it.

"Why aren't we moving? We need to get out of here," Zander yelled.

"Lower your voice. We're playing possum."

"From whom?"

"The North boat. The South boat will no longer be a problem."

"How can you be so sure?"

"Watch. It should be any time now. When something happens, it should distract the North boat. That's when we make our move."

Zander kept his mouth shut after that. He realized that Max had all the options covered, and he had become an unnecessary obstruction. He decided to shift his concentration on the reason they had come here in the first place. Aubrey still hadn't stirred, and he knew that was a blessing. He wouldn't have to worry about keeping her subdued.

Max was back on his SAT phone, and after he hung up, he started the motor. Zander expected them to move, but they just stayed in place. He could see Max's watch light up and wondered what was happening.

"Pay attention to the south boat," Max said.

Thirty seconds after Max made the comment, the sky lit up in a huge fireball. It was almost like someone lit off a huge flare, and Zander could see for miles. It was miles of open water, however. Not one thing caught his eye. Then just west of where the fireball blew, Zander saw the shrimper light up almost every light on board. They had blown the south boat out of the water. It made Zander's spirits lift for the first time all evening. He had little time to think about it, because Max had shoved the throttle and they were running full bore toward the lights of the north boat.

It was just as Max had said. The boat had stopped dead in the water. The explosion had taken down their guard, and they were deciding how to proceed. When Max was close to the boat's port bow, he cut the engine and let the momentum pushed the raft until they were even with the stern.

The boat hadn't noticed the move, and by the time they got back to tracking the raft, Max had drifted past their stern. The boat started up, and Max lifted the missile launcher to his shoulder. Zander waited for the loud report that was sure to come and closed his eyes. When he heard nothing, he opened his eyes and saw Max balancing on the seat with his left leg using the motor to stabilize his body.

The men on the boat realized that their prey had slipped past them in the confusion and were trying to turn the boat around. Zander could see men trying to grab firearms in the dim light and knew Max had to act fast or he would become a piece of Swiss cheese.

Just as the penis boat turned, Max fired the missile launcher. Zander could see the exhaust ports. It was the last thing that would ever be seen on the boat.

The explosion pushed the raft at least two feet back in the water. Zander used his body to cover Aubrey from the debris that came raining down on them. Some of it was burning, but Max had a fire extinguisher and nothing burning lasted for more than a few seconds.

When Zander looked up, he saw a ring of fire burning on the water line where the boat had been a few seconds before. Nothing was left. Whatever number there was of the crew, they had been evaporated. Max discarded the remains of the missile launcher into the ocean. He pushed down the throttle, and soon they were on a course back to Key West.

The seventy or eighty miles couldn't go fast enough for Zander.

40

The black watercraft flew through the night ocean without detection. A light was visible was from the navigation screen that Max was watching. Zander was holding onto Aubrey as tightly as he dared. He was afraid he might choke the life out of her, but he never wanted to let her go. He would never let her out of his sight again.

An hour-and-a-half had passed, but it could have been ten minutes in Zander's mind. He had no concept of time. Understanding the woman he was holding in his arms was his focus. He was facing Max and looking at him. He was seeing nothing, however. His mind was trying to sort everything that had happened over the past few weeks. Nothing was making much sense, but he tried anyway.

Max took his eyes off the navigation electronics and peered over the boat to his left.

"Zander, look to your right."

Zander heard the words but hadn't been able to focus on the present. He just looked at Max.

"Zander. Snap out of it," Max said again.

Zander looked around trying to find the present. He had heard Max's words but hadn't been able to make his brain follow any direction.

"Lights off the starboard bow."

This time Zander looked to his right and saw the lights twinkling in the darkness. It was a welcome sight.

"Key West," Max said, as he throttled back.

Zander expected him to begin veering toward the island. Max kept the boat on a straight course, however. Soon the lights were behind them.

"Where are we going?" Zander asked.

"Shark Key. I know someone there. Aubrey is going to need medical attention. We need someone who won't be reporting this to any authority. We don't want any hospital involved.

"Explain that again."

"Aubrey is dead. She no longer exists. If you want her out of her past life, that's the way it has to stay. The Feds won't be looking for her unless we give them reason."

Zander sat back realizing that Max had the situation in hand. He hadn't thought of anything other than rescuing Aubrey. Max had his back, and everything that would happen now was because he knew what he was doing.

Shark Key was just past Key West and Stock Island. Zander couldn't see much, the little island looked dark. Max cut the engine and stood up. He flashed a light a few times. Zander saw a response just up the beach from their location. Max made his way as slowly as possible to keep the engine noise down.

They rubbed up against a dock. Zander could see two silhouettes waiting with what he thought might be a gurney. Max threw one of the men a line, and soon they were tied to the wooden structure.

Max climbed over a seat and came right over to Zander.

"We're going to hand Aubrey over to these two men. They will see to all of her needs."

"I'm going with them," Zander said, not letting go of Aubrey.

"I'm afraid that won't be possible. I'm pulling in some huge favors, and you aren't part of the equation."

Max pulled Zander's arms away from Aubrey, and the two men jumped aboard and lifted Aubrey's limp body. They put her on the gurney in one fluid motion, and before Zander could turn around, they disappeared in the darkness. Max had returned to the rear of the boat and started the motor. They were headed back to Key West, before Zander had time comprehend what had just happened.

Realizing that Zander was confused, Max reacted.

"Zander, we're heading back to Sunset Key. Mona will be waiting for us. I'll explain everything to you then. Just remember that Aubrey will have the best care possible."

"Why couldn't I go with her? She needs someone close to her that she can trust."

"There's more to it than that. I told you that I would explain when we meet Mona. She'll have breakfast waiting for us. Now settle back and keep your voice down."

Zander was dismissed. He would never like it, but he had no other option.

Max beached the boat where they had boarded it earlier in the evening. Zander saw two people on the beach. He could see that one was a woman. Mona waved to them in the dim light.

"Welcome home, you two. Breakfast is ready when you are."

"Zander, go up to the house with Mona. I need to secure a few things here, and then I'll join you."

Zander stumbled from the boat and walked over to Mona. The other person was a man that Zander had never seen before. He moved toward the bow, and as Zander and Mona left the beach, he could see Max passing things to the stranger. He was putting them into the big canvas bag Max had stored away earlier.

By the time the two reached the house, Zander heard the motor start and the boat pull away from the beach. Before he could find a chair at the table Mona had set up for breakfast, Max entered the house and threw the bag he was carrying into the laundry room.

"Don't you think you should put those things someplace else?" Mona asked.

"After breakfast. Zander needs some answers, and I don't think we need to concern ourselves with anyone discovering our movements tonight. We covered our tracks."

Mona went to the stove and began to dish out breakfast. Zander wondered if he was hungry, but the omelet and sausages looked quite inviting. He had most of it gone by the time Mona poured the coffee. Max smiled up at her. She put her hand on Max's shoulder.

"Thank you," was all she said, and then turned around and put the coffee pot back on the burner.

Zander realized, at that moment, that Mona was instrumental in having Max help him. He wondered what this had cost him.

"Yes, thank you Max. I owe you Aubrey's life. I'll be at your service to make sure that I pay back this debt."

"It's always good to get back in the game now and again," Max said.

"This isn't something just anyone could pull off. What did it cost you?" Zander asked.

"I had to pull in quite a few favors. It's unfortunate that I lost my Cuban contact. But it's all good."

Zander sat back with his coffee and waited for Max to finish breakfast. Mona joined them but just had a cup of coffee. Zander wondered if she had eaten before they arrived. When Max finished, he pushed his plate away, and looked at Zander.

"You have many questions, I'm assuming. I'll try to head them off with an explanation of sorts."

"Thank you," Zander said.

"First of all, you couldn't accompany Aubrey because they are taking her someplace secure with doctors and staff on duty that no one can know about. She will get the best of care. That I can assure you."

"Do you know the extent of her injuries?"

"She is in rough shape, I'm afraid. She wasn't raped, and that's a huge relief. Rape almost always happens in these prisons. She was in solitary with the Cuban version of the CIA watching. The guards never had a chance to take advantage. She was interrogated, however. I can't begin to tell you the horrors she endured. I'll be getting word as soon as they have time to assess her situation. A prognosis should be forthcoming after that."

"As soon as you know something, I want to go to be with her," Zander said.

"We'll follow the doctor's orders. You need to prepare yourself for the possibility that you won't be having any contact with her for quite a while."

Zander wanted to argue but decided against it. Max was a formidable character, and it would not be prudent to question his authority. He decided to find out what had happened during the rescue. Many things failed to add up.

"Can you at least tell me what happened tonight? It didn't seem to follow any script that we had talked about earlier."

Max nodded.

"It was pretty fucked up. Carlos and Benedict cooked up a scheme to try and lean on me for more money. Benedict told me we would never leave the island alive if I didn't give him more money."

"How much more?" Zander asked.

"Another 500 thousand above what I was prepared to give them. Carlos made a half-hearted attempt to talk Benedict out of the threat, but I knew he was in on it from the start. I told Benedict I didn't have that kind of money at my disposal, but he said I could go get it, and they would keep Aubrey until I returned. It wasn't an acceptable option."

"I heard a gunshot," Zander said.

"It was Benedict's gun. I don't particularly like people pointing a weapon at me. I reached for it, and there was a struggle and it went off. Fortunately, Benedict was the recipient. Carlos begged to go with us, because he said his cover was compromised. It was bullshit. But I needed to control the situation, and it was easier with Carlos in tow."

Zander wasn't quite sure that Max's account was truthful. He doubted that Max would try to disarm anyone. He seemed to be a shoot first and deal with the aftermath later.

"You knew that we would run into trouble?"

"I suspected. Carlos was playing both ends. He didn't want to lose our relationship in case his plan went south, but he wanted the big payday. Benedict was just a pawn. I think Carlos would have killed him regardless of the outcome."

"The fast boats?"

"Carlos' insurance. One way or another, he was bound to get his payday. When I knew he was making his move to leave Cuba, I realized the danger we were in. That's when I contacted the shrimp boat. They were on high alert and took out the first boat leaving us with an even playing field."

Zander realized it was not close to even even but was thankful for Max's skills.

"Did you have to shoot Carlos?"

"Yes. He was a danger to the entire operation. He knew too much. Aubrey would never be safe with him alive. No honor among thieves, and a good thing for you to remember in the future." Max got up and got the coffee pot.

Mona had been silent throughout Max's monologue. Zander looked at her and noticed no surprise by any of the explanation. Her acceptance proved to Zander that she was aware of Max's past, and knew he still could play the game when he was called upon.

Max sat back down and looked at Zander waiting for questions. Zander sat back and took a sip of his coffee. It was hot and strong. It opened his sinuses.

"What happens now?" Zander asked.

"When I get word on Aubrey's condition and recovery time, I'll contact you. I've been around a few of these situations, and there is always more than meets the eye."

"I have no idea what you are talking about," Zander said.

"Aubrey went through a great deal of trauma. I don't know if we'll ever know the full extent of it. She's going to need help getting over all of this. I'm talking about psychiatric help here, and it might take time. What I'm telling you is that you are going to have to dig deep and find more patience somewhere than you've ever had to use before."

"I'm not very good at patience."

Mona put her hand on his shoulder.

"We know. This is something you'll have to deal with, because Aubrey can't get back to you and leads a normal life until she's healed. That means her body and her mind. Max assures me she'll have the best care in both areas."

Zander nodded, but he wasn't tracking.

"How much time is this going to take?"

"It's hard to make a prediction. When things appear to be getting better for Aubrey, I'll contact you, and you will return here," Max said.

The comment surprised Zander.

"Where am I supposed to go?" Zander asked.

"I believe you have some other issues that may need your attention. Go be with your family. Get to know your child. Make peace with her mother. You'll never be able to move forward until you do," Max said and put his arm around Mona.

Nothing was in Zander's control any longer. He knew he needed to talk to his friends. It was possible they could make sense of everything that happened. He doubted it, but there was always comfort being around people who were grounded.

41

Max and Mona took Zander to Key West for lunch and dinner. They found a few bars with entertainment. It was Mona's idea to get Zander's mind off things and keep him up until they went to bed later in the evening.

Sloppy Joe's was swinging with a piano player who liked to insult people who got up to use the bathroom. Zander enjoyed both the music and the comedic relief.

As they walked down Duval, Zander realized that he did enjoy the craziness of Key West. He hadn't experienced it before because of his last encounter with Sara Jane. He hadn't thought of her in a while, and he was surprised that the thought of her conjured very little pain for him.

The three lasted until 7:00 pm. Zander was nodding off over dinner, and Mona suggested they go back and turn in for the evening. They got a boat ride back to the island with a friend who happened to be at the restaurant.

Max suggested a nightcap, but Zander passed. He was dog tired and just wanted to sleep. When he woke up the next day, showered, and packed up his stuff, it was after 8:00.

Mona was making coffee when he walked into the kitchen.

"I'll get breakfast started in a bit," Mona said.

"None for me, thank you. I want to get going. I'm planning to make Cedar Key today, and it's a drive."

"Well, at least have some coffee," Mona replied.

"I can do that." Zander pulled out a stool next to the island.

When the coffee was finished, she poured two mugs and slid one in front of Zander. She sat on a stool across the island from him.

"Max talked at length about your situation last night. I'm afraid I kept him up too long. He's still asleep."

"What did you decide?" There was no irritation in his voice.

"We decided your life is complicated, and we have no answers."

"Neither do I."

"Do you want my advice?" Mona asked.

"Sure. I could use some good counseling."

"I don't know how good it is, but I think you need to get involved in your daughter's life. What was her name again?"

"Sandra."

"Sandra. Your daughter needs a father. It may be that you can't be there for her all the time, but you should be available for those times she going to need you."

"This is all new to me."

"I'm no expert, since I don't even have any kids. I am a daughter, however, and I know how important a father is in a young girl's life."

"Like you said before, everything is complicated."

"Whatever the woman is calling herself these days, she still is Sandra's mother. I can't believe I'm even saying this, since she tried to have me killed. We have no love lost between us, and if she was in front of me right now, I might shoot her."

Zander nodded. He knew the feeling.

"I think I've come to grips with whatever our relationship is right now. I know that we won't ever be together as husband and wife. It wouldn't work for either of us."

"I don't know Aubrey, but your decision to put yourself in harm's way to save her speaks volumes."

"I didn't know I was that transparent," Zander said smiling.

"She must be quite a woman," Mona said.

"She is. I hope she'll be able to become that woman again," Zander said with concern in his voice.

"She's got the best care anyone could ever hope to have. Max will follow her progress and keep you informed."

"Will you make sure he does, Mona? Max can keep things pretty close to the vest."

"Not like someone else who's sitting across from me."

Zander knew Mona was right on. He had always been one to keep things hidden when they seemed to have dire consequences. He had to do a better job of sharing with his friends.

"I'm planning on sharing everything with Herbie and Gail when I get to Cedar Key."

"How about Fats?"

"I guess I'll call him on the road. It will give me something to do."

"See that you do. These things are easily put off, but take it from me, isolation is only good for people with a communicable disease."

Zander got up and pushed his empty coffee mug toward Mona.

"Thanks for the coffee. I need to get going. I've got to get across the bay and find my car in the parking garage."

Mona got up.

"Max is going to take you over. It wouldn't serve any purpose having you leave without at least letting him do this service for you. I'll make sure he's up and ready to go."

A voice came from their bedroom.

"I'm ready. I've just been listening to you two talk. It was quite entertaining."

"Can't take the spying from the spy," Zander said.

"I'm old, and it's all I have left."

"You've got Mona," Zander said and realized it came out wrong.

"Yes, I do. You'll have Aubrey back soon as well. Trust me on this."

"I have no other choice, do I?"

"No, you don't. Are you ready to roll?"

Zander grabbed his bag and slung it over his shoulder. He was wearing the back clothing Max had given to him.

"You look like a longshoreman," Mona said laughing.

"I thought I was one last night, for sure."

"You did good Zander. Did I tell you he saved my life?" Max asked Mona.

"You did, and I thank you for that Zander," Mona said, putting her arms around Zander's neck.

"Let him go, you wench. He's got places to go and doesn't need to be thinking about a tryst with you," Max said, but they both knew he was having fun.

Zander broke away.

"Thanks for everything Mona. With any luck, I'll be seeing you soon, and you'll meet the best woman in the world."

"Present company excepted?"

"Well, there's that," Zander said and headed for the door.

"Pack our bags, Mona. I need to get away for a while," Max said.

"How long and where?"

"Just a few days. I'm thinking South Beach."

Mona screwed up her face.

"I have some other suggestions."

"I'm all ears."

"You are. You should have plastic surgery. We'll talk about it when we get back."

Zander and Max were chuckling, when they walked down to the beach. A small boat was tied to the dock. They got in, and Max started it up. They skirted Duval Street and found a place to tie up close to the parking garage where Zander had left his rental.

"Thanks for everything," Zander said as he climbed from the boat.

"No need to thank me. Someday, I might need a favor in return," Max replied.

"Who are you, The Godfather?" Zander asked with a grin.

"You can call me Don Max Kuhn."

"Just remember to keep me in the loop regarding Aubrey. When it's possible, I want to be with her."

"I will do that. Mona won't let me shirk that duty."

Zander nodded and set off for the parking structure. He never looked back. He heard the boat motor start and knew Max was heading back to Sunset key.

Zander wondered where they would be heading. Mona would make the decision and have Max in tow before he knew what happened. He liked the couple and hoped that maybe someday he and Aubrey could be like them. The thought made him anxious. Too many unanswered question made him nervous.

As he left the island, Zander decided that he needed to take care of the situation with his daughter. He knew Jayne too well, and there was no need for her to make decisions without being able to at least have input.

Traffic wasn't heavy leaving the keys, and soon he was heading west on Alligator Alley. At the rate he was going, he would be able to reach Cedar Key in nine hours. It would be in time for dinner, and he liked that. He decided to make a call to give Gail a head's up.

Gail seemed happy to hear from Zander. He told her not to make anything for dinner; he would like to take them out.

"I'll call Herbie right now. He'll want to be here to welcome you back this evening. How long will you be staying with us?"

"Just tonight, I'm afraid. I've got some decisions to make with the family concerning Sandra. I use the word family in the loosest of terms."

Gail decided not to comment.

"See you tonight," she said and hung up.

Zander threw the phone on the passenger seat and drove on. He knew he had to call Fats but was dreading the call. For some odd reason, Zander always preferred speaking with Fats. He hated the phone and never felt comfortable sharing personal things on it.

When he made the turn and headed north just past Marco Island, he looked over and picked up the phone. He pressed Fats' number hoping it would go to voicemail. No such luck. Fats answered on the fourth ring.

"Mon frère. How fortunate to receive communication as an aftermath. How will this postscript fit into your endgame?"

Fats' hippie-speak served to irritate Zander most of the time, but just hearing him sling his bullshit was a source of comfort right now. He decided to end it, because one could tolerate so much excrement.

"Keep your mouth shut and just listen, unless you want me to hang up."

There was no response from Fats on the other end of the line. Zander took it as a good omen and began his explanation of what had happened since they last talked.

He talked uninterrupted for over an hour. He made sure he left nothing out, and after he passed Sarasota, he stopped talking. It was still quiet on the other end.

"You may speak now," Zander prompted.

"Thank you. Now what transpires?" Fats asked.

"I'm heading to Gail and Herbie's place. They need to know what is going on as well."

"Then what?"

"I need to come to terms with Jayne and Millie. I want to be part of Sandra's life, but we need to find out how that's going to work."

"Just do me one main service, my man."

"What's that?

"Don't you rekindle any personal relationship with that woman."

Zander knew Fats couldn't say Jayne's name. He had such a dislike for her that he believed by not speaking of her she became nonexistent. Zander wished it worked that way.

"That has never been part of any plan that I've even considered. I've got Aubrey to worry about right now. She is my life, but that doesn't negate my responsibility to Sandra."

"It is a major conundrum, to be sure," Fats said.

"I have no idea how all of this will end. I'm going into this whole thing blind."

"As long as you are not blinded, once again, by the queen of all bitches."

Fats had a point, and Zander knew what he was trying to tell him. His decisions, when it came to Jayne, had never been good. It was as though she had some kind of extrasensory power that he couldn't navigate. He vowed to never let it control him again.

"When this entire escapade comes to a screeching halt, what are you planning?" Fats asked.

"I hadn't thought that far ahead."

"Zander, you need to come home." Fats hung up.

The comment surprised Zander. He had never thought of Frisco as home. He had been a number of places in his life, and none of them had ever seemed to have the feeling of home for him. The more thought about it, the more he realized that the Branchwater and the little cabin were the closest things to home that he had ever experienced. He had never experienced a sense of belonging to the little Iowa town of his childhood. Fats had become his best friend, and he had many other close relationships in both Frisco and Breckenridge. He decided that he and Aubrey would be returning to the little mountain village. It would be their home if Aubrey agreed.

It might have been the first time that Zander ever put someone else's wants and desires over his own. This could be the start of some renaissance but time would tell.

42

Cedar Key was a welcome sight. Zander always enjoyed the low-key atmosphere that was so unlike the rest of Florida. It reminded him of going back to Hospers, his small Iowa town. Neither place had been his home, but he felt comfortable in both.

As Zander made his way through the community on his way to Herbie's, he saw a truck moving closer to the rear of his rental. He saw it was Herbie, and his friend was giving him the finger. Zander thought it was the most welcoming gesture he had ever seen.

When they stopped at the house, Herbie grabbed Zander and put him in a huge bear hug.

"I'm so damn glad to see you, I could shit."

Zander laughed and asked Herbie to stop squeezing him to death. Herbie dropped Zander to the concrete, and just when Zander regained his balance, Gail exploded from the door and ran over and jumped on Zander almost dropping him to the pavement.

"Wait a minute. I haven't been gone all that long. These reconnections could very well be killing me."

Gail still had her arms around Zander's neck.

"We were worried, and it sounds like we had every reason."

Zander stopped and pulled her arms away from his neck.

"Let me guess, Fats called you."

Gail nodded, and Herbie smiled.

"We called him, and his phone was busy so we left a message. He called back and told us he had been on the phone with you. He wasn't shy about telling us what had happened."

"Go figure. He was never one to keep his mouth shut. I'm sorry. I wanted to explain everything in person to you both. I should have realized that Fats couldn't be entrusted with information that involved my life."

"Don't be so hard on him. He is just concerned about you, as we all are," Herbie said.

"Why don't you start at the beginning and tell us everything. We want more than the *Reader's Digest* condensed version. Come in the house. I've got dinner cooking and Herbie is about to pour the wine."

"I am?"

Gail looked at him.

"I am. I am." Herbie said, realizing his mistake.

"I thought I told you that I was taking you out for dinner this evening," Zander said trying to sound peeved.

"What do you think the chances are of that happening?" Gail said, waiting for Zander to challenge.

Zander was beaten and tactfully decided to keep his mouth shut.

The three went into the house. Zander saw that there wasn't a light on, but hundreds of candles were putting a beautiful flickering light on the living room and kitchen area.

"Gail, this is beautiful. I hope you've got your fire insurance paid up," Zander said.

"It better be impressive. It took me forever to light all these damn candles."

"I didn't even know we had this many candles in the whole place," Herbie said mesmerized by the candlelight.

"We didn't, but we do now," Gail said.

Herbie groaned but went right over and opened some wine and poured it into three glasses. It was a large pour, and there was nothing left in the bottle. Zander was amused and thought maybe Herbie needed the wine much more than he did.

"Give us the straight poop. We want to hear everything that happened in your rescue of Aubrey," Gail said.

Herbie took a drink and agreed.

Zander left out much of the detail he had shared with Fats, since they both knew most of the story. He tried to give them what he thought were the highlights if that's what you could call them. Highlights weren't what Zander would label about anything that happened the entire evening.

Both Gail and Herbie sat transfixed, as Zander told them what had happened. When he finished, Herbie got up and opened another bottle of wine. He poured the wine into the three glasses and made a comment.

"And the prodigal son returneth."

The comment surprised Zander. Herbie had never appeared to be very Biblical. In fact, Zander couldn't ever remember his family attending church growing up. Zander decided that maybe Gail had influence on him in that regard. He decided to follow up.

"And it appears that Gail has killed the fatted calf."

"You know she would do most anything for you, Zander."

The entire exchange was puzzling to Zander. He wondered if it had some meaning that he wasn't grasping. He decided that it was just religious guilt from his childhood. The feeling never went away, so he just buried it with everything else he couldn't understand.

By the time dinner was concluded, three bottles of wine had been consumed. All three amigos had a bit of a shine working.

"I've got to get to bed before I fall down," Gail said, and went to her bedroom.

"I'll help you with the dishes," Zander offered.

"Nope. We'll do those tomorrow. I've got to get to bed before the window of opportunity slams down in my face." He followed Gail into the bedroom.

Zander thought the window had already been shut and boarded up. It made him smile, and he fell into his own bed. That night he slept without dreams for the first time as long as he could remember.

The next morning he got up quietly, went down to the kitchen and cleaned up the dishes from the night before. He was finishing up, when the door opened, and both Herbie and Gail walked out together.

"Good timing," Zander said.

"We heard you making all kinds of noise but decided to let you work for your dinner," Herbie joked.

"It's the least I could do."

"Of course it is, so we let you."

Zander hung up the dishtowel.

"Zander, you did an amazing job. Herbie could take a lesson," Gail said.

"I thought I was pretty amazing last night. At least that's what you told me," Herbie replied.

Gail put a fist into the muscle in Herbie's left arm. Zander figured it hurt from the look on his face. He also realized that the window of opportunity had remained open for Herbie. It made him think of Aubrey, and it made him sad. He had no idea what their relationship would be when she got better. Maybe not so much "when" but "if" she got better.

The three went for breakfast at a local place just down the block from their home. Zander had wanted to get going, but he realized his friends wanted him to at least spend part of the morning with them. They were the kind of friends not to take their feelings into consideration.

After breakfast they took a walk. They found their way to a bench overlooking the gulf and the islands south of Cedar Key. It was a beautiful morning, and Zander wished he could spend more time with them both. He knew that Sandra's future had to be decided and that would need to include how he fit into it. He couldn't just let that to chance, especially when Jayne was involved.

Herbie broke the silence and interrupted Zander's thoughts.

"That rental must be costing you plenty. Why don't you let me drive you to the DePont estate, and then Gail and I can turn in your car at the rental in Gainesville?"

"I need to have wheels in case Max calls and wants me back down to Key West."

"Don't you think there might be transportation at the DePont's?" Herbie asked.

"I don't know how this is going to work itself out. It may not end on a amiable note."

"Well, then, they give you something to drive just to get rid of you," Herbie said smiling.

"If you need a ride, or the use of my car, you are always welcome," Gail said.

Zander knew it was a good idea. He had no need to be paying for a car that would just be sitting on the DePont property.

"Thanks for the offer. I guess I will take you up on it. But I'd like to get going, if at all possible."

They walked back to the house arm-in-arm. Zander got his things together and came down to the kitchen.

"Throw your stuff in the truck," Herbie said.

"Truck? Aren't we taking my rental?"

"No, I've got a few deliveries to make after I drop you off. Killing two birds with one stone."

The alliteration was almost too much to handle for Zander. Too much killing had happened in his life recently. He wanted to get beyond all that.

Both Herbie and Zander were quiet on the way to Perry. Zander was trying to think about how he would approach the subject of Sandra with both Millie and Jayne. Herbie was letting him. Zander was clueless about how to proceed, and thought he would let the women take the lead. It gave him a bit of relief.

"Thanks for everything, Herbie. You are a good friend. I won't forget this."

"See that you don't. No matter what happens, we're just a phone call away."

"I haven't had much luck with phones," Zander said.

"I know, but it's time you got yourself into this decade. Hell, it's time you got yourself into this century. You've got a daughter to think about."

"I've got Aubrey to think about as well."

"Did you ever think that you might be a lucky man?"

The comment floored Zander. It seemed like everything people were saying to him were full of surprises. He considered what Herbie had said.

"I don't know what you mean."

"Looking at what has happened from dark glasses gives you a pretty dark perspective on your life. Things happen for a reason. How we accept them makes us the people we are to become."

Zander wondered who this guy was sitting in the trucks driver's seat.

"You're saying that these things are positive? What planet are you from?"

"You reap what you sow."

There was that Biblical reference again. It was irritating to Zander.

"When did you become so knowledgeable in Biblical theology?"

"Gail and I have these discussion. She has turned my depressive personality around. We all have to search for the positive things in life or the negative will consume us."

"Easy to say, but not so easy to follow."

"Try getting back to your roots. Think of our life back when you didn't seem to have a care in the world," Herbie said.

"We did. We just didn't know it back then."

"Was that so bad? Every day was new, and we looked forward to what it would bring."

"You didn't have a very good childhood."

"I didn't know it. I didn't realize it until after high school. I have to admit I had some pretty blue times and some awful thoughts back then."

"So what changed?"

"It took a long time for me to realize that I was depressed for years until I reconnected with you, and then Gail came into my life. I'm happy to say that I've fought the demons and have won out over them."

"I'll consider it."

"Just remember that all your experiences become the basis of how you proceed with your life. Some terrible things have happened to you, but they are in the past. The one thing left is the here-and-now. How you deal with that will determine what your future will be like."

"When did you get so smart?"

"When I got rid of all the things that were dragging me down. Look at you. You've got a woman who thinks you are something special, and you've got the greatest gift of all, a child. How you reconcile these two things will be either the beginning of your happiness, or the creation of your own private hell. I've been to both places. I recommend the former. End of lecture."

Zander was still considering what Herbie had said when he dropped him off at the DePont's front gate.

43

Zander trudged up the long lane toward the house. He was unsure how he would approach the subject of his daughter. He thought it might have to be two separate strategies. One tactic would be needed for a more reasonable Millie DePont and another for Jayne.

He was having a difficult time trying to get rid of what Herbie had been telling him. It was all too much to think about. Zander wondered if he had been living entirely too much in the past. He had too many things on his mind to even consider all the philosophical bullshit.

When he came around the final bend in the drive, he stopped. It was like a firecracker went off in his head. Right here and right now was the proverbial crosswalk in his life. He had been going through his existence with small moments of pleasure. It wasn't what anyone would have called happiness, but it was all he knew.

He remembered a statement from his college days. "The unexamined life is not worth living." He couldn't remember who said it or where it came from. He knew it was from one of those Greek dudes, either Socrates or Plato. The exact author was of no interest to Zander. The words seemed to have meaning for him now, however. It was time to define his life with something other than his past.

A huge weight was lifting from his back. Zander thought it might be that moment of grand enlightenment. He knew that it would take work to overcome the rut he had let himself slip into. He couldn't let his guard down for even a moment. This new approach to life needed to be ingrained into his personality. He knew it would be a struggle, and he needed help. He would have to remember to thank Herbie for his insights.

Just as Zander reached the door, he stopped once again. He knew this change in his life depended on one thing. Zander and his relationship to Sara Jane, Jayne, or whoever she was at the moment, had to somehow be reconciled in order to move on with both of their lives. It could no longer be his ego versus hers. A child was involved now, and it would serve no purpose to screw up Sandra's life just because her parents were two separate assholes.

Zander smiled at the thought. If they were going to be assholes, they would be united assholes when it came to being there for Sandra. Zander used the huge knocker on the door. Rosita answered before Zander could knock again.

"Oh, Mr. Zander. It is so very good to see you. I believe Miss Amelia is in need of your assistance." Rosita pulled Zander into the foyer and shut the huge front door.

Zander gave Rosita a huge hug. The motivation for the hug puzzled him, but it seemed like the thing that he should have done long before. Rosita seemed confused.

"Rosita, thank you for what you do around here. I'm almost certain that nothing would run correctly without your influence."

Rosita smiled, and Zander thought she might have been blushing. It was difficult to tell with her beautiful brown skin.

"Thank you, Mr. Zander. I'm afraid there are things I cannot do even if I try. Please follow me. Miss Amelia will want to see you."

Zander followed Rosita into the kitchen. He wondered what she was concerned about. Rosita had never shared much concern with Zander. Zander saw Millie sitting in a rocker near the kitchen table. She was rocking and holding Zander's child. When she saw Zander enter the room, she almost jumped out of the chair.

"Just in the nick of time. I didn't think we would ever see you again."

"Why would you even say that? I know I have responsibilities, and I am not one to shirk my duty." Zander was hot.

"Is that what she is to you, a duty?"

"She is, until I get to know her. That's why I'm here. A father needs to get to know his daughter, don't you think?"

"I do. I also think her mother should do the same. It's not happening."

Millie made an attempt to hand over Sandra to Zander.

"Whoa, hold the phone. I don't know anything about babies."

"It's time you learned. I hope you're a quick study," Millie said.

She showed Zander how to hold the child. Zander looked at Sandra and was surprised to see she was awake and looking at him.

"She's beautiful." Zander was looking at Sandra and thought he could see Sara Jane as a child. "She looks like her mother."

"Yes, she does, but her eyes are yours."

"Hopefully, it won't become an albatross around her neck later in life."

"The sins of the father and the mother are not visited on the child."

There was another biblical comment. Zander knew it was incorrect, however. The actual verse said that the sins of the father were visited onto the sons of the third and fourth generations. It was of no matter. The past few days had revealed too many references like that to be any kind of coincidence. Millie told Zander to sit, and he took his place on the rocker.

"Why isn't Jayne taking care of Sandra's needs? It doesn't seem right that a grandmother should be doing this."

"I don't mind. She's such a good baby. Look at her look at you. I don't know what she is seeing. Maybe she sees movement and shapes, but she is quite inquisitive. She fusses when she is hungry and needs changing. Taking care of her is a pure joy for me."

"But the question still remains, doesn't it?"

Millie sat next to Zander at the table. Zander hadn't noticed when he walked in, but Millie seemed very tired.

"Are you okay? You seem worn out," Zander said.

"I'm fine. Just a bit tired from the nighttime feedings."

"There is something you aren't telling me?" Zander asked.

"Rosita, why don't you take Sandra and give her a bottle. When she's finished put her to bed. It's time for her nap."

Rosita took Sandra from Zander's arms. Zander could tell she was an old hand at caring for babies. He hoped with practice he could be as confident. Right now, he just had to be sure he wasn't going to hurt Sandra because of his uncoordinated movements.

"Let's go out to the pool area. We need to talk," Millie said and led the way out of the kitchen.

Millie collapsed into a chair on the pool's apron. Zander pulled another over so they could talk without having to raise their voices.

"We need a drink," Millie said.

Zander thought she might be stalling.

"It's way too early to start drinking. Why don't you just say what's on your mind."

"There's something wrong with Jayne."

Zander wanted to say, "No shit, Dick Tracy," but he kept the comment to himself.

"She's broken. No question about it. What else is wrong?"

"She has isolated herself in her room. She hasn't been out of it since you left. She takes her meals there and eats very little. She's asked for vodka a few times, but I won't bring any to her. I told her if she wants a drink she needs to come down and join me."

"She needs to go see a doctor or a shrink."

"She wouldn't go, so I brought my doctor here to the house. I thought that maybe she was going through something physical. Carol is my friend, and she was Jayne's doctor during her delivery. I thought if anyone could find the problem it would be her."

"Did Jayne let her in?"

"Well, we kind of bent the truth a bit. Carol said it was time for her post-delivery checkup, and Jayne didn't object."

"So what's wrong? Is there something wrong?"

Millie looked at Zander and just shook her head.

"You men can be so dense. Of course there's something wrong. She wants nothing to do with her daughter. The doctor called it postpartum depression or some such nonsense."

"I've never heard of it."

"I hadn't either, but Carol said it isn't all that uncommon. It's some kind of depression that mothers go through after their child is born."

"Is she seeing anyone about it?"

"What do you think? I can't get her to come out of her room. She won't even let me in. Carol told me that I should keep Sandra away from her for the time being. She might want to hurt herself and the baby."

The comment alarmed Zander.

"Do you think she's capable of doing something like that? It wouldn't be the Sara Jane I knew. She was always just about Sara Jane."

"I don't know. That's why I'm concerned, and that's why I'm so happy you showed up."

"What did the doctor think we should be doing?"

"She said we should just leave her alone, until she decides she's had enough. Rosita and I snuck into the room when she was asleep and removed anything we thought might be used to do damage to herself. But I don't think she's got enough energy to try anything like that. She hasn't eaten enough to keep a bird alive. That's why I'm so concerned."

"What do you want me to do?"

"I have no idea. I thought maybe you might have some ideas. I'm at a loss and getting more concerned by the day."

"Let me think about it. I'm sure there is some button I can push to snap her out of this funk she's in. I've never had a problem getting into her head in the past."

"Things are different. She's not the same person you once knew."

"I'm not sure I ever knew her."

"Whatever you decide, I'll support. I can't go on like this very much longer."

"Why don't you go up and get some sleep? You look terrible."

Millie looked at him.

"I'm not sure I should say thank you or just kick your ass. I suppose I do look terrible, but at least you should try to put a better spin on your comment."

Millie pulled herself out of the chair and walked away from the pool area. Zander watched her go and knew he liked this woman. He would need to do some thinking about how to proceed. Herbie's words started to ring back into his head, and now he welcomed them. This was one of the moments that would serve to shape whatever future would follow.

Zander sat back and felt calmer than he had in a very long time.

44

Zander watched and learned about his daughter from Millie, Rosita, and on the weekends, Holly. Millie had entered Holly at the University in Gainesville with the understanding that she would return on the weekends to help with Sandra. Holly decided to study child development. Zander thought that her personality would serve that major well. He hoped she could handle the other general education requirements.

Millie was looking more like her old self. Zander's presence seemed to have that desired effect. Zander did his share around the house. Mostly, he took care of Sandra, and Millie used the respite to look after the timber business.

The first week went by without even a glimpse of Jayne. She stayed in her room all day. Whether she wandered around at night, Zander had no idea. He was far too exhausted taking care of Sandra's needs to worry about it.

Zander called Max every day for the first week, until Max had to put a stop to it. He told Zander not to call. Max said he would call once a week with a progress report. Of course, Zander couldn't help himself and still tried to call. Max stopped answering the phone, and Zander took the hint.

Zander's babysitting routine led him to the park on the massive grounds surrounding the house. He would walk Sandra in her stroller for hours always talking to her. Most of the time she was sleeping, but Zander would continue speaking to her. He wanted her to always remember his voice. He starting calling her Sandy when just the two of them were alone. He liked the sound of it. Sandra was just too formal a name to suit his taste.

One day, when he was returning to the house, Zander saw a curtain move at an upstairs window. He was sure it was Jayne's room. He realized she was watching them and made a point to check it out each time the two of them left for a walk. After a week of seeing the same curtain move, Zander had enough.

"Jayne's been watching Sandy and me from her bedroom window," Zander said to Millie.

"I suppose it doesn't surprise me. You can't live in a room twenty-four hours a day without getting bored. I would have gone nuts a long time ago."

"Nuts or not, it's time she took a little responsibility around here. This shouldn't land on your shoulders."

"It's not. You're here."

"Point taken, but as soon as I hear from Max, I'll be leaving to get Aubrey."

"Are you planning to bring her here?"

Zander hadn't considered how he would balance Aubrey with his new responsibilities concerning Sandy.

"I hadn't thought about it."

"I don't think it's a good idea with Jayne being in such a fragile state."

The comment served to piss Zander off.

"She doesn't want to step up to her new-found responsibilities. When everything has always just been about her, I guess it almost be impossible to give up that exaggerated sense of self-importance." Zander handed Sandy to Millie.

"What are you going to do?'

"Something I should have done when I first got here. Someone has to deal with this. It might as well be me."

Millie looked at Zander through narrowed eyes. She was considering what he had said and wondered if she agreed with it. Since she had no other solutions, Millie said nothing and went into the kitchen with Sandy to get a bottle. Zander took it as confirmation of his handling the situation. He went to Jayne's bedroom door and knocked on it. No answer came from inside. He tried the door and found it locked. He beat on the door with both fists as hard as he could.

There was a lull, and then he heard the click of the door lock. He tried the handle and this time the door opened. He pushed the door open and looked around the room. Jayne was back in bed with her back to him. Zander took a step inside the room.

He was greeted with a stench so strong he almost gagged. It smelled like rotten food, onions, and body odor. Zander walked to a window and threw it open as far as possible. He followed suit with two other windows.

"What in the hell do you think you're doing?" Jayne asked in a raised voice.

"Trying to get the room aired out before I puke."

"No one asked you to come in here."

"And yet you unlocked the door."

Jayne said nothing.

"When is the last time you bathed?"

Jayne remained silent.

"It smells terrible in here, and it's you. I've smelled hog farms in midsummer with less stench. You're about as sexy as a wet bag of laundry."

"You don't understand."

"I understand that you have abandoned your daughter who needs you. I understand that everything seems to just be about you. I understand that you have put the burden of taking care of Sandy on Millie."

"Her name's Sandra not Sandy."

"Until you take responsibility in her care and well-being, you have no right to tell anyone what to call her. Good God, what the hell is wrong with you?"

"Get out."

"So, it's all about your desires, interests, and perceived needs. How egocentric can one person be?"

"Look in the mirror."

"I have. I'm happy to say that I'm over that part of my life, and I'm over your attention-craving love of self-infatuation. You know what all that means don't you?"

"What is it, college boy?"

The comment took Zander by surprise. He wondered if Jayne somehow felt resentful, because Zander had gone to college and she failed to have the same opportunities. He decided to oblige that feeling.

"You're a narcissist. You reconcile the narcissi with the cist."

"Don't give me any your psychological babble."

"*Narcissi* is the genus name for a daffodil. The flower has a corona sometimes called a crown. Sound familiar? The word "sist" is sometimes spelled "cist" and we all know what that is." Zander was making it up as he went.

He did have a little knowledge of things botanical. When he was in college, he took Botany class so he could avoid having to take in introductory course in physics. He remembered sitting in the physics class the first day and being totally lost. He went to the registrar's office and dropped the course. He hadn't cared much for the botany class either, but at least he could understand it, and there weren't any formulas to worry about. He had never had a chance to use anything from the class until now. He was happy to also be able to embellish on what was true.

"I have no idea what you are trying to tell me."

"A narcissist could be a beautiful flower. Instead it lets a cancer destroy itself and those around him or, in your case, Sandy."

"You need to leave. I don't want you around my daughter or family."

"Your daughter? That's rich. When is the last time you even held her? When did you cultivate this sense of entitlement that lets you feel you can take advantage of others?"

Jayne sat up and looked at Zander before she decided to speak.

"Maybe I just need some help and understanding."

"Don't expect special favors or compliments coming from me any longer. You have a lack of ability to recognize the needs or feelings of others. No one envies you. Your arrogance and haughtiness has served to exaggerate your heightened sense achievement and lack of talent." Zander was on a roll.

Jayne began to cry. Zander thought the tears might be of the crocodile variety, since he saw no actual wetness coming from her eyes.

"Trying to pull out all the stops to get sympathy. I can tell you it no longer works on me and anyone else around here. You have used up all generosity and goodwill. All that's left for you is animosity, and you are the one person who can change that."

"Tell me how I can make all this better," Jayne said and sat on the edge of the bed.

Zander decided not to get any closer to her than necessary. He thought he might be spared any feeling of remorse because of her stench. It had been easy to unload on her.

"You can start by taking a shower and cleaning yourself up. Then you can clean up the room, and just maybe, you might be able to feel better about yourself. All this narcissistic behavior is because you don't even like yourself. It's a smokescreen, and it's time you did some self-examination before it's too late," he said and left the room.

Zander had never spoken to Jayne like that, ever. He wondered how she would react now that he was out of sight. He decided to stay at the door and see if he could pick up any reaction. He hadn't liked what he had seen. Her hair was greasy and hanging in front of her eyes. Her gown was dirty, and he wondered how long she had been wearing it. Her eyes were sunken in their sockets, and there was no color in her cheeks. Her weight loss was pronounced, and she looked gaunt. It was a far cry from how she had presented herself in the past. Zander was right in calling her a narcissist. She had been one, but she had gone beyond that label right now.

Zander heard some movement and then he heard Jayne's voice.

"If I'm a narcissist, then I'd better start acting like one," she said to her image in the mirror.

He was curious what effects his lecture would have on her. He heard what she uttered and wondered if it would have a positive outcome for Sandy. He left, when Jayne started the shower.

He went down to the kitchen to find Millie. She was sitting in the rocker feeding Sandy another bottle.

"What's the prognosis?"

"Remains to be seen. I was pretty hard on her. Either she'll come out of this distress, or she'll get worse. I did hear her start the shower, so that's something I guess."

"Do you think she would have it her to harm herself?"

"I don't think she would do that. She's pretty much stuck on herself." Zander said. "If she doesn't get over this depression or whatever it's called, Sandy would be better off with you, Rosita, and Holly anyway."

"You can't believe that."

"I do. I wouldn't have said that before, but now we have Sandy to consider. If Jayne won't step up and be the mother she's supposed to be, then my daughter will be better off without her." Zander was surprised when he vocalized the thoughts he had kept to himself.

Millie and Zander spoke of "what if's" over coffee that Rosita served. It was warm in the kitchen, and it made Zander feel comfortable. The kitchen had always been his favorite place while growing up. It had been a place of good smells and good conversations. He knew he needed that after being in Jayne's bedroom.

Zander was holding a sleeping Sandy when the door to the kitchen opened. In walked Jayne with an armload of dishes, which she put in the sink.

"Rinse them off and put them in the dishwasher," Millie said, pretending nothing had happened.

Zander turned his head to hide a smile. He liked the fact that Millie was following his lead and not letting Jayne get by with her bad behavior.

Jayne finished putting all the dishes in the dishwasher, when Millie spoke to her again.

"What does your room look like?"

"It needs cleaning. Rosita would you see to it please?" Jayne asked.

"Rosita is busy. You will need to see to it yourself. Be sure to use air freshener so the rest of us can walk by and not gag at the smell."

Zander thought he could see a flash in Jayne's eyes, but she failed to respond to Millie. Instead she walked over to Zander.

"Could I hold my daughter, please?"

"Sandy is sleeping, but I think she would welcome the feel of her mother's arms even in her slumber." He handed Sandy to Jayne.

Millie caught Zander's eye, and both knew that Jayne would be back to herself. Neither knew if it would be a good or bad thing.

Epilogue

Niemand Kan Regter Zijn In Zijne Eigen Zaken
No one can be the judge in his own case.
---Dutch Proverb

Zander got the call from Max on a Tuesday. It was almost two months after they had rescued Aubrey. Zander wanted to ask him many questions, but Max was having none of it.

"You need to take care of whatever business you have up there. I want you to be ready at a moment's notice."

Zander was exasperated and wanted to know why he couldn't drop everything and just come to Key West. The question was answered when Max shared something Zander wasn't expecting.

"She doesn't want to see you right now."

"What the hell is going on?"

"She has a lot to work through. I think she's getting close but doesn't want you near her until she's ready. My guess is that she doesn't want you anywhere near Key West or southern Florida."

"I don't understand."

"Think about it. She has far too many memories around her to process. She needs a fresh start."

Zander thought about what Fats had said to him about coming home, and he made up his mind at that moment.

"I'll take her to Colorado. We can both make a fresh start there."

"I'll call you when she's ready."

"If Aubrey is serious about not having me come down there, you should deliver her to Herbie's at Cedar Key." Zander was back to making plans.

"Let's not get ahead of ourselves."

Zander thought that Max had hung up. Then he realized Max never hung up at all, but pressed a button to disconnect. Old terminologies hadn't kept up with this new cell phone business. Hanging up the phone like you used to do with the old Bakelite rotary models no longer was possible. No such thing as a line going dead. Phone lines were gone and all but nonexistent, because everything went through the air via towers and satellites. It was all very perplexing, and Zander realized that he might be stuck in another time. He would have to remedy that. Aubrey needed him in the present if they were to have any future together.

There had been no conversation with anyone in the DePont household about Zander's arrangement with Max or any strategy dealing with Aubrey. It might be better not to have to do any explaining. He would figure out some kind of arrangement involving Sandy after Aubrey's needs had been met. He wanted to avoid jinxing anything, and his track record hadn't been very good in that arena.

The next few weeks seemed to move at a snail's pace for Zander. He still spent time with Sandy by walking with her in a stroller on the grounds, but Jayne had stepped up and had seen to most of the child's needs. Zander couldn't tell if she was warming up to her daughter or just going through the motions to avoid answering to either Zander or Millie.

Zander was getting bored, and Millie noticed. One day she loaded him up into her Caddy and took him over to the business office. She showed him how the company ran and went through the paperwork. Zander was quite impressed with the bottom line.

"You don't seem to be lacking in capital."

"I make a great deal of money each year," Millie said.

Zander wondered why she was sharing her business secrets. He had no time to ask, because she took him to the logging sites and then to the mill where they processed the timber. When she was finished, Millie drove to a pub in Perry. Zander thought it might be something she failed to own or had any interest in. It wasn't a place where everyone made sure they spoke to her. They ordered beers and sat without speaking, until they had consumed half their pints.

"I took you here, because I wanted a place where we could talk without being interrupted."

"So this is one of the few places you don't own?"

Millie smiled.

"I don't own everything in Perry."

"Just most things," Zander said.

"I want to make you an offer."

Zander disliked where the conversation was headed but said nothing.

"I want you to take over the day-to-day management of the company."

It was what he had feared.

"Thank you for the offer, but I can't do that."

"I don't understand. This is a huge opportunity for you."

"It's more than I deserve. It's just something I can't do at the moment."

"It's that other woman, isn't it?"

"Her name is Aubrey, and yes, that's something I need to fix."

"What about your daughter? She needs a father in her life."

"You'll get no argument from me on that issue, and it's something I will reconcile. I just can't do it, until I can settle the future with Aubrey."

"So, you will be just another phantom father figure."

"That's just not in my nature. I will be there for Sandy, but I just haven't figured out how it will work."

"I'm giving you an option here that most people could only dream about."

"I know that. It's just that it can't include Aubrey, and that's a non-starter for my life. Why don't you offer this opportunity to Jayne?"

"She's got your daughter to worry about. I don't want to put this on her. It would just be a burden."

The comment made Zander laugh.

"You don't know your daughter very well, do you? How long do you think it will be before she gets restless doing nothing but taking care of Sandy? What happens when she goes to school? Do you think she's going to be satisfied just sitting around your pool everyday?"

The series of questions made Millie sit back. She took a drink of her beer and glanced at Zander.

"Good questions. I hadn't thought that far ahead."

"You know, you couldn't get anyone better to run your logging operation and the mill. Jayne was born to be in charge. Maybe you should let her be in charge of something legal for a change. It might change her life and make things more tolerable for Sandy. Besides, you've got enough support to see that your granddaughter gets everything she needs. Love and understanding are not the things that are lacking in your household."

"I'll consider what you've said." Millie drained her glass. "Let's go."

Zander's glass was still half-full, but he stood and left it on the table. Millie was on a mission, and it wouldn't serve anyone to stand in her way.

· · ·

Max's final call came one week after Millie's offer. Zander gave him Herbie's address in Cedar Key. Max told him that he had some loose ends to tie up concerning Aubrey's identity, and he would deliver her on Friday. That gave Zander four days to ease into his exit from Millie's estate. In truth, he was restless. He needed something to occupy both his body and mind. He knew Aubrey would consume all of his time, and he was ready for it. He was not considering taking his leave from Sandy lightly, however.

The four days would consist of the time he could spend with his daughter. It was getting harder to spend the time he wanted, because of Jayne's taking over the duties that the rest of the household had assumed. Zander knew it was the thing that should have happened, and now that it had, he was concerned about how he felt about it. Jealousy wasn't a normal emotion for him, but that's just what it was. He knew that Sandy would be relying on Jayne during her formative years, and he would be a come and go parent.

Millie must have seen a change in Zander's demeanor. On that Thursday, she took him aside.

"When were you going to announce that you are leaving?"

"How could you know that?" Zander asked.

"I've lived on this earth a long time. I've been through things that would have killed the average person, so I think it's given me a heightened sense of perception. When are you leaving?"

"Friday. Aubrey is being driven to Cedar Key. I'm to meet her at Herbie's place."

"Were you going to tell us or just leave?"

"I wouldn't do that. I just needed to work up a little courage."

"It doesn't take much courage to leave. It would take more courage to stay in my book."

"Right. The courage I needed was in telling you. My relationship with Jayne is over. Other than our mutual interest in our daughter, I no longer have feeling for her. You, on the other hand, have become my friend. I feel closer to you than I did to my own mother. That makes me regret what I might have had here with you and Sandy."

Millie looked at Zander and then did something that surprised them both; she wrapped her arms around Zander and hugged him like she would never let him go.

The hug lasted longer than either of them could have anticipated. After they both began to feel uncomfortable, Millie let him go.

"Go pack your things. You should leave right now. I'll have Hector drive you there. Let me smooth things over with Jayne."

"Are you sure? I thought this should be something I should do."

"Trust me, you'll be better off away from here when Jayne finds out. You know how she is."

Zander knew what Millie was talking about. He went to his room and threw together his things into his rucksack. When he was finished, he went down to see if he could say goodbye to Millie, but there was no one around. When he went to the door to wait for Hector, he could see Millie and Jayne pushing Sandy in her stroller as they were walking toward the park. Zander felt pangs of remorse seeing the three of them together. Walking with Sandy had always been his job. Now it was over.

There was a song by Joni Mitchell from 1970 he had always liked and one lyric just hit him like a brick wall.

"Oh, don't it seem to go,

That you don't know what you've got until it's gone."

It was the story of his life.

NOTE FROM THE AUTHOR

Word-of-mouth is crucial for any author to succeed. If you enjoyed the book, please leave a review online—anywhere you are able. Even if it's just a sentence or two. It would make all the difference and would be very much appreciated.

Thanks!
Jeff

NOTE FROM THE AUTHOR

Word of mouth is crucial for any author's success. If you enjoyed the book, please leave a review online—anywhere you read it. Even if it's just a sentence or two, it would make all the difference and would be very much appreciated.

Charles

Jeff

Thank you so much for reading one of our **Jeff Zwagerman's** novels.
If you enjoyed the experience,
please check out the beginning of the story!

South of Sideways by Jeff Zwagerman

View other Black Rose Writing titles at
www.blackrosewriting.com/books and use promo code
PRINT to receive a **20% discount** when purchasing.